Rose Tremain sa   his Magic Knot cradled in her palm. She swayed slightly, her eyes dazed and dreamy. His nerves sparked. Need for her struck like lightning. He managed to suck in air, to ruthlessly crush the feeling until his body calmed.

So, he had been right. Rose Tremain was more dangerous than she appeared. She'd been sent to enslave him by capturing his stones. If she thought he'd give in easily, she had another think coming.

Silently, he walked forward and closed his hand over hers. His vision blurred at the whip of sensation. Too late, he realized his mistake in touching her. Gritting his teeth, he fought the mental pull as she sucked his very essence through their joined hands into a deep, hidden part of her that whispered of ancient magic and mystery.

Niall snatched up his Magic Knot and stumbled back. His breath came in short gasps as he stared at her in shock. Rose was the Cornish pisky Tristan wanted. How had she stopped them from sensing the truth about her? That deception alone proved she was up to no good.

Slowly, her green eyes focused on him. Confusion set tiny creases between her delicate brows, then surprise chased them away. She slapped a hand over her mouth.

"Aye, be afraid, little thief," he whispered. "You'll pay dearly for your deception before I'm done with you."

The MAGIC KNOT

HELEN SCOTT TAYLOR

LOVE SPELL

love SPELL

NEW YORK CITY

Dedicated to my wonderful, supportive husband,
who always believed in me.

LOVE SPELL®

February 2009

Published by

Dorchester Publishing Co., Inc.
200 Madison Avenue
New York, NY 10016

ISBN 10: 0-505-52796-0
ISBN 13: 978-0-505-52796-7
E-ISBN: 1-4285-0606-3

Visit us on the web at www.dorchesterpub.com.

ACKNOWLEDGMENTS

I would like to thank all the people in many corners of the world who voted for this book in the American Title IV contest. I will be forever grateful for the enthusiastic support of so many kind people who've never met me, yet who found the time to vote to make my dream come true. A big thank-you must go to *Romantic Times*, who cosponsored the contest with Dorchester, and my editor Alicia Condon for selecting *The Magic Knot* for the final.

Special thanks to my steadfast friends Mona Risk and Joan Leacott who encourage me to produce my best work. Also, I want to mention my online friends at From The Heart Romance Writers who've cheered me on and been behind me all the way, and the members of Mary Buckham's Super Tuesday Group for their encouragement and belief in me.

Other people who've helped me along the way who I want to mention are Joyce Ellen Almond (whose critiques always gave me a boost), Trish Johnson, Alice Audrey, Jaclyn Dibono, and Barbara Turner-Vesselago for her wonderful Freefall writing workshop where my writing journey began.

Finally, my heartfelt thanks to my dear husband Glyn Taylor and my family for their support during the contest. I'm especially grateful to my mother-in-law Janet Taylor (who missed her vocation and should be working in book promotion!), and my sisters Pamela Tuckett and Angela Croudace.

The MAGIC KNOT

Chapter One

Roughly translated, the slogan on Niall O'Connor's family crest read: "We need all the help the gods can give us."

Not that he wanted help from anyone, gods or otherwise. He'd learned early on to look out for himself. Unfortunately, every now and then he had no choice.

So here he was—cap in hand, metaphorically speaking—on his way to ask for a favor from Tristan Jago. Which unfortunately entailed getting past Tristan's sidekick, Nightshade, a vampiric nightstalker with attitude problems.

Niall rode his motorcycle up the narrow drive to Tristan's rambling granite manor house, stopped on the circle of gravel outside the front door, and cut the engine.

Trevelion Manor sat alone atop the rocky Cornish cliffs overlooking the Atlantic. In the distance, purple storm clouds billowed across a gunmetal gray sea. A portent of trouble if ever he'd seen one. It looked like the gods definitely weren't smiling on him today.

As he kicked down his bike stand, the front door opened. Nightshade stepped out of the shadowy interior, folded his arms over his glistening oiled pecs, and spread his wings to block entry. Quashing a sigh, Niall pulled off his helmet and rested it on the bike's seat.

Niall flexed his hands to check the position of the two crystal knives strapped to his wrists. If he could avoid fighting Nightshade, he would. Not that he thought he'd lose. Quite the contrary: he was sure he'd win. But he'd fought enough hand-to-hand to last a lifetime.

"It's a pleasure to see you, Irish!" Nightshade hooked his thumbs in the loops of his jeans and grinned, his teeth white against ebony skin. "I've a hankering for a taste of Tuatha Dé Danaan with a seasoning of leprechaun."

"In your dreams, boyo." Niall halted a safe distance away and patted the pocket of his flight jacket containing the check. "You going to let me in? I've a wee present here for your lord and master."

Nightshade sneered, exposing the glistening points of his fangs. "I'm no one's servant. Taunt me again, Irish, and you'll live to regret it."

Obviously Tristan's sidekick had aspirations above his station. *Worth remembering.*

In the muted light of the corridor, Tristan Jago's thin, pale face appeared. "Boys, boys." He smiled urbanely as he approached and placed a restraining hand on Nightshade's shoulder. "Be a good fellow and let Niall in. I believe he comes bearing gifts." He stroked his paisley silk cravat and slid an appraising glance over Niall. "You're always welcome, my friend. Gifts or no."

Niall suppressed a shudder. The druid boasted reptilian qualities any lizard would be proud of.

"Come and play chess with me, Niall. I still have our game set up in the drawing room." As Nightshade disappeared into the house, Tristan glanced after him and sniffed. "I can't get that philistine interested in chess. Says he doesn't see the point."

Niall followed Tristan inside. The musty smell of animals long dead tainted the air of the drawing room. Niall spared a cursory glance for the multitude of stuffed wild creatures lining the walls and resisted the temptation to press his sleeve against his nose. How could anyone, even a human like Tristan, live surrounded by death?

Nightshade sat slouched across a chair before the crackling fire, his legs slung over the arm, and pointedly ignored Niall. That suited him fine. He wanted to settle his business, no hassle, and get out.

Tristan walked to the bay window overlooking the sea and lowered himself into a wing chair beside the chessboard. Lightning flashed, banishing shadows from the room for an instant and lending his pale face a ghostly appearance.

Niall withdrew the check from his pocket and held it up so the figure of twenty-five thousand pounds was clear in the pool of light beneath the table lamp.

Bony fingers shot out and plucked the check from his grasp. "You have been a busy boy." Tristan gave Niall a narrow look. "That's some return on my initial thousand. What was it this time? Equity options?"

Niall shifted uneasily. He hated discussing his trades. "Commodities, mainly. A little cocoa and oil. Some gold. Dollar and euro to finish up."

"You really do have the luck of the leprechauns."

"That scrap o' paper fulfills my half of the bargain. You'll renew the spell of protection over me brother and sister for another three months."

Inclining his head, Tristan indicated the seat opposite him. "Spare me half an hour, and we have a deal."

Niall tensed in frustration at being manipulated, even if it was only into a game of chess. "Aye, then, I suppose." He dropped into the vacant chair and scanned the chessboard to refresh his memory of where they'd left the game three months ago.

"Your move, I think," Tristan said.

Jaw clenched, Niall placed the white knight in a square to protect his queen. The irony of the move brought a grim smile to his lips. He would never return to Ireland and subjugate himself to the Irish fairy queen, even if it meant paying Tristan to protect his brother and sister from her for the rest of their lives.

The frantic jingling of a small bell pulled his attention from the chessboard. On the other side of the room, a gold hand clicked around the face of what looked like a cuckoo clock, and a figure twirled out of a little door on the front.

Tristan jumped up, grating his chair on the parquet floor, and marched across the room to stare at the dancing doll. "At last."

Pushing up from his seat, Nightshade prowled over to join him. "I thought you said they were all gone," he whispered in gruff disbelief.

Tristan shook his head. The stalker slanted Tristan an accusing look that raised the hair on Niall's neck. They both appeared to have forgotten him. "What's this all about?" he demanded.

Dragging his eyes away from the dancing figure, Tristan gave a thin smile. "This, my dear Niall, is a magical device that tells me a Cornish pisky is about to cross the River Tamar and enter Cornwall."

Niall frowned. "You told me they'd all disappeared years ago. That's why I brought me sister here. I assumed the lass'd be safe from the machinations of fairies."

"And so she is." Tristan ran his hand across his mouth, then tapped his lips. "Find this pisky for me, Niall. Find her and bring her here."

Who was this lone pisky woman? The grim set of the stalker's mouth suggested that she heralded trouble. Niall didn't want to get involved in anyone else's disagreements. He had enough problems resolving his own.

Niall leaned back and shook his head. "I've no interest in bothering meself with piskies. Find her yourself."

Tristan turned on him, pale brown eyes flaring with emotion. "That will not do, my dear Niall. Not at all. If you want me to cast another spell to shield your siblings from Ciar's pervasive gaze, bring the pisky woman here."

A flash of anger burned through Niall. He was sick of having his brother and half sister used as leverage. Niall unfolded from the chair and took a step toward the druid. He had three inches on Tristan and used every fraction of them to intimidate. "You have me money tucked away in your pocket. I advise you, don't go adding conditions now, druid. Honor the bargain." He kept a wary eye on Nightshade, ready for him to jump to his master's defense, but the stalker stayed still, watching with guarded interest.

Tristan glared. Smudges of red appeared on the taut, pale skin of his cheeks. They stared each other down for a few seconds; then Tristan shook his head. "I only want to give her directions to find her troop, Niall. You'd best do as I ask if you want my help."

Niall held himself still as death. He didn't believe that explanation for a moment, but in truth, he had no choice except to comply. The spell of protection over his brother and sister must be recast—whatever the cost.

The pisky should be easy to find. She'd be drawn to him and his brother, Michael, because, apart from Nightshade, they were the only fairies in Cornwall. All he had to do was wait for her to show up at Michael's pub and then bring her to Trevelion Manor.

Niall thumped a fist on his chest in reluctant assent, then raised a warning finger. " 'Tis a bargain, then. But no more demands after this."

Tristan flashed a triumphant grin that added to Niall's unease.

He could almost hear the gods sniggering at his latest plight. He hoped he wasn't going to live to regret this.

Rosenwyn Tremain stared through her BMW's windshield at the towering gray struts of the road bridge spanning the River Tamar. *The gateway to Cornwall.* She swallowed anxiously as the line of traffic edged closer to the bridge. In a few minutes she'd be over, on Cornish soil—or, more precisely, Cornish asphalt.

A slash of lightning cut across the leaden sky, briefly relieving the dull afternoon. She shuddered, then nervously fluffed her short hair.

Never set foot in Cornwall. Her mother's plea whispered in her memory as her car crawled forward.

Rose passed beneath the Cornish coat of arms marking the center point of the Tamar Bridge. Tension clenched her belly. She snatched a breath, held it, half expecting to be smote down by a thunderbolt.

"Oh, for goodness' sake." She slapped her palms against the steering wheel. "Pull yourself together, woman, and get over it." What was the worst that could happen? She'd get a hostile reception from the business she was due to investigate. That wouldn't be a first. No one liked being told they were insolvent.

Just over an hour later, Rose maneuvered her car along a narrow Cornish lane. She glanced at her satellite navigation system and gnawed her lip. Either the satellite was faulty, or the Elephant's Nest Public House was in the middle of nowhere. She had a nasty suspicion it was the latter.

She crawled until the road opened out at the head of an estuary. Stopping on a small humpbacked bridge, she stared at the pretty scatter of lighted cottage windows glowing in the curve of the valley. Living in London, she found it easy to forget places like this existed.

The satellite system directed her along a narrow track beside the estuary for another half a mile. Finally, an ancient building with whitewashed walls intersected by black beams shone in her headlights. She swung her car around and parked near the front door. Her watch read five thirty, nearly opening time.

The plan had been to make a start on the financial assessment this afternoon, but the drive had taken longer than expected. As she was late, the best she could do was get the preliminaries out of the way so she could make a quick start in the morning. A small review job like this should take only two days. Then she could spend the rest of the week tracing her father.

Climbing out, she slung her purse strap over her shoulder and grabbed her briefcase. A cool breeze flowed up the estuary with the incoming tide. Salty air tingled in her lungs. So, this was Cornwall—the county of her birth.

Checking out the parking lot, she noticed a red Porsche Boxster, spotless and gleaming beneath a streetlight. The license plate read, MICK. She grimaced. Maybe the problem with the business's finances was an owner who spent the working capital. She'd met a few of those in her years as an accountant. Mr. Michael O'Connor's private spending would be her first target—and he wouldn't like that. Those she investigated never did.

As she walked toward the front door, she paused and stared at the incongruous sight of a fat pink elephant with a wicked grin perched on a nest of plastic twigs. Lucky the guy who owned this place had a sense of humor. He would probably need it when he received her report.

When she reached the entrance porch, the low drone of a powerful motorcycle engine rolled through the darkness behind her. Its headlight flickered amid the trees on the riverbank as it approached. Rose suppressed a strange compulsion to go inside before it arrived. The air vibrated with the thud of the engine as the machine slowed and, with a crunch of gravel, swung into the parking lot.

The man halted beside the Porsche, dropped a brown-booted foot to the ground, and turned his head toward her. The lamplight gleamed off the visor of his helmet. When he looked at her, the three linked stones on her necklace tingled warmly against her skin. She clasped them through her shirt to stop the weird sensation.

He twisted his hand on the throttle, and the roar of the engine snapped her out of her trance. Rose shivered as she took in his green combat pants and battered leather flight jacket. She hoped he wasn't the owner of the pub.

Dragging her attention back to the pub, she cleared her throat, then strode through the door into the bar. The gentle lilt of traditional Irish music and the smell of wood smoke welcomed her in. After the plastic elephant out front, she was pleasantly surprised by the old-fashioned interior with its beamed ceiling, brass ornaments, and polished oak bar.

A middle-aged woman, with a mass of fair hair secured atop her head by an orange flower, looked up from where she was restocking the shelves behind the bar.

"We're not open till six, m' love." She poked her thumb behind her. "Boss is still out back working his magic."

Rose suspected the magic had something to do with the delicious smell of food emanating from the back. So Michael O'Connor cooked. He probably couldn't afford to pay a chef.

Rose slipped a business card from the leather case in her pocket and held it out. "Sorry to call so late. Mr. O'Connor is expecting me. I just want to introduce myself tonight and get the lay of the land. I'll be back to start work in the morning."

The woman took the card and read out loud. " 'Rose Tremain. Francis Marchant Partnership.' You got yourself an impressive list of letters after your name, but it don't tell me what you're here for."

Rose assumed a neutral expression. Keeping the reason for her presence secret from the staff was always difficult. But it was necessary when investigating a business facing bankruptcy.

She gave the woman a reassuring smile. "Mr. O'Connor is expecting me. If you'd just give him my card, I'm sure he can spare me a few minutes tonight."

The woman flicked the card between her fingers thoughtfully. "Now, which Mr. O'Connor would you be wanting?"

There were two? Rose cast her mind back to the job file. She was certain the Elephant's Nest belonged to a sole proprietor. "My call is in connection with the pub." Rose indicated the empty room. "Michael O'Connor's the owner, I believe."

The woman's face split into a warm grin. "Our Mick. Right you are, then. Won't be a mo." She disappeared up the three steps leading into the back, and Rose glanced around, suddenly uneasy. She usually dealt with large organizations. She had an inkling this job was going to be very different.

The fair-haired woman scuttled back down the stairs, giggling, and Rose watched expectantly for her latest client to appear. If he were the cooperative sort, her job would be a lot easier.

Michael O'Connor ran down the three steps with the grace of a dancer, flicked back his wealth of chestnut curls, and flashed her a seductive grin.

Rose felt her jaw go slack. He was the prettiest man she'd ever seen. From his cobalt blue eyes to his perfect lips, everything about his face was finely formed and faultless. As he sauntered out from behind the bar, he hooked his thumbs in the front pockets of well-worn, skintight jeans and tilted his lips into a smile that could probably melt hearts at fifty paces.

Oh, my God. She eyed his body—she couldn't help herself. He might be pretty, but there was nothing feminine about the muscles outlined beneath his scarlet

T-shirt. She felt her mouth slip into a flirty smile and mentally slapped herself. *Get a grip.* But she couldn't. She was intoxicated, losing her senses.

He halted before her and extended his hand. " 'Tis a pleasure to meet you, Rose Tremain." He rolled her name off his tongue like an endearment. She caught a whiff of spicy fragrance and felt a liquid tug of arousal deep in her belly.

She closed her eyes and swallowed. This was certainly a new technique for impeding her investigation. She'd faced clients who were hostile, unhelpful, and obstructive, but never before had a client dazzled her with sex appeal.

Opening her eyes, she struggled for control. She bit the inside of her lip hard enough to hurt as she shook his hand. His eyes glittered between spiky dark lashes like the warm blue waters of the Mediterranean, tempting her in for a dip. What heaven she would find if she slid into that water. Let it flow over her. Immersed herself. Gave in to the pleasure waiting to—

A crash of breaking glass behind the bar snapped her back to the room as though she'd been yanked out of sleep. She blinked. For a second her mind swam; then her head cleared. Michael O'Connor still looked pretty, but now her normal good sense kicked in. He was exactly the type of man she always avoided. She'd learned as a child that the beautiful people who hung around her mother were all gloss and no substance.

Professional distance, she repeated in her head. Realizing she still held his hand, she dropped it like a hot brick.

His eyes flickered with confusion. Tilting his head to one side, he pouted. "You're a strong-willed lass. What's your business with me, Rose Tremain?"

Rose straightened her back. "I assumed you were expecting me, Mr. O'Connor. You signed my firm's letter of engagement and agreed to the appointment date." Although the bank he was in debt to would have given him no choice in the matter.

He shrugged, pulled a squashed packet of cigarettes from his back pocket, and flipped one out. "Not sure I be remembering that."

Okay, she had encountered this tactic before: denial. "Well, as luck would have it"—she gave him a polite smile, propped her briefcase on a table, and pulled out a copy of the letter he'd returned—"I have a copy here."

He scowled at her, jabbed the cigarette between his lips, and lit it with a gold lighter.

"Grand," he said in a tone suggesting her presence was anything but. "Me office is this way."

He led her behind the bar. As he passed the display of cigarettes, he tossed his half-full squashed pack into the trash and grabbed a new one. Okay, so he was extravagant and wasteful. Rose made a mental note to add those to the list of things he could correct to save money.

They mounted the steps, and she followed him along a short corridor with a kitchen off to one side. He took her through to a back entrance hall with a small reception desk in the corner. They must have rooms to let. Perhaps she could stay here?

"I don't suppose you have any vacancies?"

He glanced back at her and his lips stretched into a grin. The hot, seductive glint in his eyes started to dissolve her brain again until she stamped on the feeling. How the hell did he do that when she had no interest in him?

"You after staying with me, darlin'? That can be arranged."

Maybe staying here wasn't such a brilliant idea. "No, forget it. I don't want to inconvenience you. I should have booked ahead. I'll find somewhere—"

" 'Tis no inconvenience. You'll have a room on the house."

"I'd prefer to pay." She refrained from telling him he needed all the revenue he could get.

He showed her through a door marked OFFICE behind the reception desk.

Rose paused on the threshold and glanced into the room expectantly. For the second time that evening, her mouth dropped open. The massive oak desk in the corner was hidden beneath piles of documents. Cardboard boxes were stacked beside it, also full of documents. But the thing that sent a chill of foreboding through her was not what she saw, but what she didn't see.

"Where's your computer?" She glanced behind the door and found nothing but a chair with a slat missing from its back.

Michael O'Connor laughed. She'd heard contagious laughs before, the sort that made you smile, even when you hadn't heard the joke. Michael's laugh had her grinning like a fool—at a problem.

"I can't be doing with all those shenanigans. I like the old-fashioned ways."

A sense of doom settled heavily in the pit of her stomach. She eyed the heaps of documents. The easy two-day job she'd expected took on mammoth proportions. It was vital to get the investigation out of the way quickly, or there wouldn't be enough time to find her father. "Are your accounts recorded manually,

13

then?" She searched for any sign of an analysis book but couldn't see one.

"You'll be needing me brother, Niall, if it's computers and accounts you're after. He's the one with the gift in this family."

Oh, thank God. Relief melted through her like the effect of a good cup of coffee. "Can you ask him if he'll spare me a few hours in the morning to go through the records? From then on I'll be fine alone, providing one of you remains available to answer questions."

"Your wish is my command, darlin'." Michael beamed his bone-melting smile at her again.

This time Rose caught herself before she responded inappropriately.

"I'm always available for a pretty girl," he said with a wink.

Rose shrank inside from embarrassment. False flattery was one of her pet peeves. She hadn't been a girl for many years, and her mother had made certain Rose had no illusions about her looks.

With a tight grip on her briefcase, she heaved a determined breath. This job wouldn't be a problem. She'd complete her report on the Elephant's Nest as fast as possible, then concentrate on the real reason for her visit to Cornwall. Niall O'Connor would be her point of contact. Hopefully he'd be easier to work with than Michael. Anyone logical enough to keep the financial records must be normal and down-to-earth.

The following morning, Rose checked her lipstick in the dressing table mirror in the room she'd taken at the Elephant's Nest.

When she was served breakfast at seven, there'd

been no sign of Michael O'Connor, thank goodness. He would probably be like strong spirits—too much to swallow until later in the day. She turned away from her reflection with a sigh. Imagine having to wake up in bed with him. How soul destroying to be faced with a man prettier than yourself every morning.

She checked her watch and wondered what time Niall O'Connor would be available. Until he showed her where he kept the accounts, there was nothing for her to do. She cast a sideways glance at her running outfit laid out on the chair. There would have been time to do a few miles after all, but it was too late to change her plans now. She'd already showered and dressed in a navy suit.

Rose wandered across to the window and fiddled with the three stone rings hung on a chain around her neck as she stared at the river. What could she do to fill the time?

Rose.

The whispered call in her head made her squeeze her eyes closed. She couldn't read the cards now. What would Niall O'Connor think if he came to the room looking for her and saw them?

Rose.

She glanced at her pack of Magic Knot tarot cards in their black velvet bag on the nightstand. Taking them out of her case had been a mistake. Rose rubbed her temples to try to banish the quietly whispered entreaties in her head.

We only want to help.

After all her years living a normal life, why did she still have this ridiculous urge to ask advice from the cards?

Why do you deny us?

15

"Talk about emotional blackmail." Rose swung around and snatched up the cards that had been designed and given to her by her mother.

She pushed her cell phone and makeup bag aside and laid out on the dressing table the square of purple silk she kept with her cards. Then she sat on the stool, feet flat on the floor, closed her eyes, and took three deep breaths to ground herself. After gathering the seventy-eight cards in her hands, she shuffled, their familiar smooth feel a balm to her soul.

Today she wouldn't read for herself. After years of depending on the cards to tell her how to live her life, she'd finally weaned herself off the need for her morning reading. What she really required was more information on the two O'Connor brothers. Understanding their characters would help her deal with them.

She pictured Michael and fanned the cards in her hand. Eyes closed, she ran the tips of her fingers along the top of the pack.

When a corner dug into her skin, she opened her eyes, drew the card, and placed it faceup on the silk. *The Moon.* "Oh." She bit her lip. The pale circle of the moon glowed behind the veiled face of the woman portrayed on the card. "The pale light masks a dark and secret nature," Rose whispered, repeating the words her mother had recited many times when she'd taught her to divine with the tarot cards. Michael was not what he seemed.

She touched the card's image. *Illusion,* whispered into her mind. *Hidden truths.*

A shiver ran through her. That didn't bode well for her investigation. She needed a more precise idea of how he would behave as her client. Fanning the cards, she closed her eyes and drew another. The Seven of

Cups. After laying it beside the Moon, she scanned the image of the golden-haired man lying beside a stream in a grassy glade, a misty dream bubble full of riches and beautiful women above his head.

"Dreams invade reality." Michael lived in a fantasy world and probably wasn't able to cope with reality. Two escapism cards together were worrying. They suggested an addiction. Maybe the smoking? With the tip of her finger, she traced the man's golden hair down the back of his cloak. Sizzling lust burst through her.

"Yowee!" Rose snatched her hand back and pressed it against her chest to calm her pounding heart. With Michael's looks, he probably had no trouble feeding *that* addiction.

After thanking the cards, she slid them into the deck. Anything Michael told her about the business should be treated with extreme caution.

Perhaps his brother would prove more helpful. "Niall O'Connor," she whispered. "Show me the heart of the man." The name Niall tasted strange and sharp on her tongue. She didn't know what he looked like, so she concentrated on his name and let a feel for him float into her mind. With slow, precise movements, she reshuffled the cards, fanned them, and pulled one. "Justice." She breathed a sigh of relief. In his heart, Niall O'Connor was a just and fair man. If she stayed on the right side of him, he'd probably help her.

As Niall seemed more promising, she decided to choose two more cards for him. Shuffling, she asked to be shown how he would help her and then drew the King of Coins. "Money?" Surely if he had any capital, he'd have bailed out his brother. This card must indicate that his advice would be reliable. She touched the dark-haired man who sat on a throne of twisted branches, a huge gold coin clutched in his hand. A warm breath of suggestion whispered in her ear, the words unclear but soft and beguiling.

Bewildered by the feeling, she took a deep breath to clear her head and moved on. Shuffling again she asked, "How will Niall work against me?" then selected a card. *Ten of Swords!* Her hand fisted against the silk as she stared at the young man lying facedown with ten swords thrust into his back.

Rose closed her eyes and massaged her temples, her belly queasy with remembered humiliation. She'd pulled the same card during her personal reading on the day her mother betrayed her. After all these years, the nightmare scenario was as clear as ever.

She drew a breath and tried to stay open to the card's meaning for this reading. It could represent the successful conclusion of her investigation. But she'd asked to be shown how Niall would work against her. Reluctantly, she touched the image of the prone man and waited for the voice in her head.

Sacrifice, the whisper hissed.

She ached to withdraw her hand, hardly able to bear the feelings.

Betrayal, separation, pain—

She yanked her hand away with a groan and stared wide-eyed into the mirror, her ragged breaths filling the silence.

The memory of finding her mother with Tom burned in her mind. She'd been so terribly naive and trusting. How could she ever have believed Tom loved *her* when she knew she was nothing special?

She crushed the memory down. Her life was exactly as she wanted it now, and when she located her father, maybe she'd finally have a parent who valued her achievements—and valued her.

After squaring off the pack, she pressed the cool cards against her forehead. What did the Ten of Swords mean? How would Niall stab her in the back? The prediction filled her with disquiet, but it wasn't the card's fault.

"Thank you," she whispered. The characters on the Magic Knot tarot cards had been her companions from her earliest memories. When her mother went on a binge, Rose had always turned to the cards for comfort. For a sad, lonely little girl, the characters had been her only family.

With a sigh, she slid the pack into its velvet bag and cinched the drawstring. She checked her face, then grabbed her purse and briefcase. When she stood, she straightened her body into professional mode. Let Niall O'Connor try to stab her in the back. Forewarned was forearmed. She had plenty of experience dealing with difficult people, from the uncooperative to the downright rude. "Bring it on, Mr. O'Connor. I'm ready for you."

Chapter Two

At nine o'clock, Rose steeled herself and entered the small, untidy office Michael had shown her the previous evening. She felt deflated when there was no sign of Niall O'Connor.

Using a duster and polish borrowed from the woman cleaning the bar, she kept busy while she waited by tidying herself a workspace. At nine twenty, when she had the surface of the desk clear and gleaming with lemon-scented beeswax, Niall still hadn't appeared.

She set her briefcase on the corner of the desk and took out the file from the bank. Then she arranged neatly around the space her cell phone, which had no signal in this back-of-beyond place, her calculator, her PalmPilot, and her pencils and pen. She leaned back in the rickety swivel chair and surveyed her handiwork.

Awareness tickled the back of her neck. She swung the squeaky chair around and checked the door.

A man stood in the open doorway, shoulder against the door frame, arms crossed over his chest in a relaxed pose at odds with his alert expression. Rose had a strange moment in which reality twisted into a different shape. He looked like Michael O'Connor, only the oozing charm had been replaced by a faint air of menace that fluttered dark thrills of anticipation through her.

Every feature of his face matched Michael's, from the startlingly blue eyes to the perfect lips. How was it possible for two men to look the same and yet so different? This man had short hair and wore a loose brown shirt, green combat pants, and brown leather hiking boots. Of course, the man on the motorcycle had been Niall.

"You and Michael are identical twins."

"I know," he said flatly as he appraised her, his eyes blank, his face expressionless. "Who might you be?"

"Rose Tremain. Michael didn't tell you?"

"Obviously not." He raised one eyebrow slightly. "What're you doing in the office?"

"Waiting for you."

"Me?" A hint of a frown creased his forehead and then was gone.

She'd managed to surprise him. For some reason, it felt like a minor victory.

Rose stood, slipped a business card from her pocket, and held it out. "I'm hoping you'll take me through the last three years' accounts, Mr. O'Connor. Your brother told me you keep the books for the pub."

Niall pushed away from the door frame, took a stride forward, and pulled the card from her fingers. He stared at the words for a moment, then tapped the card's side against his palm.

"Don't go telling me Michael's bankrupt." He glanced down and swore under his breath.

She was surprised he recognized the letters after her name that indicated her insolvency qualification. "I'm afraid he's missed the last six months' loan payments to his bank. I'm here to do a report."

Niall placed her card on top of the filing cabinet

beside the door and shook his head. "Michael's misled you, Ms. Tremain. I don't get involved in running the Nest. This here's me brother's passion."

Rose stared at him, a knot of dread tightening her belly. "Then who does keep the books?"

Niall glanced at the dusty heaps of documents piled against the wall. "I'm guessing nobody."

Rose gripped the back of her chair so tightly her fingers hurt. "Someone must have prepared the accounts in previous years. What about paying the taxes? He must account for tax when he pays his staff."

Niall shrugged, a .brief flick of his shoulders, as though he objected to responding. "Employees get paid cash out of the till. I've seen him do it."

"Didn't you say anything? Tell him he needs records?"

Niall stared at her, his penetrating blue gaze probing. His eyes were the same color as Michael's, but they didn't make her think of inviting Mediterranean seas. There were sharks swimming within these waters.

"I don't go wasting me breath." He turned to leave, and a little spurt of desperation surged through her.

"I can't do this job without the records. No way am I starting from scratch with source documents."

He paused in the doorway and gave her a challenging glance. "Leave it then. Take yourself back to London. I'll sort matters here."

"If I walk away, I'll have to notify Inland Revenue." Technically, she shouldn't inform him of that fact, but he'd have to be stupid not to realize. And she was certain Niall O'Connor was not stupid. "Do you think he really wants a tax inspector on his doorstep?"

"What about if the arrears are paid off?"

Rose watched him rest his long fingers against the

door frame. With a strange tingle in her belly, she remembered the old wives' tale comparing the length of a certain male body part with the span between thumb and index finger. She blinked and swallowed awkwardly. What the hell was the matter with her? Exposure to Niall's brother must have addled her brain.

"I'm sorry. Once the instruction's been issued, we've got to continue with the investigation unless the bank cancels the request. Even if you pay the arrears, it'll take a few weeks to filter through the system."

Anyway, how did he intend to pay off the loan? Unless . . . She remembered the King of Coins from the tarot reading. Maybe Niall had money. She considered his scruffy clothes and thought of the old motorcycle. If he was wealthy, he did a damn good job of disguising the fact.

Niall slapped his hand against the doorframe, making her start. "All righty, I'll get you the old accounts. Radcliffs in Lostwithiel prepared them until last year. For the current year you'll have to work with these." He nodded toward the heaped documents.

Her heart dropped. "What about a computer? Michael mentioned you're the computer expert."

"No computer. Michael doesn't like them."

Great. Wonderful. What century were they living in? She shook her head. "He's obviously not averse to modern technology when it comes on four wheels with a Porsche logo stuck on the front. Maybe he could sell that and pay the bank. Or is it on finance as well?"

The expression on Niall's face didn't change, but she got an inkling that he was uncomfortable. "Ask Michael. I'm not his keeper."

As he walked away, she moved to the doorway and

her eyes strayed from the width of his shoulders to the play of muscles in his tight backside as, with determined strides, he disappeared down the hall by the kitchen. She bit her lip. *How are you going to stab me in the back, Niall O'Connor?* She knew with certainty that he wasn't being completely honest. Michael had told her Niall was the computer expert, yet he claimed there was no computer. And she'd been forced to drag every bit of information out of him. Niall was hiding something that affected her investigation. His name might not be listed as an owner of the business, but she was certain he had his long, sexy fingers in the pie. And he didn't want her to find out.

Nightshade left the bright morning sun behind in the upper rooms of Trevelion Manor and descended the twisting stairway into the warren of caves and tunnels that riddled the ground below.

The previous evening, Tristan had been tight-lipped about the identity of the pisky female who'd crossed into Cornwall. Maybe a few hours working alone had loosened the man's tongue, and he would be ready to confirm Nightshade's suspicion that Princess Ailla Tremain had returned. Thirty years ago, he'd yearned for her and she'd rejected him. If she had returned, he would find her, forge a blood bond, and take her for his mate.

Holding an oil lamp aloft, Nightshade walked on silent feet through the cavernous underground chamber that had once been the meeting place for his people. Remembered laughter from his childhood among the Cornish piskies rang in his head and echoed hollowly in his heart, happy memories from a time before he'd matured and they'd cast him out. It was natural, his pisky mother told him; nightstalkers were meant to be solitary creatures.

Raising the lamp, he cast a sideways glance at the paintings illuminated by the flickering circle of light. Ailla had decorated the walls with art nouveau murals in jewel-bright colors celebrating Samhain and Beltane, the two hinges of the year.

He paused and recited words he had not spoken for many moons.

"Earth be my foundation,
Air be my inspiration,
Fire be my passion,
Water cleanse my pain."

In his mind's eye, he saw Ailla, copper curls caught in a ribbon behind her delicate neck, paintbrush in hand. Such a talented artist—talent Tristan had forced her to use in a terrible way. Guilt scraped Nightshade's conscience and he pushed it away. She had been as bad as the rest of the piskies, rejecting him, forcing him out, even though he'd risked Tristan's anger protecting her little girl.

He passed down a short hallway and halted at Tristan's workroom. As he pushed open the carved oak door, the stench of decay and death made him gag. In the muted light from six black candles, he watched Tristan push the nozzle of a hot-glue gun in the back-side of a baby rabbit. The rabbit's lifeless glass eyes stared back at him in despair.

Tristan glanced up, a thin smile of satisfaction stretching his lips. "What do you think?" He balanced the rabbit kit on its wooden stand and tipped his head to one side. "Pretty good, if I do say so myself. Not many people have a delicate enough touch to mount the smallest animals."

Nightshade could not imagine why anyone in his right mind would mount a carcass that should be returned to the earth. Over the years, he had learned to keep that opinion to himself. He grunted in acknowledgment; even one as accursed as he could not offer praise for such blasphemy.

As he walked into the room, the sense of death was swept from his awareness by the sizzling presence of spiritual energy so pure and concentrated it flashed along his nerves like lightning. "Curse you," he ground out. Pressing fingers to his throbbing temples, he scoured the room for the source.

Racks of animal skins filled the space: the chestnut fur of fox, the black and white stripes of badger. Nightshade swung his gaze the other way. In the farthest corner, he spied the two globes that haunted his nightmares, full of dancing golden lights that fluttered within their glass prison like trapped fireflies. He shielded his eyes from the glare. "Cover them. Now."

Tristan's lips peeled back in a smile. "They know you're here. They'll never forget your betrayal."

"As if I need reminding." With an arm shielding his face, he stumbled forward, ripped a fur from its rack, and covered the sparkling globes. Immediately, the pain in his body eased back to a dull ache. He rounded on Tristan. "Why not just stick me with one of your bloody dissection tools if you want to hurt me?"

"I have no intention of hurting you, silly boy. I feed on them. You feed on me. We're all part of the circle of life."

Nightshade stared at the packed earth beneath his feet, grimacing at the twisted analogy. There were times when he loathed Tristan so deeply he wanted to crush the life from his frail body. He looked up at the druid's white mask of a face. "I don't know why I ever let you use me." How naive he'd been in his blind need for revenge on the people who'd cast him out.

"We used each other," Tristan said matter-of-factly, and placed the rabbit on the bench behind him. A nimbus of black fire shimmered around Tristan's hand as he walked forward and laid his deadly palm against Nightshade's chest. "We still do. I need you. You need me."

In the flickering light cast by the candles, Nightshade gazed at the paper-thin skin clinging to Tristan's emaciated flesh. "If I smash those globes and release the piskies' spirits, you'll wither and die, old man."

"Free them, and they'll torment you for your treachery. They may hate me for trapping them, but you betrayed your own kind."

Grief and despair pierced his soul. Nightshade snapped his wings angrily and stepped back.

Tristan's hands darted out and gripped clawlike into Nightshade's biceps. "Bite me," he coaxed. "You know you want to." He angled his head, loosening the silk cravat to expose his neck. "Renew our bond. It's been too long."

Pain lanced Nightshade's gums as he gritted his teeth to stop his canines from lengthening. The yearning for Tristan's blood rode him every minute of every day like an alcoholic's thirst for drink. He turned his head away as his stomach clenched with a mixture of hunger and nausea. He needed blood, but feeding on Tristan disgusted him.

Nightshade's only hope of forging a new blood bond was the pisky woman. Faking a conciliatory smile, he raised a hand to caress the dry skin of Tristan's cheek.

"I don't wish to feed now, master. Maybe later." He eased back and tried to sound indifferent. "Who is this pisky female, anyway?"

Fingering his cravat, Tristan sighed, then turned back to his work. "No one you know."

Frustration warred with Nightshade's need for composure. Silently, he counted to ten. "I knew all who lived with the Cornish troop."

Tristan struck a match and lit some fresh candles, then raised the baby rabbit to eye level and stroked its face. When he placed the carcass back on the bench, he gave Nightshade a sideways glance. "She was born shortly before we imprisoned the piskies."

Born thirty years ago? Surprise lanced him. The woman must be Ailla Tremain's child, Tristan's daughter, Rosenwyn. Nightshade stared into the golden candle flames licking the darkness. He shuddered at the memory of the little girl's screams, when day after day Tristan locked her in the dark and threatened to starve her unless Ailla finished the portraits.

"Rosenwyn," he whispered, and caught a flash of vicious anticipation in Tristan's eyes. He hoped Rosenwyn's mother had warned her about her father. "Why would your daughter come back after thirty years?"

"Who knows?" Tristan shrugged and started sliding his tools into their case. "It's good timing, though." With a sly smile he added, "I have plans for her."

Nightshade no longer wanted any part of Tristan's plans. He needed someone to feed on to replace Tristan, and if it couldn't be Ailla . . . Rosenwyn had been his friend when she was a child. Now that she was a woman, he'd make her much more.

For the first time in years, life held promise. Night-shade smiled to himself. After dusk fell, he'd go a-huntin' and catch himself a mate.

Niall strode down the short corridor to the pub's kitchen, pushed open the door, and paused on the threshold. Of all the irresponsible idiots . . . How could Michael have let himself get into so much debt that the bank would send a snoop to poke into the business and put Ana at risk of exposure?

Michael sat brooding at the pine table in the center of the room, cradling a mug of coffee between his hands. A woman unloading the dishwasher looked up and gave a tentative smile. There were always too many damn people about the place when he needed to speak to Michael privately. They'd have to take this little discussion outside.

"I believe you have something to tell me," he said as he grabbed a fistful of Michael's shirt, hauled him out of his seat, and shoved him toward the back door.

"Hey, watch the coffee, boyo," Michael grumbled as Niall propelled him outside into the sharp, clear autumn morning. Michael fussed with his shirt and shot Niall an irritated glance. "You got out of an empty bed again, I'll wager."

Niall grabbed a breath of cold air to calm himself, walked to the corner of the building, and then stared at the glassy surface of the river. "Sex is not the answer to every question."

Michael came up beside him and flashed a grin. "Naw. But get enough sex, and all those troublesome little questions float out of your mind entirely."

When would his brother grow up? With a resigned

sigh, Niall let go of his anger. He eased back against the wall. "Why did you not tell me you'd defaulted on the loan? You surely knew I'd help."

Michael shrugged, lit his cigarette, and blew a stream of blue smoke into the crisp morning air. " 'Tis always the same with you, Mr. High-and-Mighty-Everything-I-Touch-Turns-to-Bloody-Gold. You're always after being in control."

"How do you intend to rid us of the lass poking around in the office? 'Tis a genuine miracle if you know where your last three years' accounts are."

"Don't need them, boyo. Don't need them. I'm going to work a little magic on the lass. After a few nights in me bed, she won't give a jot for the accounts."

Niall stared at Michael incredulously. Was his brother really as stupid as he sounded? "Rose Tremain is not some starry-eyed tourist you can bounce on your bed and pack off home with a sparkle in her eye. Don't even think about using your glamour on her."

Michael stared at his feet and kicked a tuft of grass. "Truth be told, I gave the lass a taste when she first stepped foot in the place."

"Great Danu!" Niall pushed away from the wall and gripped Michael's arm. "Please tell me you weren't fool enough to take it too far?"

Michael looked at the glowing tip of his cigarette, then flicked it into the water. "I gave her the twinkle of me eye and nothing happened. That lass has a will of iron, to be sure."

That wasn't possible. Michael's glamour was infamous in the Irish fairy court. He could enthrall all humans and even weak fairies. "If Rose Tremain wasn't mesmerized, there has to be a reason. Either the lass knows you're of the Good People and protected herself with a charm, or she carries fairy blood. And I'll wager that woman is no fairy. We'd have sensed it." Niall tapped his fist against the wall. "Only one conclusion comes to mind: Ciar is behind this visit in some way. Aye, Rose Tremain is not to be trusted."

Michael made a derisive noise. "Is it sure you are?" He rolled his eyes heavenward. "Sweet bejesus, Niall. You see the Queen of Nightmares around every corner. Rose Tremain's nothing grander than a glorified bean counter in a boring blue suit with a boring, practical haircut."

Niall thought of the stately lass he'd seen in the office that morning, with moss green eyes and short auburn hair—practical, yes, boring, no. She had plenty of spark in her. Although when he considered the questions she'd asked, it was obvious Michael was right: she gave no indication she was anything more than an accountant.

Rose Tremain's visit might be innocent, but he couldn't risk the chance that she would rout out financial details about Hedgehog Cottage that would lead to his sister. "Whatever she is, I'm after getting rid of her as soon as possible. I don't want her finding out about Ana. If Ciar ever discovered where she is—"

"Saints in heaven preserve us!" Michael tossed down another cigarette butt and stamped it into the grass. " 'Tis always about Ana. You dragged me out of me beloved Ireland because of Ana."

"Ciar could easily have taken it into her head to hurt you as well. When I rejected her, her curses could have stripped the fur off a cat."

Michael stamped his foot like an angry child. "My queen would never hurt me. Anyway, Troy would not see me harmed."

The bitter taste of rejection rose like bile in Niall's throat. Troy might be their father, but from personal experience, Niall knew he would turn his back on them if it suited him.

"Ciar has probably long since forgotten you," Michael said. "What makes you think you're so fine a fellow she'll bother with you now you're gone?"

Niall didn't think he was fine or important. But he was certain Ciar's pride would prompt her to hunt him down and punish him for spurning her. No one turned down the fairy queen and survived unscathed. And if Niall wasn't available, Ciar had left him in no doubt that she'd delight in hurting those he loved.

Niall straightened his cuffs to ensure that his knives were concealed. "Here's what's going to happen. I'll transfer enough money to pay off your loan. Then I'll take a ride to Lostwithiel and fetch accounting copies from Radcliffs. That should be enough to satisfy Rose Tremain, if the lass is genuine."

Niall grasped his brother's shoulder. "While I'm gone, be mindful of how you answer her questions. Don't go telling her about me computer, nor that I gave you the Porsche. If she asks about the money I've paid into the business, tell the lass to speak to me when I get back."

Michael frowned. "What money might that be?"

Niall resisted the urge to shake his brother; it wasn't Michael's fault he'd been mollycoddled. Sometimes Niall thought his father had done him a favor when he'd abandoned him. "No matter. Tell you what: don't answer any questions. When I get back from me jaunt, I'll speak with her."

After striding into the kitchen, Niall made a quick phone call to transfer money, and then fetched his helmet and jacket. He'd stop briefly at Hedgehog Cottage to check on Ana, then go to Lostwithiel. He glanced at the clock above the fridge. If he got the accounts to Rose Tremain by lunchtime, then gave her a hand in the afternoon, they should be rid of her by evening.

Rose froze beside her car in the parking lot, the packet of mints she'd come to fetch clutched against her chest. Her mind was buzzing with the snatches of Niall and Michael's conversation that the breeze had carried from behind the pub. With his own words, Niall O'Connor had confirmed that he was hiding facts from her. Where did he get his money? Why was he hiding it? Maybe he was a criminal on the run. He did have an air of danger about him. She shivered with a mixture of fear and fascination.

Michael had told her the truth last night. Niall owned a computer, and he didn't want her to check it. Part of her wanted to confront him, but direct confrontation might not be the most effective tactic, especially when she wasn't sure of her facts. She rubbed at a spot of tension in her neck. If she checked his computer, she'd have a better idea what she was dealing with.

What if she discovered he was on the wrong side of the law? Rose glanced at the back corner of the pub. A chill trickled down her spine. She'd just have to contact the police.

After closing her car door quietly, she thumbed the remote lock on her key and returned to the office. Next, she had to find Niall's computer. As if thinking of the man conjured him up, the roar of his motorcycle engine outside rattled the office window.

She checked her watch. The round trip to Lostwithiel

and a visit to the accountant shouldn't take him longer than an hour. There was no time to waste.

With notebook in hand, she headed through the reception hall and climbed two flights of stairs to the swing door marked, PRIVATE. She knocked, hoping Michael was busy downstairs. After thirty seconds with no response, she pushed open the door and called his name. Her heart beat a dull thud in her ears as she listened to the silence.

Rose crept up the steps to the top floor, then gazed down the hallway. Four doors stood ajar, two on either side. The first two led into a small sitting room and a bathroom, respectively. A stifling cocktail of women's perfumes and cigarettes emanated from the third room. She wrinkled her nose and risked a peek. Black satin sheets and a gold headboard made her think of a bordello—so probably Michael's bedroom. She closed the door and headed for the fourth room.

Panic pulsed in her throat as she eased the door open. Although she knew Niall was out, her hand trembled on the knob. This wasn't her usual modus operandi. But then, Niall O'Connor wasn't the usual type of client.

Drawing a deep breath, she willed herself to be calm. The room was plain and reasonably tidy. No clothes lay on the tan carpet, and the bed was neatly covered with a navy bedspread. "Bingo," she whispered at the sight of the laptop computer on the pine desk beneath the window on the far side of the bed.

After a glance at her watch, she took a seat and twitched the mouse to bring the screen to life. A password request flashed up. Rose tapped her nails on the desk. She should have expected Niall to be security-conscious. Now she was stumped.

On impulse, she typed in *Elephant's Nest* and hit enter. When that didn't work, she tried *Niall O'Connor* backward, then a few name combinations without success.

Frustrated, she fluffed her hair and glanced around for inspiration. Wintry sun glittered off the top of a small wooden box on the windowsill. *Pick it up*, a voice said in her head. Trusting her intuition, she did so. The top was decorated with a silver shield bearing the heraldic symbols of an oak tree and two lions. Beneath the coat of arms an inscription read, *O Dhia gach an cabhair*.

An instinct she'd learned to trust as a child made her type the phrase. A picture opened of a strange brown-skinned child by a thatched cottage. Rose squinted at the screen. The building appeared to be scaled down to fit the child, like an elaborate playhouse. After puzzling over the image for a few seconds, she dismissed it and checked the list of programs. There was no accounting software.

"Darn," she whispered to herself. She checked Excel and found a spreadsheet that purported to show payments Niall had made to the Elephant's Nest. Some were rent, but a number of large amounts were described as Hedgehog Cottage expenses. Could this be a money-laundering scam? Rose looked over her shoulder at the door, bit her lip, and hit print.

Her heart pounded in time with the click of the printer, until the machine spit out three sheets of paper and fell silent. She jammed the sheets into her notebook and pressed a hand to her heart. She was fast realizing she was not cut out for sleuthing.

A quick glance at the open windows minimized at the bottom of the screen revealed an online stockbroking service. That must be how he made his money—at least, she hoped so. Although there was something scary about Niall O'Connor, he fascinated her. She'd be disappointed to discover he was a crook.

She hadn't found much, but at least the printout gave her a starting point for her questions. After setting the computer to standby, she tucked the notebook beneath her arm, then picked up the wooden box to return it to the windowsill. Tingles ran across her skin. She blinked, trying to clear her mind as drowsiness tugged down her eyelids. A dreamy sensation fluttered through her mind, whispering of secrets and dark delights.

She must put the box down. And she would in a minute, when she could summon the strength to place it back on . . . A wave of heat shimmered up through her body. *Oh, God.* She dropped back onto the seat. What on earth did Niall keep in the box? With trembling fingers, she eased up the lid.

Rose's breath caught. Three small linked circles of pale stone nestled in black velvet. The strange jewelry was similar to the piece her mother had given her when she was a child. She touched her chest and felt the earthy brown stones she always wore underneath her blouse. Her mother had told her never to take the stone pendant off. Obviously, nobody had given Niall the same advice.

"Niall." Her voice quavered on his name. The urge to touch his stones filled her with sharp longing. "Get a grip, woman." Rose tried to drag her gaze away.

She blinked and shook her head. How long had she been in the room? All she had to do was close the lid and place the box back on the windowsill. Her fingertip slipped into the box, grazed across the top stone.

Everything smoothed out inside her; worries drifted away. Between her breasts, the stone pendent she'd worn against her heart all her life resonated with the elemental beat of the stones beneath her fingers. Her eyelids lowered, and she toppled down, down into a place of dark, hazy pleasure.

Chapter Three

Wind rustled the last dry leaves clinging to the oak trees around Hedgehog Cottage. Niall knelt on the damp earth before his tiny half sister and pushed her dark curls behind her ears. She shook her head and the wiry twists of hair bounced free around her nut-brown face.

"Are you sure there's nothing you're wanting?" he asked.

She studied him with large brown eyes and shook her head. "You and me, lad, we don't need much."

"Aye, that's for sure. But I like to get you things, Ana. You must indulge me fancy to spoil you on occasion."

She clutched the sheepskin collar of his jacket, pulled him forward, and kissed his cheek. He breathed in the fragrance of newly baked bread that clung to her clothes and his sister's earthy scent—familiar since she'd tended him as a babe. He gathered her chunky little body in his arms and closed his eyes. It was his turn to care for her now. Instead, he'd put her in danger by rebuffing Ciar and bringing her vengeance down on Ana. He should have let the fairy queen have her way with him. He'd suffered worse indignities.

Ana pulled away and patted his cheek with a small, warm hand. "Don't you go worrying about me, darling boy. Take a leaf out of your brother's book and go have yourself a good time."

Niall's guilty heart ached as she crouched, placed her palm on the damp soil, and whispered a leprechaun earth-magic blessing for him. A wrinkle of power shivered up through his knees.

She grinned. "Be off with you now, lad, and let me get back to me baking."

He stood, reluctant to leave. "Look after yourself, Ana."

She flapped her hand dismissively. "A worrywart you are, and no mistake. Begone."

Niall mounted his bike, pulled on his helmet, and raised a hand in farewell when he left the clearing in front of Hedgehog Cottage. As he maneuvered along the narrow track hidden among the trees, he glanced toward the Elephant's Nest just visible through the bare branches two hundred yards to his left.

A stunning jolt of pleasure swept through him. His heart pounded. Blood flashed. All strength left his body. The bike slewed over on the wet track, throwing him into the dirt. The roar of the engine sputtered, died. He lay on the soft leaf litter, panting with shock as he tried to clear the fuzziness from his mind.

After a few seconds, he flipped up the visor on his helmet, dragged in a shuddering breath, and stared at the gently swaying branches. What in the Furies had just happened?

He sat up and brushed the dead leaves and mud from his clothes. His whole body hummed with awareness. A subtle thread of connection pulled at his mind. He looked around, confused. Someone was messing with him psychically. Fear pricked. Maybe one of Ciar's people had found him or—

"Dagda!" Realization hit like a punch in the gut. Someone had touched his Magic Knot. If the person broke it, Niall's mind, body, and spirit would be rent asunder, each to flounder alone in the shadowy in-between world. Such a punishment would appeal to Ciar.

Niall surged to his feet, ignoring the sick swell of nausea in his gut, and sprinted through the trees toward the Elephant's Nest.

After racing through the front door, he mounted the stairs two at a time. The humming in his head befuddled him as though he'd drunk one tot of whiskey too many. He grabbed the handrail on the second-floor landing to steady himself before he yanked open the swinging door to the private flat and climbed the last stairs.

His bedroom door stood wide. As he approached, he flexed his fingers, ready to palm a knife. He hesitated for a heartbeat, then stepped into the open doorway.

Rose Tremain sat on the chair before his desk, his Magic Knot cradled in her palm. She swayed slightly, her eyes dazed and dreamy. His nerves sparked. Need for her struck like lightning. He managed to suck in air, to ruthlessly crush the feeling until his body calmed.

So, he had been right: Rose Tremain was more dangerous than she appeared. She'd been sent to enslave him by capturing his stones. If she thought he'd give in easily, she had another think coming.

Silently, he walked forward and closed his hand over hers. His vision blurred at the whip of sensation. Too late, he realized his mistake in touching her. Gritting his teeth, he fought the mental pull as she sucked his very essence through their joined hands into a deep, hidden part of her that whispered of ancient magic and mystery.

Niall snatched up his Magic Knot and stumbled back. His breath came in short gasps as he stared at her in shock. Rose was the Cornish pisky Tristan wanted. How had she stopped them from sensing the truth about her? That deception alone proved she was up to no good.

Slowly, her green eyes focused on him. Confusion set tiny creases between her delicate brows; then surprise chased them away. She slapped a hand over her mouth.

"Aye, be afraid, little thief," he whispered. "You'll pay dearly for your deception before I'm done with you."

"Oh, my God." Rose stared at the flinty expression in Niall's eyes, then down at her empty palm. She clenched her fist and pressed it against her pounding heart. How the hell had she let him catch her?

"I didn't mean . . . I'm sorry." There was no adequate way to apologize. Most of the time, she thought of her own stones as nothing more than peculiar jewelry, but she hated people touching them. "I saw the box and . . . I know it sounds daft, but it's as if they called to me."

Niall's features hardened. "Don't be thinking you'll bind me to you, lass. I'm stronger than Ciar imagines."

"Ciar?" Rose shook her head. "Who's Ciar? I don't know what you mean. I came up here for . . ." She glanced at his laptop, her memory fuzzy. She'd checked out his computer . . . then what? Had she found anything?

41

"Go on." He crossed his arms. "Let's hear your excuses."

"You lied to me about there being no computer—"

"No, lass. You didn't listen properly. I told you Michael didn't have a computer."

Rose felt her dander rise at his condescending tone. She had *not* misunderstood what she'd overheard him say in the parking lot. "Semantics. It doesn't matter who owns the computer. If the machine's used in the business, I need access."

"And did you find anything useful with your prying?"

"In the course of undertaking a *legitimate investigation*, I checked for accounting software and looked at Excel."

"Legitimate." He laughed, but there was no humor in the sound. "So tell me, what incriminating evidence did you find?"

His eyes gleamed coldly fierce. Now was not the time to confront him about the spreadsheet. She stood, retrieved her notebook from his desk and twisted it between her hands. "We'll discuss my findings when I've had longer to investigate the pub finances. Now I need to get on with it."

Niall turned, dropped his stones into the box, and put it back on the windowsill. Rose took the opportunity to try to sidle between him and the bed to reach the door.

With a casual stride, he widened his stance to block her escape route. Rose jumped back, notebook clutched to her chest like a shield.

He fixed her with an implacable stare. " 'Tis time to cut to the chase. Who sent you?"

"Who sent me?" She backed up another step. "Didn't you read the card I gave you this morning?"

He became inhumanly still, his face an unreadable mask more unnerving than anger. "Cut the crap. Who really sent you? Queen Ciar?"

"Queen Ciar?" Rose repeated the name in an incredulous whisper. What was he involved in, an international crime ring? Did someone have a contract out on him? That would explain why he hid the fact that he had money. Fear slithered through her, and she edged farther back. "I don't know what sort of trouble you're in, but it's nothing to do with me. I'm from Francis Marchant."

"Lies." He jerked a thumb toward the box containing his stones. "You know full well the Knot revealed who you are and why you're here. Drop the innocent act, lass, and answer me questions. Otherwise I'll have to make you talk." His expression hardened, and he took a step closer.

Rose threw up a hand to stop him and backed into the nightstand. "I'm warning you: I know self-defense."

He flexed his hands at his sides like a man about to draw a gun. Fear sent adrenaline spurting through her, setting every sense on high alert. She must get away. Niall O'Connor was dangerous. Her colleagues weren't expecting her back in the office until the following week. If he hurt her, no one would miss her until it was too late.

Instinctive self-preservation cut in. She glanced across his bed and leaped onto the mattress heading for the door. The second she moved, he came after her. His fingers closed around her ankles. With a yank, he dragged her legs from under her and flipped her onto her back. She crashed down on the mattress, the air knocked from her lungs. The back of her head thumped the pillow with a whack that sent stars spiraling across her vision.

Faster than seemed possible, his body landed on hers, pinning her to the bed. After a moment of shock, she dropped her notebook and slapped at his face and shoulders. He caught her wrists easily and cuffed them above her head in one hand. Bucking and twisting, she tried to knee him in the groin and dislodge him. He didn't budge. Solid and unyielding, the hard length of his body pressed hers against the mattress.

Finally, lungs aching, Rose stilled with exhaustion. She squeezed her eyes closed and turned her face away. A mix of anger and fear burned inside her. What would he do? "Let . . . me . . . up," she said in a gasp.

He didn't speak, didn't move. His hot breath brushed her cheek. The fragrance of the woods, earth, and fresh air filled her nose. Gradually, Rose became aware of every place his body touched hers, especially the hand-span of hard male flesh crushed against her pubic bone. Beneath her skin, tingling nerves awakened and thrummed to life. Her breath caught halfway in. She snapped open her eyes and stared at the wall. Her hormones had to be kidding.

The woodsy scent of him slithered through her like a drug. A sparking ball of lust tangled with the fear in her belly. Slowly she turned her head on the pillow to face him. Derision shimmered in his vivid blue eyes, his beautiful face etched in uncompromising lines by the wintry sun filtering through the window.

"Get off me," she ground out, and tried to yank her hands free. Their eyes locked for one scorching beat. Rose blinked and snatched a breath. "If you'd damned well cooperated, I wouldn't have needed to come up here."

He arched a brow and stared at her challengingly. She stared right back, something inside her feeding on the confrontation.

"If you'd had the patience to wait an hour, I'd have fetched the accounts," he said in a tight voice. "But that's not your true business with us, is it? Who sent you, Rose Tremain?"

Rose glanced away and cursed under her breath, then met his gaze again. "Don't you understand English? Watch my lips. Francis Marchant."

At her command, his gaze shifted to her mouth. His eyes narrowed to burning blue slits. Suddenly Rose couldn't get enough air. Time paused between heartbeats. Niall flexed his hips against her, lowered his face, and parted his lips, then sighed and shook his head. "You've not the faintest idea what I'm speaking of, lass, have you?"

Angry with him for thinking about kissing her and, inexplicably, even angrier because he hadn't followed through, she jerked on her wrists. "Let go. And stop poking me with your hard-on."

His eyes widened; then he released her and leaped back off the bed. Stunned at the speed and impossibility of his move, she lay staring up at him like a fool for a few seconds before she got her brain in gear. After grabbing her notebook, she scrambled off the bed. Breathless, hot, and shaky, she staggered toward the door and caught hold of the doorframe.

Hesitating, she glanced back, her heart skittering as she scanned the hard male body that had so recently been pressed against her. She covered her face with her notebook to hide a slightly hysterical grin. It appeared the old wives' tale was true. Niall's long, sexy fingers did indeed indicate how another part measured up.

He shifted uncomfortably beneath her scrutiny. "Me reaction means nothing. Friction is all it was, right enough. Aye, friction."

The heat in her belly cooled and she averted her gaze. He probably didn't think she was pretty enough for him because he was so damn perfect.

As she turned to leave, the glint of silver decorating the top of Niall's box caught her eye. A shimmer of re-membered pleasure swept across her skin and hummed through the stone pendant nestled between her breasts. Whether Niall liked it or not, something very strange had just happened between them.

Niall stared at the photo of Ana on his computer screen and closed his eyes against a dark rush of guilt. Rose must have seen the picture. He hoped her knowl-edge wouldn't put his little leprechaun sister at risk of discovery.

Although Rose must be the Cornish pisky Tristan wanted, she obviously thought she was human. The fairy part of her was buried so deeply, Niall would never have sensed it if she hadn't touched his Magic Knot.

He glanced at the rumpled bed and remembered the soft heat of her body. Now that she'd touched his stones, the two of them were linked by a spirit bond normally shared only by lovers. Intimate parts of him throbbed in memory, craving physical connection to complete the union. Thank Danu he had fought the desire to kiss her. The last thing he needed was to get involved with Rose and make her a target for Ciar's revenge. He had his hands full protecting Ana.

Niall touched the picture of his sister's beautiful, wrinkled brown face. To keep her safe, Tristan must recast the spell of protection over Ana in the next few days. That meant Niall had no choice but to take Rose to the druid to ensure his cooperation.

He ground his teeth. He'd rather avoid involving Rose in his problems. She wasn't looking for fairies. Left alone, she'd return to London none the wiser and live out the rest of her life as a human.

Maybe if he explained the situation to Tristan . . . He reached for the phone, but paused as he remembered the crafty gleam in the druid's eyes when he'd heard about the pisky woman. Had the Cornish piskies really emigrated to America? Desperate for the druid's help, he'd accepted that explanation without question. Now he wasn't so sure.

Tomorrow he'd ride over to visit Tristan and explain that Rose thought she was human and knew nothing of the Good People. Niall sat back, opened his Internet stockbroking service, and watched the share values scroll across the screen. Tristan Jago was a greedy man. Surely he wouldn't jeopardize the regular checks Niall paid him by refusing to cast the protection spell?

As evening approached, Rose ran down the stairs from her room at the Elephant's Nest humming. Just when she'd been ready to tear out her hair with frustration at trying to make sense of the business records, the senior partner from her firm had rung. Michael's loan had been cleared and the investigation called off. The King of Pentacles had spoken true. Whatever Niall was involved in, he had money and connections.

But she didn't want to think about him. One more night at the pub, and she'd be on her way to find her father.

When she jumped off the last stair into the hallway, Michael stepped out from behind the reception desk. He slid his eyes down her body as though he were imagining sliding her into his bed. Typical. Michael had been conspicuously absent when she wanted to question him. As soon as she changed into Lycra shorts and a sports bra, he miraculously appeared.

"Well, well." He ambled up and waggled his eyebrows. "What a grand little body you were hiding beneath that sober suit."

His attraction dragged at her. Rose stilled, clinging to her common sense. As he stepped closer and the smell of his aftershave wafted around, she noted the thud of her heart. Interesting: he affected her physically, but mentally she remained detached.

He moved closer, lips tilted into an appealingly wicked grin, and brushed his fingertips down her arm. "How about you and me celebrate my reprieve after I close up, darlin'? Me room's on the top floor."

"I know," she said innocently, trying for a straight face and nearly making it. "The black-and-gold one, right? I saw it earlier when I was up there with Niall."

"Niall?" Michael's perfect, dark, winged eyebrows scrunched together. "What were you doing up in the flat with me brother?"

"Nothing you need to know about." She patted him on the cheek. "I promise you, *darlin'*, I'm not your type."

"Aye, that's as may be. But are you me brother's is what I'm asking meself."

Rose turned away from the sudden flash of curiosity in Michael's eyes. She attempted a casual shrug, but it came out as a nervous jerk.

The memory of Niall's body pressed against hers

had plagued her all afternoon. Rose halted and rubbed her temples. She could feel him close by. *Darn.* Why was she so sensitive to him?

She stomped out the door, halted beside the low wall that divided the parking lot from the riverbank, and started stretching out her muscles. Forget Niall. Forget Michael. She stared into the dark water swirling against the reeds and planned the first steps she'd take to locate her father. She had five days to find him. Five days to make sense of her life.

Bending forward, she grabbed her ankles and stretched the backs of her thighs. As she stared at the pub between her legs, Niall strolled around the corner and stopped beside his bike, staring at her backside.

Rose straightened so fast the blood rushed out of her head, leaving it spinning. "Heck. You gave me a scare creeping up like that."

He gazed at her for a moment, then pulled an oily rag from his pocket and turned to his bike. "If that's what you call creeping, lass, you're deaf."

Rose finished her stretches, watching him out of the corner of her eye to check whether he looked at her. He didn't. *Damn Niall O'Connor.* She jogged toward him, slapping her arms to warm up. He knelt in the dirt next to his bike, unscrewed a metal ring from the engine, and rested it on a rock.

"I wanted to ask you about your stone rings." However hard she tried, Rose couldn't stop thinking about how weird she'd felt when she touched them. And it was too much of a coincidence that they both had them. "What are they?"

He gave her a shuttered glance and shrugged. "A knickknack. Nothing more."

She didn't believe that for a moment. How could she

make him open up? On inspiration, she hooked her finger in the chain around her neck, pulled her three linked stones out, and cradled them in her palm. "I don't like anyone touching mine, either." Normally she kept them hidden. But with Niall it was different, as though they shared a secret.

Niall glanced up from his task, his eyes wary. He dropped the rag and slowly rose to his feet. When he stared down at her stones, his eyes flashed with heat, then blanked.

"Don't be foolish, lass," he said, his voice strained. "Keep them hidden."

The tang of engine oil blended with the woodsy scent of him. She tried to ignore the flush of her skin as she remembered the weight of his body on top of her. "Mother advised me to wear them. Weren't you told the same?"

He turned, crunching the gravel beneath his boots, and went back to his bike. "Mine live in their box." His curt tone suggested the discussion was over.

Rose fluffed her hair in frustration. Maybe she should just forget the stones and concentrate on what she'd come for. "Listen, you seem to know all the right people; maybe you can help me. I want to track down my father. I don't have an address, but I've got a name. . . ." She faltered, suddenly uneasy. After all the years of planning, she finally had a chance to find her father. Why was she hesitating? She shook away the feeling of foreboding. "He's called Tristan Jago. Ever heard the name?"

Niall's hands stilled their fiddling for a moment; then he shook his head without looking up. "Doesn't ring any bells." He hunched closer to the engine, and she got the message loud and clear. As far as he was concerned, their conversation was over.

"Fine. Never mind. I'm going to Truro tomorrow to check the electoral roll. Hopefully . . ." She stared at the back of his head. What was the point in wasting her breath? He wasn't interested. "Well . . . I'm off for my run."

Rose jogged away along the riverside path and didn't let herself look back. After she left tomorrow, she would never see Niall again. What did it matter if he wasn't interested in her? The only thing they had in common was the wretched stones. And that was probably a coincidence.

She found her rhythm, enjoying the satisfying slap of her feet and the building tension of muscle. The chill evening air invigorated her body, and the gentle swish of the river calmed her mind. When she returned to the pub, she'd read the tarot cards and ask questions about her father. She'd put off the reading for long enough. Rose had never been like her mother; she'd always felt her father must be the key to her identity.

Rose glanced around. Dusk spread dark, misty fingers beneath the overhanging branches of the woodland. The river glowed, a ribbon of moonbeams beside the path. Deep peace filled a hollow place inside her that she hadn't noticed was empty.

After a couple of miles, Rose stopped where the path climbed away from the river into the trees. Night came faster in the country, and she didn't want to be running beside water in the pitch-black. Retracing her steps, she rehearsed what to say when she introduced herself to her father.

Would he look like her? Rose hadn't resembled her

mother, who was extraordinarily beautiful until drugs and alcohol ravaged her looks.

With a startled squawk, a bird shot out of the woods before her. Shock stabbed her chest. Silly. It was nothing. No doubt she was far safer here than pounding the streets in London, and yet . . .

The fragrance of almonds drifted incongruously on the cool autumn air, raising the tiny hairs on her body. Rose increased her pace. She forgot about finding her father. With every scrap of awareness focused on the path, she watched for the welcoming lights of the pub.

Beside the path, a whip crack of sound reverberated through the thick darkness beneath the trees. Deep, primeval fear shot through her. She slowed, scanned the blackness wildly. Looking for something. Hoping for nothing. A patch of shadow detached itself from a tree trunk and moved toward her. Dragging her gaze away, she sprinted forward, muscles burning. The pub must be close. Would Niall still be outside? Would he hear if she shouted?

Sticky warmth brushed her shoulder. Rose screamed, ducked her head, spun around, flailed her arms. The track behind her stretched away quiet and empty. *I'm going mad.*

Gulping three deep breaths, she struggled to ground herself. "Calm down, woman. *Calm down.*" This was her mother's fault, spooking her about Cornwall, making her imagine things. Rose flexed her shoulders, forcing herself to stand still and face the murky woodland to prove she wasn't scared. She counted to three in her head, then moved forward, recovered her rhythm, and ran on toward the pub. "There's nothing there, nothing there," she chanted under her breath.

A sudden blast of air made her duck and throw her

arms over her head. A monstrous black beast hung in the sky, blotting out the pale hook of the moon. Cold air sliced her throat as she gasped. Gagging on the cloying fragrance of almonds, she staggered back. Her shoe sank in wet mud. Arms wheeling, she scrambled to catch her balance.

The beast swooped down. Strong arms pulled her against a warm, oil-slicked chest. Rose screamed and battered the taut muscular arms circling her.

His long hair fluttered against her face in the draft from his wing beats. Rose gulped and tried to shout for help. Nothing came out but a terrified whimper.

He pressed his cheek to hers. Lips brushed her ear. "Welcome back, Rosenwyn," a deep, gravelly voice whispered. "Remember me, sweet one? I remember you."

The madness of fear gave Rose strength. As the devil man lifted her from the ground, she pounded with her fists, jabbed with her elbows.

"Shh, my love, don't panic," the dark voice crooned hot against her ear as he caught her arms to her sides. "I'm not going to hurt you. I've come to take you home."

Home! Where was home—hell? Through the black, mind-numbing wash of terror one word of hope burned: *Niall*. She wasn't sure if she screamed his name out loud or only in her thoughts, but somehow she sensed Niall's startled response—his catch of breath and jolt of heart—as if they were her own.

Niall was her only chance.

Chapter Four

How could Rose be Tristan's daughter?

Niall sat on the low wall beside the pub and stared at his bike as he pondered what he'd learned.

Now she planned to stay until she found her father. So much for his hope that if he paid off Michael's loan she'd leave. How could Niall maintain his calm when every cell in his body was attuned to her? The only way to weaken the bond was physical distance. And the quickest way to achieve that was to introduce her to Tristan. One look at the decrepit druid and Rose would hightail it back to London.

Unable to resist the draw of an intimacy he'd never expected to experience, he closed his eyes and opened his senses to Rose. She twanged the invisible thread joining them with little flashes of emotion that tingled around the periphery of his awareness. A yearning for physical contact burned in his belly, the intimate spiritual bond more addictive than a drug and just as deadly. However much he wanted Rose, he must not give in to the desire. If Ciar discovered their relationship, she'd harm Rose to punish him.

He smiled as he sensed the emotions flowing from

her thoughts: pleasure, satisfaction, curiosity, anticipation, then a jolt—a burn of fear. Niall snapped his eyes open and stared sightlessly as he concentrated on Rose. The fear subsided; the heat faded. Niall relaxed a notch. Then her terror flared so hotly, he clutched his head in pain as her voice reverberated inside his skull, screaming his name.

"Rose," he hissed in an agonized whisper as he struggled to regain control.

He surged to his feet and sprinted away from the pub on the path she'd taken. Maybe Ciar had already discovered his bond with Rose and sent shade warriors to frighten her. Shades he could handle. With their bodies left so far away in Ireland, the shadows would be weak.

He might not be able to acknowledge his bond with Rose, but he would give her his strength and his protection.

Rose peered over her abductor's arm to the rapidly retreating safety of solid ground below. Hope flashed as she saw Niall sprinting toward them along the path, limned by moonlight, his face inhumanly perfect and determined.

She tried to shout his name. But the devil man tightened his grip around her chest and beat his wings. They were too high. Niall would never reach her.

He leaped with the grace of a stag, long, lean muscles extended to the limit, defying gravity. His fingers locked around her ankle. Her body ached, bone and muscle stretched to the breaking point as both men hung onto her. Then the arm around her chest slipped.

A scream ripped from her throat as she plummeted down. Rose tensed, ready for a jarring impact, but

Niall swung around and caught her against his body. While her head was still spinning, he gently deposited her in a heap of musty leaf litter.

As soon as she gathered her wits, Rose scrambled backward until her head hit a tree. She huddled against the rough bark, clutching her knees.

Niall positioned himself between her and the winged man, his stance wide, combative. Although common sense screamed at her to run, the tremors of shock in her muscles robbed her of the strength to do so. She couldn't take her eyes off Niall, his lithe body tense, ready to defend her. With a flick of his wrists a gleaming blade appeared in each of his hands. The edges of reality blurred.

Her would-be abductor beat large black wings and lowered himself to the ground, head bowed, arms crossed over his chest like a fallen angel. He touched down on the toes of one foot with the grace of a ballet dancer and raised glowing silver eyes.

"She belongs with me," the dark angel said. His voice was deep, resonant . . . frighteningly familiar.

Rose pressed her forehead against her knees and rubbed her temples. A door to the past cracked open in her mind. Memories of childhood stirred like dust in a tomb. She remembered sobbing against the winged man's chest as he rocked her in his arms.

"No way!" Niall's firm reply pierced her thoughts. "Leave her be, Nightshade. She has no knowledge of the Good People."

Niall was acquainted with this devil man . . . Nightshade? And who were *these good people*?

Nightshade faced her, eyes narrowed to glittering silver slits. His wings snapped closed against his back;

then he took a step forward. "Rosenwyn," he demanded, "you remember nothing about me?"

Rose shook her head in denial. Nightshade knew her *real* name. No one had ever called her Rosenwyn except her mother. Rose's carefully cultivated normal world fractured, and flashes of childhood memory escaped. *Mother singing and dancing with strange people. The drowsy scent of fragrant candles. Alone in the dark. So alone . . . until . . . Nightshade came for her.*

She pressed her hands over her face and shook her head to clear the images. *I'm a senior manager with Francis Marchant.* Fear was making her imagine things—that was all.

Niall stood watching intently as Nightshade approached her. She groped among the fallen leaves for something to use as a weapon. Her fingers closed around a broken branch. Pushing herself up on shaky legs, she held it out, but strangely, her heart wasn't in the threat. "Keep away. I . . . I'm sure I don't know you."

She expected him to react angrily or, if she was lucky, fall back at her threat. She wasn't prepared for the flash of hurt in his eyes before he dropped his head and hid his face behind the veil of dark hair. With his wings folded and invisible from the front, Nightshade resembled an ordinary man. An extraordinarily beautiful man, his ebony skin sculpted into perfect curves and hollows by the moonlight.

Slouching off, Nightshade beckoned Niall, then halted a short distance away beside the river. She could just make out the shadowy outline of Nightshade's wings folded against his back as the two men spoke. *His wings are soft.* She remembered the feel of running her hand over them. Tickling him?

Oh, God. She stared into the shadows beneath the trees, and the branch dropped from her fingers. Nightshade had said he wanted to take her home. The only home she could ever have had in Cornwall was with her father.

All her life she'd believed her mother was the weird one—her father was supposed to be her anchor to normality. Rubbing her arms against the cold, she summoned her self-control. It didn't matter. If she didn't like the truth about her father, she had her career, her life in London.

Rose ignored the creeping chill of disillusionment and channeled it into annoyance. What were the men talking about? She reached out her senses to Niall as she did to her tarot people, but felt nothing. Had she imagined the connection with him earlier? Well, she'd learned one thing from doing her job: the best way to get answers was to ask.

With a determined stride, she walked toward the men. They glanced up and fell silent as she approached. "Nightshade." His name felt awkward in her mouth, like a foreign word. "I've come to Cornwall to find my father." She paused and swallowed. "Do you know a man called Tristan Jago?"

Nightshade grimaced, and the two men shared a meaningful glance. Denial whirled inside Rose's head as Nightshade flicked back his hair and tilted his chin defiantly. "I do."

Shock jolted her body. His terse reply left no room for doubt, no room for hope. She had to face facts. If her father was involved with Nightshade, he wasn't the normal dad she'd built her childhood fantasies around.

Out of the corner of her eye, she saw Niall slip his

knives inside the cuffs of his shirt. He'd been mighty quick to come to her rescue, almost as though he'd expected trouble. He knew Nightshade, and he'd obviously lied to her about not knowing Tristan Jago. Add that to his deceit over the pub accounts and she didn't trust him as far as she could throw him.

In the moonlight, she glanced from one man's evasive expression to the other and anger fired her determination. This was no different from an insolvency investigation. If she wanted to root out the truth, she'd have to be firm. "I'd like to talk to you both back at the pub. I'm freezing my butt off out here, and I've got questions about my father. After putting me through this"—she plucked at her ripped, dirty shorts—"I think you both owe me some answers."

The look of surprise the two men exchanged before they pasted on emotionless expressions gave her a shot of satisfaction that boosted her resolve.

On weary legs, she made her way back toward the pub, acutely aware of the two men at her back. Niall carried knives up his sleeves, and Nightshade had wings and silver eyes. *Shit!* The hairs on the back of her neck prickled and she fought the overwhelming urge to look around.

Now that she'd gotten their measure, she wouldn't let them intimidate her again. Difficult situations had never beaten her before. She would get one of these two men to answer her questions about her father. Rose just prayed they were answers she wanted to hear.

Feeling more composed after a ten-minute walk, Rose went through the back door into the Elephant's Nest kitchen. Michael was leaning against the counter dressed in skintight scarlet silk pants, a multicolored shirt, and a pixie hat with a tassel and bell on the end. He held a cigarette in one hand and a glass of amber liquid in the other.

He looked like an X-rated Santa's elf.

Rose smiled and some of her tension fell away. Winking, he held up his glass. "Want one, darlin'?" He glanced at Nightshade hovering in the doorway behind Niall. "You've had a shock, I'll wager."

She nodded. "I usually steer clear of alcohol, but tonight you can make mine a double and stick a little parasol in it."

Michael filled a tumbler, strolled over, and pressed it into her hand. He clinked his glass against hers. "*Sláinte.*" This time the look in his eyes only warmed her. Odd that she had become immune to his attraction just when she was starting to like him.

Niall walked up and raked his gaze over Michael, and a muscle jerked in his cheek. "Who you got working tonight?"

Michael grinned, mischief bright in his vivid blue eyes. "The lovely Marie. She's out front now stocking the bar. Me fans will soon be arriving to hear more tall tales."

Niall sighed as though the worries of the world weighed on his shoulders. He crossed to the door into the hall and locked it. "The nightstalker cannot stay long," he said, glancing toward Rose. "Marie will need to use the kitchen."

At Niall's signal, the extraordinary dark angel sauntered into the brightly lit kitchen. Rose tried not to stare. She didn't know whether to think of him as man or beast. Niall had called him a nightstalker, whatever that was. He was over six feet of well-packed muscle, with everything above the waistband of his jeans on display. Her gaze trailed up and down his body; then she cleared her throat and looked away. *Definitely all man.*

In her peripheral vision she caught Niall watching her, eyes narrowed, mouth tight. She sensed him like heat, warming the edges of her mind. He averted his gaze, straightened his cuffs, and the heat faded, leaving her cold.

So, she hadn't imagined the link with Niall. After years sensing only her tarot people, why the sudden connection with Niall?

Michael tilted his glass at Nightshade and gave him a cheeky grin. "Come join us in the bar. Tonight I'll reveal one of the secrets of the fairies." He sucked on his cigarette and blew a perfect smoke ring. "'Tis a tale about a nightstalker who creeps around watching lasses in their underdrawers. I'm thinking you'll add some spice to the telling."

Nightshade raised his chin. "Don't mock me, bard, or I'll crush your scrawny neck."

Michael shrugged innocently. "What's biting him?"

"For Dagda's sake." Niall stared at Michael, frustration shimmering in his eyes. "Don't tread on his toes. We have little enough time as it is."

Nightshade folded his arms and leaned against the door frame. "I believe Rosenwyn wished to ask *me* some questions."

Under the fluorescent light, his silver eyes gleamed, and his black hair slid over his shoulders like ebony water. Rose tried to suppress the little frisson of excitement that buzzed through her every time she looked at him. Any normal person would be running in the opposite direction screaming.

Gradually she became aware of the heavy silence

and glanced at Niall and Michael. They were both watching her: Niall with his mouth set in a tight line of disapproval, Michael with an indignant pout. Michael clicked his tongue. "Now, why does she not look at me that way? I have the glamour."

Niall rounded on Michael. "Button your lip. We're not here to stroke your ego." Niall turned back to Rose, eyes veiled. "If you have questions about your father, lass, now's your chance."

Rose had lots of questions about her father, but first she wanted to discover what Niall was so eager to hide from her.

"Michael, what do you mean, that you have the glamour?"

Niall gave Michael a dirty look. "You could not keep your mouth shut."

Michael shrugged. "Makes no difference." He pointed his cigarette at Nightshade. "Exhibit one in the freak show. Meself, I'm just small fry."

Nightshade growled low in his throat, raising the hairs on Rose's body.

Niall smacked his palm on the kitchen counter. "Show her, Michael, if you must. But make it snappy."

After depositing his glass on the counter, Michael held his hands before his face and wiggled his fingers. "Abracadabra."

Niall rolled his eyes, drawing Rose's gaze for an instant. When she looked back, Michael was different. It took a moment for her to work out what had changed. His face was the same, but the gloss had gone. His hair was no longer as thick and luxuriant, his complexion less glowing. The whites of his eyes were bloodshot. He was still good-looking, but in a more normal way, and he was clearly a little worse for wear.

Rose hadn't thought of it for years, but whenever her mother looked awful after a drinking binge, she'd go to her room to refresh herself and return looking perfect. "I could use some of that. What is it? Some kind of illusion?"

Michael opened his mouth, but Niall beat him to it. "Something like that."

Niall didn't seem the type of man to use deceit to improve his looks, so she passed over him and stared expectantly at Nightshade. "I bet you use it too."

The nightstalker grinned and arched a brow at Niall. "I'm naturally beautiful. My gift is different."

"Your gift?" Presumably he meant his wings. She glanced at Niall, remembering his superhuman leap to rescue her. "Do you have a gift?"

"We have no time for this now." He stared pointedly at the clock above the fridge. "What is it you be wanting to know about Tristan?"

Tristan. Niall's familiar use of her father's Christian name jolted her back to reality. She was avoiding the very questions she craved answers for, frightened of what she'd discover. Reluctantly, she met Nightshade's disconcerting silver gaze. "You said you know my father?"

"That's right."

"In what context?"

"They live together," Michael chipped in as he clicked his lighter and lit another cigarette.

"Live together?" Rose studied Nightshade, who shifted uneasily. She glanced toward Niall, who avoided eye contact, then Michael, who grinned wickedly. The penny dropped with the thud of a lead ball. "Ah."

Rose clutched the back of a chair. Her father had a *relationship* with this . . . this . . . The room suddenly seemed too bright. She covered her eyes with a hand. When Rose's mother had railed at her for being boring and plain, Rose had clung to her fantasy of a normal dad who would think as she did and value her academic achievements. She'd been ready to accept that her father might not be quite as she imagined, but this was beyond anything . . .

"Lass, are you feeling all right?" Niall's gentle inquiry brought tears to her eyes for the disillusioned child inside her. She blinked them away before uncovering her face.

"Yes, yes, I'm fine. It's just a surprise."

"You must come home with me, Rosenwyn," Nightshade said in his dark, gravelly voice. "You and I belong together. We're the last—"

"Enough!" Niall stepped between Rose and Nightshade, as if blocking her view of him would prevent her from hearing his words. "She doesn't need this." He touched her arm, and comfort flowed from his fingertips. "Me advice to you, lass: forget about Tristan. Take yourself back to London and get on with your life."

"Your destiny lies with me, Rosenwyn," Nightshade said, stepping up beside Niall. "I'm the last of your people."

Shock jolted her. "You're not related to me." God, she hoped there weren't wings in her gene pool. "I'm looking for my father. Not you."

"Stop this now." Niall shoved Nightshade in the chest.

He staggered back, but kept speaking. "Your father is not of the Good People like us. He's human."

"Human?" Rose gaped at Nightshade. Reality stopped and flipped over like a negative image. So that meant . . . Her usually quick brain stalled. "I don't understand . . ." She refused to believe she was anything like Nightshade. And Niall and Michael were human—weren't they? They looked human, apart from Michael's glamour and the way Niall jumped higher than any man should be able to jump. Her brain juggled the implications, but she couldn't keep all the balls in the air.

"Oh, my God." She dropped into a chair, closed her eyes, and tried to focus her mind.

She clutched her three stones through her sports top and took comfort from the familiar smooth circles. A suspicion trickled into her brain. Niall had similar stones. What about the other two men?

Rose glanced up to see Niall shepherding Nightshade out the back door. "Wait," she called. Both men jerked around. She pulled her stones out and cupped them in her palm. She remembered Niall's reaction when she'd mentioned her stones earlier. Somehow they were the answer to an important question, but she didn't know what the question was.

Nightshade smiled, a slow curl of lips revealing pearly white teeth like a crescent moon in a night sky. "My sweet, you offer them to me?"

"No, you bloody don't!" Niall jumped between them and struck out, the action so swift Nightshade was on his back before Rose realized Niall had hit him.

Surely they weren't fighting over her?

"Well, well." Michael pushed away from his safe spot on the opposite side of the kitchen and ambled toward her. "Me brother, the grand protector, strikes again." He gazed at Rose's stones cradled in her palm. "Let me see what you have there, lass."

All three men seemed interested in her stones, so

they must be significant. Niall had advised her to keep them hidden. Her mother had given her the same warning years earlier, but men had never shown any interest in them before.

Niall backed up and glanced at Michael over his shoulder. "You'll keep your hands off her as well if you know what's good for you."

Michael angled his head and scrutinized his brother. "If I didn't know better—"

"Shut it."

Michael shrugged. "Denial will not go changing the facts, boyo." He pulled a leather thong bearing stones similar to Niall's out of his shirt and then swung them in front of Rose. "Snap. Nightshade, show her yours."

Nightshade had risen and stood in the doorway, lip swollen, nostrils flared like an angry bull. He glared at Niall as he pulled a key chain from his pocket and unclipped it from the loop on his jeans. Three earth-colored stones hung from the chain.

"Nearly a complete showing," Michael said. "Except Niall, of course, who dares not wear his in case someone should steal away his soul."

Niall kept a watchful eye on Nightshade, ignoring Michael's taunt.

Rose hid her stones beneath her top, and pressed her hand over them. Whoever these people were, she was one of them. She'd blamed the fact that she had never quite fit in at school on her mother's weird influence, but maybe the reason went deeper. Maybe she really was different. "Who are you? Or maybe I should be asking, what are you?"

Niall glanced over his shoulder at her. "Leave it. Best you forget we said anything, lass."

She passed her gaze over each man in turn. A revelation hovered at the edge of her awareness. Something so momentous there'd be no turning back. Should she walk away and forget or take a risk? "I need to know."

With a resigned sigh, Niall dropped into a chair and rubbed his face. "Your father's human."

"And my mother?"

Niall glanced at her, then looked at Michael, who shrugged.

"Your mother was of another race."

"What race?"

"Fairy."

"Fairy?" Rose stilled and waited for the burst of shock and disbelief that didn't come. Had she always known? Had she spent her life running away from the truth?

Rose took three deep breaths and grounded herself. She could handle this if she had facts to focus on. "Give me details."

Niall relaxed the fist clenched against his thigh. "There are many types of fairy." He jerked a thumb toward Nightshade. "You'll find everything from the nightstalker to tiny people no bigger than me hand."

Rose's control wobbled as tiny picturebook fairies chased around inside her head on a repeating video loop.

Niall gripped her hand with cool, strong fingers. "We're the same species as humans; otherwise we couldn't interbreed."

She sensed his presence surrounding her, protective, strong, calm. "You're the same as me?" she whispered.

"Similar, lass. You're human and Cornish pisky. Michael and meself are Tuatha Dé Danaan and"—he cast a warning look at Nightshade—"leprechaun."

"Leprechaun!" The word burst out before she could stop it.

He pulled his hand back, eyes flaring defensively.

She missed the reassurance of his touch instantly. "I thought leprechauns were . . . well, small?" She scanned Niall's lean body—obviously not.

His fierce expression softened and he raised one eyebrow slightly. "They are small, but Tuatha Dé Danaan are tall, descended from the gods who traveled to Ireland in the mists of the past."

"And praise be to the ancient gods' dominant genes," Michael added with a wink.

She tried to smile, but confusion swirled inside her head until she thought she'd drown in the feeling. What should she do? Pursue her father and face the truth, or take Niall's advice, return to London, and continue as if nothing had changed?

How could she live the rest of her life wondering about her father, about her heritage, about fairies? But if she explored this new world, how would she ever return to her normal life?

Rose rubbed her temples and became aware of Niall's gaze on her. His presence surrounded her, caressed the edges of her mind.

How could she possibly return to London without exploring the mystical connection she had with this man?

Chapter Five

Nightshade crouched in the vee between two massive branches of an ancient oak tree overhanging the rear of the Elephant's Nest.

Raucous laughter rang out through the open bar windows, and the hypnotic timbre of Michael's voice floated into the cool autumn evening as he recited another of his tall tales to the crowd.

The smell of fried chicken issued from the spinning kitchen vent on a burst of warm air. Nightshade's stomach rumbled, but he had more important matters on his mind than food.

He fixed his gaze on the second-floor window where he'd seen Rosenwyn close the curtains half an hour earlier. As he imagined her peeling off her tight shorts and top, revealing her fragrant skin, his fangs ached and his body throbbed. Soon she would be his in every way.

Shifting uncomfortably on his perch, he snatched a breath of chilly air. *Hurry up and sleep, sweet one.* In darkness, while the O'Connor brothers were occupied in the bar, Nightshade would swoop into Rose's room, carry her to the manor, and hide her in the maze of tunnels and caves beneath.

There had been a flash of heat and curiosity in her eyes when she looked at him. She might have lived with humans these past thirty years, but with his guidance, she would soon adjust to the life she had been born for.

Nightshade jumped from the tree, touched ground briefly on silent feet, and with a powerful sweep of his wings rose into the air beside her window. Through the crack between the curtains, he saw the outline of her body beneath the bedcovers.

There was no way into the room without breaking the glass, and he didn't want to frighten her again. Moving to the hall window next to her room, he used fingernails strong as shards of steel to prize open the rotten window frame. A flap of his wings propelled him onto the windowsill and he climbed inside. One dim light illuminated the landing at the top of the stairs.

He crept forward, turned into the short hallway that led to Rose's room, and stilled. Conversation hummed in the pub below, punctuated now and then by the dissonant clamor of drunken laughter. A car door slammed outside. An engine roared to life. Placing the sole of his boot carefully against the wooden panel beside the lock on Rose's door, he tensed, ready to deliver a sharp kick.

"I would prefer you not wreck the door." The softly spoken comment from the shadows beside the stairs jerked Nightshade around into a defensive crouch.

He could still taste blood from his split lip where Niall had punched him, and he welcomed a chance for retribution. "Half-breed scut. Step out and face me if you dare."

"I thought I had," Niall said flatly as he halted just out of reach. "Return home, stalker. This lass is not for you."

The hint of sympathy in Niall's voice fired Nightshade's indignation. "How dare you pity me. You're nothing. Even your own queen hates you."

Niall didn't respond, his perfect face cold as a mask of stone. As always, lust for the Irish fairy's blood beat hot in Nightshade's veins. He ached to crack Niall's shell, make the proud Tuatha Dé Danaan swoon as he bit into the warm, musky skin of his neck.

Nightshade growled in frustration. "I'll relinquish my right to her, if you give yourself to me."

Niall's eyes scraped him. "You're wasting your breath, stalker. 'Tis never going to happen."

"Then I'll take Rosenwyn. She and I are the last of pisky blood. We belong together."

"What about the piskies who went to America?"

Nightshade hesitated. Lies and deception had become his truth. In his eagerness, he'd forgotten to watch what he said. "The others are lost to me. I want Rose."

"No. The lass returns whence she came," Niall said, shaking his head. "She's more human than pisky. 'Tis not fair to wrench her from her career and home because you're bored with Tristan."

The animal inside Nightshade rattled its cage, and he took a step forward. "Don't tell me what I can and can't do. You want her as well, but you know she won't want you."

Darkness swam within the vibrant blue of Niall's eyes. Nightshade tensed, ready to fight; then with surprise, he sensed Niall relax.

"Nay, stalker. I do not want her." Niall looked at Rosenwyn's door and released a lingering breath. "Me cup of worry overflows with Ana."

At Niall's mention of his leprechaun sister, Nightshade had an idea. Niall would not let him take Rosenwyn from her bed that night, but maybe with the right inducement . . . "Agree to bring Rosenwyn to Trevelion Manor tomorrow, and I'll leave now."

With a snort of disbelief, Niall said, "No way."

Nightshade knew what the Irish's weak spot was. "Bring her, or I'll tell Tristan you had the pisky and let her go. He'll never renew the spell protecting your sister then."

"The druid's greedy. He'll be willing to play things my way when his money runs out."

"Maybe. But how long will it take him to spend that latest installment? Longer than you have before the spell dissipates, I bet."

Niall's gaze remained fixed on him, eyes cold and fierce. A muscle in his cheek jumped. "I'll not go exposing Rose to harm."

"Tristan doesn't want to hurt her; he's her father."

"I trust neither of you." Niall flexed his hands.

Nightshade stepped back. He didn't want Niall drawing weapons. The balance was delicate. Push him far enough to achieve the purpose, but not far enough to start a fight. "If I promise I won't let Tristan harm her, will you bring her to Trevelion Manor?"

Niall clenched his jaws, shifting his feet slightly.

Sensing victory, Nightshade leaned a shoulder against the wall. "Come on now, Irish. She wants to meet her dad. Give the girl her heart's desire." Nightshade looked down and scraped some rotten wood from beneath his fingernails. "I'll make sure Tristan casts the spell of protection over Ana."

The flicker of interest in Niall's eyes told Nightshade he'd gotten him.

"I take Rose away with me when I leave," Niall said.

Nightshade inclined his head. No lie would pass his lips, but once he had the pisky in Trevelion Manor, he did not intend to let her go.

" 'Tis not clear to me what you hope to gain from this visit, stalker."

Happiness. The pleasure of a woman's company. The chance to rid himself of Tristan forever. "If she decides to stay of her own free will, you will honor her wish?"

Niall gave a sharp nod.

Nightshade had Niall where he wanted him: caught between the rock of his independence and the hard place of his honor. Nightshade would enjoy watching him squirm.

Niall stood in the dim corridor outside Rose's bedroom door. The bass beat of music in the bar thumped beneath his feet. Michael must have finished telling tales and was probably now dancing between the tables, making a fool of himself prior to cajoling an entranced female up to his bed.

When he was certain Nightshade had gone, Niall slipped the key from his pocket and quietly unlocked the door.

Nightshade had assumed Niall was keeping watch over Rose. In reality, he'd been on his way to her room. Unlike the stalker, he was there only to check that Rose was safely asleep, and not too disturbed by the strange events of the evening.

Pushing the door open, he slipped through and closed it softly behind him. He held still until he heard the gentle rhythm of her breathing and was certain she slept.

He walked silently to the side of the bed. Her mask of humanity had slipped away with her consciousness. His breath caught as, in the cool light of the moon, he looked upon her inner fairy beauty for the first time.

She rolled onto her side. Her Magic Knot slipped from beneath her yellow nightdress and lay against the exposed curve of her breast. Niall froze. He tried to tell himself he hadn't wanted to see her Magic Knot, but his mind refused the lie. Hunkering down, he gazed at the three linked circles of stone.

Her warm floral fragrance enticed him as he stared at the top of her breast gleaming in the moonlight like the surface of a pearl. Niall licked his lips, battling the almost irresistible urge to touch her Magic Knot—and her skin.

She moaned in her sleep. The sound flared inside him. He fought to keep control. After his reaction to her that morning on his bed, he should have known to stay away.

Small creases furrowed her forehead. She mumbled and struggled with the sheet. "Shh," he whispered, and touched her cheek. Need to complete their bond pulsed through him. His fingertips drifted featherlight across her skin and brushed the corner of her mouth. He leaned down, drugging himself with her scent. Knots of lust tightened in his belly. Sighing, he pressed his lips gently against the soft fullness of hers. Even as he kissed her, his fingers itched to feel the weight of her Magic Knot.

All his life he had hidden his stones, guarded them from people who wanted to control him. Now a half-human pisky had stumbled upon them and would forever own a part of him, and she didn't even realize it.

He remembered the way she had looked at him that morning in his room, and his gaze turned inward.

Bitter memories cracked the moment, and his pleasure faded away. She wouldn't want him even if she knew of their bond. Nobody had ever wanted him. He raised himself slowly to his feet and stared at her face. It was too late to stop her from becoming involved in his problems. If he were to keep Ana safe, he had no choice but to take Rose to Tristan in the morning.

Nightshade expected to persuade Rose to stay with him, but Niall was certain the stalker underestimated her. As long as Nightshade didn't bite her, Niall was sure she would be strong willed enough to leave Trevelion Manor.

The curtains to his right fluttered. Whispered words rose and fell as if carried from a distance on the wind. Nagging compulsion drew his gaze toward the dressing table. A sharp chill of warning raced up his spine. *Magic.* Palming both blades, he moved silently across the room and watched his shadowy reflection approach the mirror.

An ethereal figure flowed into the glass, surrounded by glowing smoke. Long black hair cloaked her shoulders, a circlet of gold around her head. She held out a massive black book and pulsing crystal ball. His blades slipped forgotten from his hands as he clutched uselessly at the shadowy gifts.

"Niall O'Connor, son of the ancient gods. Know your past and your future. Trust your inner voice, my king. Follow your destiny."

The woman smiled, then dispersed like mist in the wind.

Gradually, he became aware of air expanding his lungs. He blinked, tensing his muscles. Shocked at how easily he'd lost his instinct for self-preservation, he snatched up his knives from the carpet and turned three hundred sixty degrees, checking the dark corners of the room. When he was sure nothing lurked there, he stared in disgust at his reflection and secured his blades to his wrists.

What ancient magic was strong enough to overcome his instincts, strong enough to lead him like a hornless goat to the slaughter? Had the woman in the mirror been one of the ancient goddesses? He concentrated on the shadow of feeling she'd left in him. Not fear, but a restless disquiet.

A discordant murmur of many voices rose in his mind. He glanced down and saw a pack of tarot cards stacked neatly on the dressing table. The voice of the woman from the mirror rose from the cacophony and he heard her clearly inside his head. *Choose a card.* Niall never used divination tools, preferring to seek guidance from nature spirits. And he knew the unwritten rule: never touch another practitioner's tools.

Despite this, the compulsion to obey made him reach out, cut the deck, and place his choice faceup on the polished wood. The same woman who had appeared in the mirror stared up at him from the card. The High Priestess.

Niall was not easily led by portent and prediction, but none of the Good People could ignore such an obvious prophecy. He just wasn't sure what to make of it. He knew enough to recognize that the book the woman held represented his past and the crystal ball his future, but her reference to him as "my king" must have symbolic significance that eluded him.

He glanced over his shoulder at Rose's sleeping form and frowned. An accountant who carried a pack of enchanted tarot cards to assignments? The lass was not as ignorant of her nonhuman heritage as she pretended.

This vision from Rose's tarot cards was another thread joining him to her. Were they pawns in some greater magic?

He turned toward the door. Although Rose obviously didn't want him and he couldn't accept responsibility for her, he knew better than to disregard the hand of fate. In the morning he would question her on the significance of the High Priestess and try to make sense of the vision.

Whatever transpired, he must still take Rose to visit Tristan. He wouldn't allow any harm to come to her, but his first priority had to be renewing the spell of protection over Ana and Michael.

Rose woke to the pale glow of wintry sunlight painting a streak across her face. Rolling over, she gazed at the rosebud-sprigged curtains and wondered where she was. It took a few moments for the blissful fog of sleep to roll back beneath the onslaught of reality.

She got up and showered, mulling over her plans for the day. There were two choices: visit her father and face reality or forget her search, return to London, and leave her childhood fantasies about her father intact. In a few weeks the memories of last night would fade, and she could continue her old life as if nothing had changed.

Except everything she believed about herself had changed.

And she'd met Niall.

Rose closed her eyes, turned her face into the warm spray, and concentrated on Niall. He rumbled at the edge of her awareness like a distant storm that promised a violent cleansing of all her old misconceptions. But could she face that?

She dried, dressed in jeans, and packed her bag. She was long past the childish need for an idealized father who had never existed anyway. Rose folded her nightdress and clutched it to her chest. For a second, lost dreams tightened her throat. If both her parents were strange, what did that make her? The taunts of the school bullies echoed in her mind. She'd been fighting a losing battle trying to fit in.

Rose jammed her hairbrush, makeup bag, and tarot cards into her case and snapped the clips shut. No way could she risk her colleagues from work discovering she was part fairy. She'd spent fourteen years developing a career that depended on integrity and trust. When she returned to London, she'd tell everyone she'd been unable to trace her dad and carry on as usual.

Eager to leave now that she'd made her decision, she left her case in her room and went in search of breakfast and her bill.

The kitchen was empty. The six-slice toaster sat on the counter, taunting her with its presence. She slipped through the door, found the bread, and set two slices to toast. No wonder Michael O'Connor was in financial difficulties if he made the guests cook their own breakfast. After switching the electric kettle on to boil, she stared out of the kitchen window across the backyard.

Niall stood at the far side of the lawn, his palms braced against the trunk of a huge gnarled oak. Rose's breath caught as she took in his tall, lean body. She wriggled, her clothes suddenly tight against sensitive places. The kettle boiled and switched off with a click, drawing her attention back to the room.

A few minutes later, with black coffee and buttered toast, she wandered back to the window. Niall stood perfectly still, long, sexy fingers splayed against the tree. He appeared to be meditating or praying.

Michael she could read like a book—a kid's book, with large colored illustrations. Niall she couldn't get straight in her mind. Last night he'd rescued her from Nightshade and almost seemed possessive, but he'd lied about knowing her father and made no secret of the fact that he thought she should leave. Although the connection between them fascinated her, she couldn't get the Ten of Swords out of her mind.

Curiosity got the better of her. She brushed the toast crumbs from her hands, picked up her coffee, and headed across the grass.

She stopped a few yards behind him and gave herself a moment to admire the view. Niall's green combat pants were awful, but they couldn't disguise his gorgeous backside. "You're up with the lark."

Dropping his hands from the tree, he turned to face her. "Good morning to you." He glanced at her bedroom window and frowned. "You weren't disturbed, I hope?"

"No. I'm usually up early because I run before work. Why would you think I was disturbed?"

He shook his head and rubbed his palms on his thighs. "No matter." He glanced at her cup. "Someone made you breakfast?"

Rose grinned. "Yeah, me. Hope you don't mind?"

"I've been out here for a while. I could have helped you."

"I know. I saw you from the window." She sipped her coffee and debated whether to pry. "What were you doing?"

He looked at her thoughtfully, then reached out and patted the tree trunk. "Seeking counsel."

"Ah." She pursed her lips. "From God?" she asked tentatively, not sure what sort of god a fairy-leprechaun cross might pray to.

" 'Tis something like that." He met her eyes, a hint of challenge in his. "When some matter confuses me, I seek advice from the tree deva."

"Right, I see." She didn't see at all. Did something live in the tree? This was getting weird again. The taunts of the school bullies echoed in her head. Then the voices transformed into those of her work colleagues. She turned away. "I'll leave you to it then."

"Stay . . . Rose." He stepped forward and grasped her wrist.

Annoyance snapped through her at the impersonal touch. Why couldn't he take her hand like a normal man?

"Let me show you."

"No, thanks." She pulled on her arm, but he didn't release her.

"Wait, lass. Don't you ever seek advice?"

Rose gave an irritated shrug. She did not intend to mention her tarot cards to him.

"I'll wager you have a question in mind that's confusing you."

"No." She had lots, but none she wanted to share.

"What about the problem of whether to visit your father?" he asked gently.

The question touched raw nerves. Rose fisted her

hand and yanked it out of his grip. "I'm going back to London and forgetting him."

"Is it sure you are?"

She rounded on him. "Last night *you* told me I should go back to London."

He raised his perfect dark brows. " 'Tis only sense to check you're doing the right thing. Ask the tree deva."

Rose stared at the coarse bark.

"This tree has dwelled here for many hundreds of years. Its spirit holds the wisdom of ages."

Her cards worked; why shouldn't the tree? She'd come a long way to find her father. Maybe she should check whether she was right to abandon her search. "Oh, hell." Rose deposited her coffee mug on a garden bench. "Okay, show me."

He reached for her wrist again. "You must be relaxed."

"Then don't hang on to me as though I'm about to run off."

His jaw tightened. He held up his hands palm out and stepped back.

She walked forward to the spot he indicated beside the tree and threw a questioning glance over her shoulder.

"Place your hands on the trunk."

She smacked her palms flat against the tree. The slight sting where the coarse bark bit into her skin satisfied a part of her that wanted punishment for doing this stupid thing.

"Relax, lass."

"Stop telling me"—she paused, then took her voice down a few decibels—"to relax. I'm relaxed." She let her shoulders droop. "See? Floppy as a rag doll."

He made a strange noise, and she glanced around. It took her a moment to realize he was chuckling at her. His eyes twinkled and, for the first time, she caught a glimpse of his softer side.

"Close your eyes, Rose," he said, a smile still flirting with his mouth. "I'll talk you through me own way of connecting."

Rose let her eyelids fall. Immediately her other senses kicked in. A gentle breeze that she hadn't noticed ruffled her hair. The fresh autumn air carried the tang of salt water from the estuary. The woodsy scent of the tree reminded her of Niall's smell, causing little flutters of excitement in her stomach.

"Feel the tree beneath your hands."

The bark prickled her skin.

"You feel it?"

"Hmm."

"Feel the earth beneath your feet. You be one with the earth, Rose. Your element is earth. Like you, 'tis strong, dependable, solid."

"Hmm." She wasn't sure about the solid bit. She filed away the element thing as a question for later.

"Breathe thrice, deep into your belly."

"I know how to ground myself. I do it—" She snapped her mouth shut. She'd nearly given away that she used tarot cards.

"Take the breaths, lass," he said, a hint of exasperation in his tone.

She grinned at the trunk and followed his instructions.

After her third breath he said, "On the next breath imagine yourself flowing out through your fingertips and palms into the tree. Let go of your senses."

Rose concentrated on her hands, felt the rough trunk, then imagined herself flowing into the wood.

"Visualize the narrow passages running through the trunk, fetching water and nutrients from the roots up to feed the branches. Extend yourself, plunge down, down through the passages into the cool, moist earth. Let it cradle you in the darkness, lass. Soft and safe."

Rose fell into dark nothingness. It was strangely peaceful in the cool oblivion beneath the ground. She had never visited this place before, but knew instinctively that she belonged.

"Let part of your essence remain in the darkness, while part flows with the sap into the branches. Spread out and fill every living cell that basks beneath the autumn sun, preparing for the cold winter. Each cell contains the tiny promise of life waiting to burst forth in the spring." Niall's voice was lower now, barely a whisper. His breath stirred the tiny hairs on her neck. His nearness sent tingles racing up her back.

Rose let her barriers fall with a sigh, opened herself, spread out to fill every cell of the tree.

Niall flowed with her like oil on water, mixing and separating. Together and apart. The solid presence of his body guarded her back. His warmth banished the chill of the autumn morning. His arms enclosed her. The gentle press of his hands covered hers on the tree.

"Feel the energy of the tree, boundless, eternal," he whispered into her ear. "Dwell in this place older than time and wiser than the ages. Ask your question."

Rose drifted in peace on the edge of the infinite, Niall's presence anchoring her like soft, silky ribbons. *Ask your question,* he repeated inside her mind.

"Should I go and see my father?" Rose whispered.

Energy spewed out of the tree, singing through her limbs, tingling everywhere Niall touched her.

Be at peace, earth child. The words whispered inside her head. *Stay with your king*.

For a moment the world spun. Rose grabbed a shuddering breath, suddenly conscious of how close Niall was. She pulled away and braced her forearm against the tree. Heat surged into her cheeks. She glanced at Niall over her shoulder.

Surprise crossed his face. "Does this word *king* have meaning for you?"

Rose shook her head. "Unless it's something to do with the tarot cards." *Damn*. She bit her lip and hoped he didn't ask more about the tarot. She fiddled with the gold stud in her ear and stared into the woodland. "That didn't help at all. Now I'm even more confused."

"If it's a trustworthy opinion you're after, why not ask your tarot cards? Surely you trust them?"

Darn, he didn't miss a thing. "Don't think I'll bother. I'm packed already. I'll just go home."

"Ask the cards, Rose. Be sure."

He was right. She should check. She looked at his inscrutable blue eyes and wondered what went on in the mind behind them. She visualized the picture on the Justice card, the scales weighing up, balancing. Fair and evenhanded. If it weren't for the Ten of Swords, she'd trust him, but that hint of doubt remained. "Okay. I'll do a quick reading."

"May I watch?"

"Watch?" She'd never done a reading in front of anyone but her mother. The thought made her heart race. "I don't know if I can do it with an audience."

" 'Tis interesting. Would you read for me?"

Rose rubbed at the tension in her neck. "You can watch, but I don't read for anyone else."

He shrugged as if it didn't matter, but when he turned toward the pub, she sensed determination in his stride. Why had Niall changed his mind about her leaving? The previous night he'd been adamant that she should return to London. Now he seemed to want her to stay. Could he be interested in exploring the psychic bond they'd developed? Taking it further? A strange feeling skittered through her. Maybe she should read the cards for him and discover whether his future included her.

Chapter Six

Rose collected her tarot cards from her bedroom; then Niall led her up to the private rooms he shared with Michael.

As they reached the top of the stairs the frantic babbling of cartoon characters filled the hallway. Niall pushed open the door to the sitting room and stood aside for her to pass.

Michael slouched in a saggy chair, feet crossed on the coffee table. He held a cigarette in one hand and the television remote in the other. Rose tried not to stare, but it was impossible to avoid looking at him. He wore blue silk boxer shorts exactly the same color as his eyes and nothing else. Unless one counted the supersize bag of potato chips balanced on his hard, muscular belly.

He bellowed with laughter as the sound of an explosion boomed out of the television. The chip bag rocked dangerously, depositing flakes of potato over the front of his shorts. He grinned at Rose, plucked one up, and popped it into his mouth.

Niall made a strangled noise, brushed past her, and snatched the remote out of Michael's hand. The television fell silent.

"Hey! Give me that." Michael jumped up—leaving a trail of chips in his wake—and made a grab for the remote control.

Niall evaded him with ease and cast a critical look at his shorts. "Go get yourself some clothes on. We have company."

" 'Tis not the company I hear complaining." Michael waggled his eyebrows at Rose, and she had to fight a laugh.

"Cut the blarney and do as I say."

Michael sauntered forward, slanting her a seductive glance as he brushed past to reach the door. He hooked a thumb beneath the elastic of his boxers and snapped it against his belly. "Me room's the third door, if you be wanting to see the rest."

Niall grumbled something in a language she didn't understand.

"Don't go taking the old gods' names in vain, Niall; otherwise you'll get a thunderbolt up your arse."

Rose couldn't resist a quick look over her shoulder. Michael's rear view was as perfect as the front. She turned back to face Niall's thunderous expression. Although nothing much seemed to shake Niall's cool, Michael obviously knew which buttons to press.

"Sorry, he's full o' the devil." Niall turned and gathered the remnants of food, fetched a cloth from the small kitchen area, and wiped the coffee table. As Rose watched him fold his lean body to complete the menial task, she wondered what he wore beneath the combat pants. Now that she'd seen Michael nearly naked, she had a fair idea what Niall looked like without clothes.

She remembered the feel of his body pressed intimately to hers when he'd caught her on the bed, and imagined him in the same position wearing nothing but silk boxers. Heat spiraled through her.

Snatching a breath, she pushed the feeling away. "That's clean enough. I always lay the cards out on this fabric to protect them anyway."

She sat on the sofa, shook out her square of purple silk, and let the material float down onto the coffee table.

Niall took the chair Michael had vacated opposite and watched quietly as she tipped the cards into her hand, breathed to ground herself, and started to shuffle. He obviously understood that she needed silence to prepare.

"I'll read for myself first. I usually choose three cards. Sometimes I draw them; sometimes I cut the deck." Rose finished shuffling, placed the deck on the table, and squared off the corners. "I'll cut today."

"What makes you vary the way you select the cards?"

Rose paused and chewed her lip. "I don't know. Sometimes one way just feels right. Mother taught me to go with my intuition." For the first time in many years, she felt a small flash of gratitude for the insights her mother had passed on. Fairy insights.

She gazed down at her pack, took a breath to focus her thoughts, and concentrated on her father's name. "The first cut will be what my father means to me, the second, my relationship with him, and the third, what I mean to him." Rose made the cuts and stared down at the three stacks, suddenly hesitant to reveal the cards to Niall.

Looking up, she searched his face for any hint of censure. There was nothing but curiosity in his eyes. The tension in her neck eased. Of course he would accept the tarot. He'd just taught her to consult the spirit of a tree, for heaven's sake. She was so used to hiding this aspect of herself, she couldn't adjust to the fact that he thought it acceptable.

Rose turned over the first card that showed what her father meant to her, the Eight of Cups. A slender man with a cloud of ash blond hair walked alone down a track into a forest, leaving eight cups lying on the path behind him.

"What does this mean?" Niall asked softly.

Rose glanced up. For a moment she'd forgotten he was watching. "My mother said this means severing emotional ties. But I can't sever ties with my father because I haven't got any. Although I did have expectations for the future." Rose chewed the side of her finger.

"Perhaps 'tis telling you to look for a new relationship to replace the one that never really existed?"

Rose glanced at him, surprised. "It could indicate that." He seemed to understand the cards instinctively. Maybe divination came naturally to all fairies.

Turning over the top card from the second stack, she stared at the Moon. A little chip of her self-image, carefully shaped and crafted to present an acceptable face to the world, snapped away.

Everything she'd imagined about her father had been false. This card representing her relationship with him spoke of deception, trickery, and lies. The fantasy that had kept her going most of her life dissolved before her.

" 'Tis a bad card, Rose?"

"There are no bad cards."

"But the meaning for you is not good?"

She swallowed the knot in her throat before she

could answer. "I've definitely been deceiving myself about my father. I don't think he'll want to meet me."

A flash of concern crossed Niall's face. "Is it possible you're wrong? You said the cards could be interpreted in different ways."

"Possible, but I've got a really bad feeling about him. This final card represents what I am to my father. Let's see what it says." Foreboding crawled through her as she turned the top card on the third pile and revealed the Five of Swords. To win by deceit.

Rose closed her eyes and tried to banish the image of the taunting face on the card. For some reason her father held something against her. At best, he would be indifferent. At worst, he'd blame her for some old hurt.

"I can't go and visit my father." Rose shook her head slowly. "This is a terrible reading."

Niall rubbed his mouth and glanced up at her from beneath his lashes. "Were I you, lass, I'd want to face this before I moved on with me life."

"I can't."

"'Tis up to you, but if you bury a problem, it spreads rot through your mind." He spoke with conviction, as though he knew from experience.

She couldn't deny that it made sense to meet her father and get closure on the issue. Rose gathered the cards together and thanked them inside her head. Before she made any decisions on her own future, she was curious to see what her cards told Niall.

"Let's do the reading for you; then I'll decide what I'm going to do." Banishing all thoughts of her own reading, she concentrated on Niall as she shuffled. The sparkle of interest in his eyes made her feel the reading was something worthy, rather than a silly habit. "I always work with three cards." For the first time in her life, she wished she'd taken the trouble to learn some more complex spreads than the simple three cards her mother had taught her.

"I'll cut the pack into three again. They represent body, mind, and spirit."

Once he nodded his agreement, Rose cut the pack and revealed the top card on the first pile. "You've got the Four of Swords for body. This suggests you need to rest and recover from something. Or it could represent the calm before the storm." She glanced up and caught him frowning. "You're fairly isolated here; have you come to escape from something?"

He laced his fingers and then pressed them to his mouth.

"Does this mean anything to you?" she prompted, trying not to sound too eager.

"Aye."

Obviously he wasn't going to satisfy her curiosity, so she moved on to the next card.

"For mind you have the Three of Wands. This one suggests a new project or opportunity."

He looked doubtful.

"Setting new goals?"

He shook his head.

The only way to help him discover the card's meaning was to connect with the character. She touched her fingertips to the picture of a man standing on a rocky crag, staring out to sea. Words flowed into her mind and she repeated them for Niall. "You're on the right path. Allow yourself to see the goal. Destiny awaits." Withdrawing her hand, she watched for his reaction.

After a sharp shake of his head he said, "Naw. Not going anywhere. No goals. No destiny."

"I'll pull the card from the bottom. This shows what's hidden or unconscious."

She turned the bottom card faceup. "Ten of Pentacles." The family card. This one was a surprise. "You want a family to bring you happiness. Maybe to pass on your experience and wealth?"

He laughed, the sound short and sharp in the silence of the room. "So you're telling me I have a subconscious desire to play happy families?" He cringed. "You're wrong entirely." He jumped up from the chair, went to the small kitchen, and poured himself a glass of apple juice. Holding it up he asked, "Want one?"

"Yes." She watched him fill another glass. What had happened to make Niall so antifamily? His reaction seemed strange, considering he lived with his brother.

"Either the cards are wrong," he said as he dropped back into his seat, "or you've misinterpreted them. Families are nothing but trouble."

Rose thought it sensible not to pursue the matter. But before she moved on to the next card, she brushed her fingertips across the jovial old man and child on the Ten of Pentacles and one word whispered into her mind.

Dynasty.

Niall wanted to be head of a dynasty? If he did, he was doing a damn good job of hiding his aspirations.

She turned her attention to the final pile and flipped over the top card. The Magician. This had always been her favorite card. The fact hadn't occurred to her before, but the man depicted in the woodland glade resembled Niall. His hair was a little longer, but the eyes were the right color, and he had the same intense expression on his face that said both so much and so little. "Your spirit card says you are independent, master of your own fate. You have everything you need to achieve your goals. You're adaptable, skillful, and in touch with nature."

When he bent closer to examine the card, the autumn sun picked up chestnut highlights in his hair. His thick, dark lashes accentuated the blueness of his eyes. Need for him tightened around her heart, stole her breath. The feeling expanded and ran through her like a shock wave. For a moment, she wondered if he was using glamour on her.

He looked up, a smile on his face. "This card I like. It feels right."

She fell into the endless blue of his eyes—not sea, but a cloudless sky where she could fly free. "Yes, right . . . Niall." His name hung between them. It no longer felt sharp, but rolled off her tongue. Full of Irish mystery—like him.

"Will you show me the rest of the cards?"

Rose nodded, a burst of pleasure bringing a smile to her lips. "They're my mother's design. Reproduced from portraits she painted."

She hadn't known how good she'd feel, sharing this part of herself with someone else. She leafed through the cards, giving him a few seconds to examine each one.

"Hold your horses." He leaned forward when she laid the High Priestess on the table. "What's the meaning of this one?"

"Spiritual enlightenment. When I draw this card, I interpret it to mean I should trust my feelings, look inside myself for guidance. Maybe dig deep to find the talents I need to succeed."

Niall tapped his hand against his thigh and stared at the card, apparently lost in thought.

"Why are you interested in this one?"

He shook his head. "Just a feeling."

Rose pointed to the card. "The book she's holding represents past life and the crystal ball the future. The gray cat curled on her lap represents wisdom and curiosity."

"Hmm." Niall drew in a deep breath and sat back. "Have you made a decision about visiting your father?"

Rose gathered up her cards and cradled them in her palm. She stared at the bare branches of a tree outside the window. The thought of visiting her father dragged through her like a spike through mud. Niall was right. She must clear away the dross of her illusions about her father if she were to move on. "Yes. Can you give me directions to where he lives?"

"I can do better than that." He brushed a fingertip across the back of her hand. "I shall take you to Trevelion Manor meself."

Rose blinked, amazed that the line of fire he'd traced on her skin wasn't visible. If she must face the death of her dreams, it would help to have Niall there to give her moral support.

Nightshade stood in the doorway of the summer kitchen at Trevelion Manor. With his back to the sweeping lawn that ran down to the cliffs, he watched Tristan prepare to slice open the belly of a dead rabbit.

It was vital he discover what Tristan's plans for Rosenwyn were before Niall brought her to the manor.

Sunlight glinted off the scalpel blade as the druid drew a scarlet line through the gray fur. The metallic tang of warm blood filled the room, making Nightshade's gums sting.

With the methodical strokes of a skilled surgeon,

Tristan widened the incision. The intense scarlet of fresh blood coated the druid's yellow rubber gloves as he pulled the wound apart and eased the animal's entrails out onto a plastic tray.

"Whatever happened to traditional divination tools? Don't the rubber gloves destroy the message in the entrails?"

"Shh, I'm concentrating." Tristan held up a hand, and blood trickled down the glove and dripped onto the cracked brown linoleum. Humming tunelessly, he started to poke about in the guts.

Nightshade folded his arms and leaned a shoulder against the door frame, content to be patient, because he already knew what Tristan would discover from the reading.

"The portents are good." Red flags of excitement blazed on Tristan's cheeks. "I think Niall will bring the pisky here today."

Nightshade examined his fingernails, contemplating how much of his nocturnal visit to the Elephant's Nest he should reveal. He smiled in anticipation of the druid's surprise. "I could have told you that."

Tristan looked up, a length of small intestine dangling from his hand. "What's that?"

Nightshade wandered across to the dirty window framed with rotten wood. He stared at the waves rolling across the English Channel toward France. Let the bastard wait.

"Tell me, stalker, or you'll suffer."

From the tone of Tristan's voice, an empty threat— for now. Nightshade cocked a hip against the counter and examined Tristan's frustrated expression with satisfaction. "I visited the Nest last night. She's staying there."

Tristan dumped the handful of entrails back on the plastic tray. "Bloody Niall. I should know better than to trust him."

"He didn't realize who she was."

"How's that possible? Niall would sense one of the Good People."

"She is half human." Nightshade watched carefully for Tristan's reaction to the reminder that Rosenwyn was his daughter.

"So?" Tristan turned away, ripped off the gloves, and dumped them in the trash.

"She's been living as a human for years. You'd never know she has mixed blood unless you were looking for it."

"Sounds like you picked her out easily enough."

"I remember her."

"Ahh." Tristan walked out to the terrace and stared at the sea.

Nightshade followed him, squinting in the sunlight. "Niall's bringing her today. Will you ask her to stay?"

If Tristan persuaded Niall that Rosenwyn should stay, it would make Nightshade's life easier. Then, with her under the same roof, it would be only a matter of time before he made her his own. He suppressed a growl at the thought of her warm blood flooding his mouth, and her sweet, healthy flesh beneath his teeth.

"She won't be staying here," Tristan announced.

Nightshade snapped back to reality with a jolt. "Why not? She's your flesh and blood."

"I know you want her. Forget the idea. You have me."

Nightshade bit down on his retort. "Why do you want to see her then?"

"She has some things of mine. I intend to retrieve them."

"What things?" Before the words faded, Nightshade answered his own question. "The Magic Knot paintings," he whispered, queasy with horror at the thought of seeing the imprisoned bodies of the piskies.

Tristan faced him. In the brisk sea breeze, clumps of his hair flapped against his skull like bird's wings. "You do have a brain in that magnificent head of yours after all." He grasped Nightshade's forearm, a glint of madness in his eyes. "I want to bring the pictures back here, let the piskies see I have their ancestral home. They'll wish they'd been kinder to me when they had the chance." Tristan's fingernails bit into Nightshade's arm. "If the girl was raised as human, she won't realize the paintings are anything more than oil on canvas. I'll persuade her to let me have them."

He slapped Nightshade's cheek, harder than an affectionate pat, but not hard enough to stir the need to retaliate. Nightshade curled his lip at the sting.

Tristan grinned darkly. "Revenge will at last be ours. I'll force the troop to watch from their painted prisons while I sacrifice the last member of their royal line. Then they'll know they're trapped for all eternity."

Tristan plans to kill Rosenwyn.

Only years of practice held Nightshade steady as the shock of Tristan's words crashed through him, shattering his brittle new hopes. Thirty years ago he'd craved revenge on the piskies. He'd believed alliance with Tristan gave him a future. Instead, Tristan had destroyed everything that mattered to him. He wouldn't let the druid kill Rosenwyn.

Rosenwyn is my queen.

The thought of watching Tristan slice open Rose's belly as he had the rabbit's weighed sickly in his gut.

Tristan gave him a searching look.

Nightshade smiled slowly, precisely, judging the exact stretch of lips and curve of mouth to indicate pleasure and acceptance. "Wonderful."

"Come, let's discuss our strategy for this meeting with my daughter." Tristan ambled toward the house.

Nightshade stared after him. He already knew his strategy: bite Rosenwyn, bind her to him with bloodlust, then kill Tristan. And if the delicious Niall O'Connor got in the way, Nightshade would be only too happy to bite him as well.

Later that day, Rose drove her car along a narrow Cornish lane, following the arousing sight of Niall's tight backside straddling his motorcycle.

He signaled and turned left between two massive granite pillars topped with statues of slender dancing figures. She slowed her car and glanced up at their frozen smiles with a hint of disquiet.

The drive ran for half a mile between rambling, unkempt banks of rhododendrons, crossed a bridge spanning a stream, and climbed a hill through stubby woodland buffeted by the sea winds.

As they emerged from the wood onto a drive circling a fountain, Trevelion Manor stood before her, a rambling old structure that looked as though it had grown out of the cliffs. The front of the building was wreathed in ropes of creeper bearing withered yellow leaves that fluttered in the sea breeze.

She shivered. Her father certainly liked his privacy. The Elephant's Nest seemed isolated, but it was nothing compared to this place.

On climbing out of her car, she wrinkled her nose at the smelly, stagnant water and rotting leaves in the fountain. Clumps of yellow and gray lichen clung to the nymph dancing above the bowl, turning what must have once been a pretty statue into a monster.

A tingle of familiarity ran along her nerves. She stared at the nymph's face, imagined it clean, imagined water spraying jewel-like drops from the shell in its hand. Had she ever lived here? Her mother had been so secretive about her father, she'd never mentioned where they lived.

Niall came over to her as the front door opened. "Good luck," he said softly, and they walked toward the house.

Nightshade stood in the doorway grinning. "Good afternoon, Rosenwyn. I knew you wouldn't be able to keep away from me."

"Hello, Nightshade." Arrogant, conceited, and proud, she thought as she took in his silky hair trailing over rock-hard pecs. But, boy, could he carry it off.

"Half-breed." Nightshade acknowledged Niall with a grin that verged on a leer.

Face blank, Niall made no response to the insult. "The lass's here to see her father."

"And her father is delighted to see her." A slender, almost frail man stepped out and smiled at her.

Rose tried to smile back but her lips wouldn't cooperate. With his waxy skin and obviously dyed black hair, he resembled a walking corpse who'd been prepared by the undertaker and then risen from the slab. She hadn't taken after her mother, but God help her if she looked like her father.

"Hello, Mr. Jago." Now that the time of the meeting was here, she had no idea what to say. She didn't even know what to call him.

He stepped closer and extended his hand. "Welcome, my dear. Do come in out of the cold wind. November has brought winter at last."

Up close, he smelled of musty fabric and chemicals. When she grasped his hand, a ripple of cold shot up her arm. Retrieving her hand, she rubbed life back into her fingers. Every instinct she possessed told her not to venture inside.

He inclined his head and indicated that she should precede him through the door. "Please do come in."

Rose glanced at Niall for encouragement and met the blank wall of his unreadable gaze.

Damn. She'd come this far. . . .

With a quiver of trepidation, she stepped over the threshold into the dark hallway. The decorative wooden paneling and plasterwork inside had obviously once been grand but, like the outside of the house, had fallen into disrepair. Her father led her along the corridor to a large drawing room dominated by eerie stuffed animals. A bay window looked out over a large garden toward the sea. Although the house was in poor condition, the place must be worth a fortune.

Nightshade wandered across to the massive granite fireplace and spread his wings toward the heat. Niall entered last and positioned himself by the doorway. Reaching out mentally, Rose sensed Niall as if he were an anchor for her sanity. She released her breath, glad of the support.

"A drink, my dear." Tristan held up a decanter of golden liquid.

"I don't drink."

"A cup of tea, perhaps."

"No, thank you." She looked around at the yellowing teeth and glassy eyes of the dead animals. The idea of consuming anything in this place made her nauseated.

"I hope you don't mind if I do." He poured for himself and indicated a seat by the window. "Make yourself comfortable. We'll talk. Catch up on the years we've missed."

Rose sat stiffly facing her father, and noticed Nightshade and Niall eyeing each other like pit bulls.

"If you two boys are going to fight, please take it outside so I can talk to my daughter in peace. Otherwise sit down and behave," Tristan said, his casual tone at odds with his words.

Niall dropped into a straight-backed chair by the door. Nightshade flopped across an easy chair, legs over one arm, wings over the other. Furniture was not designed for people with wings.

Tristan placed his glass on a side table and steepled his fingers. "Now, Rosenwyn, tell me about your mother."

Her mother's words echoed in her mind: *Never go to Cornwall. Never search for your father.* A flash of guilt stung her and lingered, a burning pain in her chest. Rose had always assumed her mother was just bitter and paranoid, but if she'd been a fairy, something terrible must have happened to drive her out alone into the human world.

"There isn't much to tell. She died eleven months ago."

"Was she happy?"

Rose stared out the window toward the sea. Had her mother been happy? For as long as she remembered, her mother had frantically tried to enjoy herself. The men. The drink and drugs. But her behavior had been a search for oblivion more than happiness.

If Rose had felt out of place, her mother must have been desperate—only she'd used a different method of escape.

Rose clenched her hands. She had always judged her mother harshly. Maybe she should have tried to understand. "In her own way, I'm sure she was happy."

"But it wasn't your way?"

Even if he were her biological father, discussing her mother with this stranger felt like a betrayal. He was nothing like the father she'd pictured in her dreams. She had no wish to reveal her hopes and worries to him.

"Mother was an artist. I'm an accountant." Rose forced a smile. "And never the twain shall meet."

Tristan Jago smiled back. "I have a knack for figures. You must get that from me." His eyes lost focus. "Your mother was a free spirit. She and I didn't see eye to eye on many things. It sounds to me as though you two had the same problem."

Out of the corner of her eye, Rose noticed Nightshade watching her. She glanced over, expecting his arrogant grin, but he averted his gaze. Unease fluttered in her chest.

"Ailla painted much of the time when I knew her," Tristan continued. "During the years we lived together here she painted the Magic Knot tarot paintings." He smiled sadly. "Such wonderful paintings. I have a strong emotional attachment to those works. My dear Ailla left me when they were finished and took you with her."

"How old was I when we left?"

"It's so long ago, I'm not quite sure. Believe me when I tell you I searched for you and your mother. But it was not to be."

Rose stared at Tristan and fished the depths of her

mind. A memory skittered back. Nightshade bending over her, tall and dark. She was frightened, screaming. He lifted her, cradled her in his arms. In her mind, she heard the echo of his deep voice, repeating her name, soothing her.

Rose gasped, clutched the arms of her chair, and jerked her head around to meet the nightstalker's silver gaze. "You're the only one I remember. You were . . ." She shook her head in frustration as the recollection faded.

Tristan cleared his throat. "That's not surprising. He's lived here for years. At one time, I think, he was even a little in love with your mother."

Nightshade must be older than he looked, but that didn't seem strange. Something else she already knew?

"Tell me, Rosenwyn," Tristan said, "whatever happened to the Magic Knot collection? I would love to view the paintings again. They hold so many cherished memories for me."

Rose glanced at Niall's taut expression, tried to sense him, found nothing. She dragged her gaze back to Tristan. Why was he so interested in the wretched paintings? Blinking, Rose gathered her thoughts. "Mother had them put in storage." Tristan's eyes widened with alarm, and she added quickly, "It's a specialized facility for fine art, with humidity and temperature controls. Mother left instructions in her will that the paintings were to be cared for."

"Perhaps . . . if you have no use for them, you could return them to their original home. I'd love to hang them here."

In the crowded drawing room, every spare patch of wall was decorated with a glass case containing a dead animal. "Are you planning to redecorate then?"

"This is a large house, my dear. I have many bare walls, and it would give me much pleasure to see them back where they belong."

Tristan's attempt to appear sentimental didn't convince her for a moment. He had an ulterior motive for wanting the paintings. Considering the state of the decrepit manor house, his motive wasn't hard to figure out. It was her stock-in-trade—money.

Rose shook her head. "I'm sorry, Mr. Jago; my hands are tied. Mother left instructions in her will that I mustn't part with them."

Tristan's face tightened until his head resembled a polished skull. "Your hands are tied, are they?" He stood, faced the window, and knocked back the last of his drink. "I was hoping you'd make this easy, my dear. Now we're going to have to do it the hard way."

Alarmed by Tristan's clipped tone, Rose glanced at Niall, who'd risen from his chair and taken a step forward. His flinty gaze flicked between Tristan and Nightshade.

"Nightshade," Tristan said without looking around. "It's time for you to earn your keep."

Nightshade pushed out of his seat with a sigh, stood before the fire, and snapped his wings closed.

Rose stood cautiously, watching Nightshade. He avoided her gaze. The first chill of fear quivered inside her.

Niall strode forward. "Come, Rose," he said, taking her arm. "I think your cards spoke true. 'Tis time to leave."

"I advise you not to get involved, Niall." Tristan turned to face him. "Remember what you've got to lose, my friend."

"I've paid generously for your service, druid. This is not part of the deal."

"What service?" Rose cut Niall a wary sideways glance as he released her arm.

Stepping in front of her, he raised one of his blades. "Me and the lass are walking out of here now."

Tristan sighed theatrically. "How disappointingly predictable you are, Niall." In a quick movement, Tristan placed a wooden tube between his lips and blew.

"What in the Furies?" Even as Niall slapped a hand to his throat and plucked out a small black-feathered dart, he stumbled forward. He moved his lips, but no sound came out.

Horror surged through her. As she grasped for Niall's arm, his eyes rolled back and he collapsed to the floor.

She knelt by him and felt his pulse still beating strongly. "You madman," she shouted at Tristan. "What the hell are you playing at?"

"I assure you, I'm deadly serious. I will have those paintings."

Heart thumping in her ears, Rose jumped up and put a chair between them. "Hurting Niall isn't going to make me cooperate." She pulled her cell phone from her jacket pocket. "Let's see what the police have to say, shall we?" Taking her eyes off Tristan for a second, she checked the display. No signal. "Shit!"

Tristan's thin lips peeled back in a parody of a smile. She backed toward the door. Nightshade circled behind her. Cut off her escape. Icy claws of fear raked her belly. Glancing around wildly, she realized she was stranded in the middle of the room with no escape.

"Admit defeat, girl. You can't evade the stalker. If

you did escape, he'd follow you and bring you home." Tristan took a step closer. "This *is* your home, you know. The property passed to your mother on the king's death, so technically it belongs to you."

Rose glanced at Niall's knife, which had dropped beneath a table when he fell, but the weapon was out of reach. "You can't keep me here. I have a job. People will miss me."

He shrugged. "Does anyone really care? You'll become another statistic." He nudged Niall's arm with the toe of his leather carpet slipper. "When our handsome Irish fairy wakes up, he'll fetch me the Magic Knot paintings to protect his sister. And I'll finally be able to finish what I started thirty years ago."

Rose had no idea what he was talking about, and at the moment, she didn't care. He took another step toward her. She backed into the solid bulk of Nightshade. He clamped her arms at her sides as Tristan approached. The blood drained from her head, leaving her dizzy.

"I won't tell you where the paintings are. You don't scare me," she said with more conviction than she felt.

Her father smiled, a vicious anticipation gleaming in his eyes.

"I assure you, I will when you see the tools I keep in my workroom."

Chapter Seven

Niall's head throbbed as though a banshee had wailed in his ear. He swallowed the sour taste in his mouth and tried to raise a hand to his eyes. He couldn't.

With effort, he forced open his eyelids and stared down at his lap. His wrists were tied to the arms of a chair. He yanked on his legs and discovered his ankles were bound as well.

The events that had occurred before he'd lost consciousness flashed back. Pain spiked in his temples as he jerked his head up. Tristan faced him at the far end of a yellow Formica table in a faded 1950s kitchen.

Where was Rose? Niall couldn't feel her. He twisted his aching neck and scanned the room. Nightshade leaned against the wall by the door, but Rose was nowhere in sight.

"What have you done with the lass?"

Tristan placed his bone-china cup into its saucer with a barely audible clink. "Always so direct, Niall. Didn't it occur to you to introduce your inquiry in a more delicate manner? To work up to it? You could possibly have tricked me into telling you."

Niall's head pounded harder. "What was on that bloody dart?"

Tristan smiled with pride. "Ah, now, that is my own little concoction. A combination of plant toxins quite deadly to the animals I trap. But for you, I used only a trace. It shouldn't cause any lasting damage."

Tristan lifted one of Niall's smoky quartz daggers off the table in front of him. The druid turned the blade toward the sun slanting through the kitchen window. "A perfect edge. Did you fashion these yourself?"

Niall fought to keep his expression neutral while outrage at having another person handle his sacred blades boiled in his gut. But he would die before he gave Tristan the satisfaction of seeing his discomfort.

Tristan sighed and laid the knife carefully beside the other. "You're going to do a little something for me, my friend. I apologize for your present indisposition, but I had to make sure you'd listen to me."

"Where's Rose?"

Tristan flicked him an irritated glance. "Forget the girl."

Niall's neck stung, and he hoped the only piercing was from the dart. He glanced warily at Nightshade, who grinned, flashing the tips of his canines.

"Wondering if I had a taste of you, half-breed?"

"The stalker didn't bite you," Tristan snapped. He gave Nightshade a warning look. "I've forbidden it."

Nightshade rattled his thumbnail along his teeth in a derisive gesture, turned away, and stared out the window.

The tension in Niall's body eased a bit. "What are you planning to do with me?"

Tristan leaned back in his seat and sipped his tea. "Release you. When you've heard my terms and agreed."

"Then speak."

"Very well. You'll go to London and fetch me the Magic Knot tarot paintings—"

"What about Rose?"

Tristan cursed under his breath. "Hear me out, damn you. Rose will be my guest for a few days. When you deliver the paintings, I'll release her."

Niall studied the shadow of insincerity in the man's pale brown eyes, the forced casualness of his pose, the white knuckles through the teacup handle. Tristan Jago was lying through his teeth.

"As an added incentive, Nightshade will keep an eye on your little sister until you return."

Niall's belly filled with ice. Those with power always resorted to threatening the most vulnerable. Tristan was no better than Ciar. Instead of facing the strong and fighting a fair fight, both used the weak as pawns to get their way. Any respect he'd ever had for the druid disappeared. Somehow he had to rescue Rose and still protect Ana.

"Rose will have to accompany me. I've no idea where these paintings are stored."

Tristan ran his hand along the edge of the table and smiled. "My daughter and I are about to have a little chat about that. Nightshade will come to the Elephant's Nest tonight and give you the address."

The chill in Niall's belly spread. Rose was unlikely to give the location willingly. Ten minutes alone, and he'd slip his binding and find her, but with two sets of eyes on him, he didn't stand a chance.

"If you choose to take your sister and run, Ana will, of course, be safe for the moment . . . until Ciar finds her, but Rose's fate will be on your head."

Niall raged behind his rigid expression. The bastard had him either way. He should never have encouraged Rose to visit her father when the cards had so obviously warned her off. He'd been a fool to trust Nightshade and a fool for believing Tristan would deal fairly.

His own selfish pride lay at the root of all the problems. How many would he make suffer because he'd rejected Ciar? He was no better than his father, betraying those who trusted him.

Niall closed his eyes and spiraled down toward the dark pit of defeat. He must give up his freedom, return to Ireland, and submit to the Irish fairy queen. Then the threat to Ana would be lifted, and Tristan would no longer have any hold over him. But first, Rose needed rescuing.

"Very well, druid. Release me and I shall leave for London when Nightshade brings the address."

Tristan gave a tight smile of victory. "Eminently sensible, my friend. When you return, I'll free Rose and cast the spell to protect Ana. Nightshade." He beckoned. "Untie our guest." Tristan stood and carried his cup to the sink.

Nightshade stalked closer. He blocked Tristan's view with his body and bent to unfasten the ropes.

"Wait for me by the stream," Nightshade whispered. "I must speak with you."

As the ropes dropped from Niall's wrists, he met the stalker's silver gaze. Was this a trick? There was only one way to find out.

With a slight tilt of his head, Niall agreed to the

meeting. One way or another he would discover where Rose was being held, even if he had to beat it out of Nightshade.

Niall twisted his hand on his motorcycle's throttle, making the machine roar between his legs. He looked at the front door of Trevelion Manor and gave Tristan a final derisive glance. Then he snapped down his visor, gunned the engine, and took off, spraying dirty gravel in his wake.

As the road dipped, he glanced in his mirror and saw Tristan go inside. He rode on for a few hundred yards. When he reached the bridge over the river in the valley he pulled up and cut his engine.

Niall kicked down the bike stand and pulled off his helmet, all his senses sharp, ready to face the night-stalker.

He waited beside the bridge, listening to the trickle of water over rocks as the light faded and darkness crept up on him. After a while, the branches rustled and Nightshade dropped from the canopy, landing silently ten feet away.

"What's this about? Changing sides, are you?"

Nightshade shook his wings and snapped them closed. "You mustn't bring the paintings to Cornwall."

Cutting his hand through the air in frustration, Niall said, "Forget the paintings. Tell me where Tristan's holding Rose."

"If she escapes, Tristan will know I helped. Leave her to me. I'll look after her."

Niall barked a derisive laugh that was swallowed by the damp woodland. "I'll not fall for that one again. No, I'll not be leaving the lass with you. Tell me where she is, or do I have to beat it out of you?" He advanced on the stalker, instinctively flexed his fingers, and then remembered he had no blades.

"Wait. Let me explain."

"Cut the blarney." He'd been poisoned, tied up, and something was hammering inside his head. Niall prided himself on his control, but it had limits. He slammed the side of his hand beneath Nightshade's ribs. With a grunt, the nightstalker retreated against the side of the bridge.

"Rosenwyn's mine. I won't . . . let Tristan . . . hurt her," Nightshade spluttered as Niall jumped on him and squeezed a pressure point in the stalker's neck.

It took Niall a moment to register that Nightshade wasn't defending himself. Niall stared into the stalker's eyes. Desperation stared back at him.

Easing away, Niall raised his palms. "Talk."

Nightshade sat, flexed his shoulders, and shook his wings. He touched his ribs and winced. "Rosenwyn and I are the last of the Cornish troop. She belongs with me."

"If you're so desperate for company, take yourself off to America and find the others."

Nightshade shook his head and stared at the ground. "They didn't go to America."

"Then what? They're all dead? The whole troop?" Niall said, half joking.

Nightshade nodded. "As good as."

Shock left Niall cold, empty. "How?"

"Tristan—"

"Not possible. The druid doesn't have the power to kill them all. 'Tis the truth I want."

Nightshade curled his lip, revealing a hint of his usual attitude. "Be quiet, Irish, and listen. Tristan broke their Magic Knots and used Ailla Tremain's paintings of them to trap their bodies. She could render a portrait in such detail . . ." He gazed into the distance, a look of longing on his face.

"And?"

"When the link between body, mind, and spirit was broken, Tristan cast a spell to bind each in his or her portrait. Then he trapped their minds and spirits in glass globes."

"Great Danu." The horror of existing in the endless oblivion of in-between, neither dead nor alive, swamped Niall's mind. The stalker flicked his gaze at Niall, then squeezed his eyes closed. Realization dawned. "What part of this betrayal was yours?"

"I was young." Nightshade rubbed a hand over his face. "The piskies ordered me out. They didn't want me."

"They only followed tradition. Stalkers are solitary wanderers."

Anger flashed silver fire in Nightshade's eyes. "Why should I be bound by tradition?"

Such a terrible crime could not be easily forgiven, but a reluctant trace of sympathy flitted through Niall. He knew exactly how it felt to be isolated and unwanted. He'd dealt with his feelings in a different way, but he had also hurt those he loved.

"Tristan spun such tales," Nightshade said. "He seduced me with magic and the lure of his blood, freely offered. Now he sickens me."

Niall's sympathy died when he remembered the danger Rose faced because of Nightshade and Tristan's schemes. "Would you punish the lass as well? Keep her imprisoned here because you've grown tired of your blood bond?"

Nightshade jumped up. "Tristan's a walking

corpse. Feeding on the piskies' spiritual energy has burned him out. It's like sucking blood from a dead body."

"Then surely 'tis a good thing if the paintings are brought back. You have a chance to make amends. Retie body, mind, and spirit and bring your troop back to life."

"How could I ever face them?" Nightshade paced across the bridge. "Tristan plans to stand the portraits around the great hall. They'll be able to look out from the paintings and see me. You mustn't bring them."

Anger bubbled inside Niall. "You deserve to be isolated with Tristan if you'd sacrifice the chance of restoring life to the piskies for your own feelings. Rose will not be suffering their fate. Tell me where she is."

Nightshade braced his arms on the wall and hung his head. "What'll you tell her about me?"

"I've not the remotest idea."

"Don't tell her I was involved in the fall of our people. I'll kneel before my queen and reveal all when she's safe."

"Your what?" Niall blinked. His brain swam in his skull as if he'd been whacked on the head.

Nightshade raised his eyes. "My queen. Didn't you know? Rosenwyn's mother was the king's daughter."

The vision of the High Priestess in the mirror filled Niall's mind. She was one of the piskies in the portraits, and she'd called him her king. Did that mean he and Rose . . . ?

Niall shook his head to dislodge the thought. He was in no position to take on responsibility for the Cornish piskies. He had to return to Ireland and placate his queen, Ciar, before she took revenge on Ana.

"Where's Tristan holding Rose?"

"There's a maze of rooms beneath the manor that used to be home to the troop. He has her in his workroom down there. But he may be with her."

Niall clenched his fists and felt the absence of his blades like the loss of a limb. "Where are me knives?"

"I don't know. Probably still in the kitchen."

"I'll retrieve me blades, and then you'll show me the room."

"Let me distract Tristan, give you some time."

Was Nightshade trustworthy? He didn't have a good track record, but it would be easier if Niall didn't have to face Tristan when he rescued Rose. "Very well then. You draw Tristan away, and I'll get Rose out of the place."

Niall would send her back to the safety of London. Then he'd return to the Wicklow Mountains and give himself up to his queen. But whatever Ciar subjected him to, she'd never break his spirit.

Rose lay on a hard wooden table, her wrists and ankles pinched beneath thick leather straps, which Tristan had nailed down to restrain her. Her chest ached, full to bursting with her pounding heart and heaving breath as though she'd run a marathon. Every muscle in her body quivered after the strain of fighting Nightshade when he carried her down into the dark tunnels beneath the manor house.

The nightstalker had gone, but Tristan remained, leaning against a workbench smoking a small, foul-smelling cigar. Even that smell was better than the fetid stink of gore that filled the dark underground room.

Rose watched Tristan, waiting for him to make his move, terrified of what it would be. He tapped the cigar and a blob of ash tumbled from the glowing end.

"It's only a matter of time before you tell me what I want to know."

"Get lost," Rose retorted automatically, and glared at him, amazed at her bravado when her whole body trembled with fear.

"Where do you store the paintings? It's such a simple question, my dear. All I want is an address. Even the company name will do. I can look it up."

The flickering light from black candles danced across animal skins. Terrible flashes of what he might do to her stabbed through her mind. Clenching her teeth, she forced the images away. She must concentrate on the present moment. Keep her wits about her. How could she persuade him to release her? Maybe Nightshade was her best chance. Although he'd carried her down, she'd sensed his reluctance. "Where's Nightshade?"

Irritation flashed across Tristan's face. "Don't pin your hopes on our winged friend." He picked up a pen and tapped the point on a notepad. "Give me an address. Come on, Rosenwyn. Don't be a foolish girl like your mother."

Her mother. Guilt flooded through her, spilling tears into her eyes. She'd thought her mother was ridiculous with her silly fantasies and hang-ups. Now she realized they weren't fantasies. Her father was deranged.

"An address?" Tristan enunciated.

A flash of anger burst through Rose. "No way. Whatever you did to Mom, she suffered for it her whole life. I won't give you her paintings."

He sighed and stubbed his cigar on a plate. "You're like her, you know. Bloody minded."

Tears trickled down Rose's face for herself and her mother as she watched Tristan unfold a roll of cloth and extract a thin metal implement from the fabric. He held it up. The candlelight flickered across the short blade of a scalpel. Terror screamed in her head. She grabbed a breath, her chest trembled, and the air sobbed out.

He took a step closer. Rose jerked at the straps anchoring her wrists and ankles. "Mr. Jago, I'm your daughter. Your own flesh and blood."

Tristan shuffled closer. She fought to slide her body away from him, but she was pinned like an animal for dissection.

"You most certainly are flesh . . . and blood," he said, looking down at her.

Gluing her eyes on the blade in his hand, Rose twisted her head to keep it in view.

"If you're so keen to be my daughter, tell me where the paintings are. For goodness' sake, girl. They mean nothing to you."

The slight edge of desperation in his voice made her drag her eyes from the blade and glance at his face. What was so special about the paintings? Flashing images of the characters from the Magic Knot tarot flitted across her memory. She couldn't make sense of his desire for them.

Rose gulped air, struggling to control her breath well enough to speak. "Let me go. I'll fetch them for you."

He laughed, a light sound filled with genuine amusement. "Rosenwyn, my dear. Do you take me for a fool? If I let you go, I'll never see you again."

"Come to London with me." She'd make sure the police were waiting for him.

His amusement died. He stared toward a golden glow in the corner of the room. "That would be impossible."

Returning his attention to her, he tapped the scalpel on his palm. "I've enlisted Niall's services to collect my paintings. Nightshade is useful, but he does, unfortunately, have his drawbacks when it comes to mixing with humans."

"Niall won't help you after you poisoned him."

"On the contrary, my dear, Niall's only too happy to help me. He has his own dark secrets, you know. Ones he'd rather keep hidden."

The image of the Ten of Swords flashed into her mind. Was this the betrayal the card spoke of? She couldn't believe Niall would do this to her.

"You don't think he was here by accident, do you? Niall's been in my pocket all along. I asked him to bring you to me."

Her stomach clenched in mortification. Niall had made a fool of her. Built her trust with the tree deva thing, then made her think he was interested in her with the tarot reading. Even though the cards warned her off visiting her father, Niall had persuaded her to come.

Rose squeezed her eyes closed and swallowed the burn of bile. How could she have been so stupid?

"Don't tell me you had hopes in that direction? I think you'd be wasting your time. Our beautiful Tuatha Dé Danaan is so proud, he even turned down his own queen. He wouldn't be interested in you." Tristan flicked a finger through Rose's hair and she cringed away. "I'd expected you to have your mother's looks, but you've missed out on the fairy beauty. I suspect that's my fault. Inferior human genes polluting the bloodlines of the Good People."

"Shut up!" She'd had enough of Tristan, enough of Niall. Why hadn't she just gone back to London? She yanked on her bindings. "Let me go. I don't want anything to do with fairies. I've got a good job. I'm in line for a partnership."

Tristan tutted and traced the flat of the scalpel blade across the back of her hand. It burned as though it were hot.

Fear locked her muscles. She lay rigid, breathless, waiting for pain.

"I'm sure you're an excellent accountant. If you tell me where the paintings are, Niall will fetch them for me and you can return to your human life and forget all about us."

Why should she suffer for a bunch of paintings her mother had kept locked away in a vault? Her mother would never have wanted her to risk her life for them. "Cobe Denton in Bexley Heath."

Tristan exhaled slowly, walked across to his workbench, and scratched pen on paper.

Rose melted against the hard wooden surface, quivering with relief.

When he'd finished writing, he looked back at her. "That was easy, now, wasn't it?" He glanced toward the door and frowned. "When Nightshade deigns to grace us with his company, I'll have him take you to your room. He can bring your bag back from the Elephant's Nest later. I'm not heartless. I'll make your few days with me comfortable."

"When Niall brings the paintings, you'll let me go?"

He stared at her for a moment, as though debating with himself what to say. Finally, he shook his head. "No, Rosenwyn. I lied. This is your home. I'm afraid you won't be leaving again."

Chapter Eight

After Tristan left, Rose kept a silent vigil, staring at the door of the workroom, waiting for Nightshade. She was certain she could persuade him to help her get away. If only he'd come back.

When her neck muscles cramped, she rolled her head into a more comfortable position and stared at the dancing shadows cast on the granite ceiling by the candles. Physically and mentally exhausted, she allowed her eyelids to droop, and she drifted. Images of the tarot people filled her head. She sat at her mother's feet as the familiar characters passed before her, smiling and bowing.

"Who are you?" she mumbled.

" 'Tis me," a voice whispered, and someone touched her hand.

Rose jolted back to consciousness.

Niall stood beside the table, scanning her critically from head to foot. "Are you hurt?"

The wild thumping of her heart eased, and a heady cocktail of anger and relief sharpened her senses. "Shit, Niall. You scared me half to death."

He ignored her comment and tugged experimentally

at the strap holding her right wrist. "Are you hurt, lass?"

"That depends on your definition of *hurt*."

He paced around the room, searching for something.

Outrage simmered. He'd made a fool of her with the tree deva and the tarot reading. No doubt he'd picked up on the signs that she was attracted to him and manipulated her to get his way.

"I didn't expect to see you again," she snapped. "Tristan told me you work for him."

"And you believe that?" He raised an eyebrow as he hefted a claw hammer from the workbench. "No man owns me, lass, nor woman neither. And none ever will."

Niall returned to her and started pulling out the nails securing her bindings.

With a frustrated breath, Rose pushed her confusion over Niall aside. Now wasn't the time to argue with him, not when he was about to get her out of this hellhole. "Did you see Tristan?"

He shook his head as he worked the nails loose carefully without bruising her wrists. "Nightshade's keeping him busy for a while."

"You're working with Nightshade?"

He glanced up, his eyes glittering slits of blue in the candlelight. "Something along those lines."

After he released her second hand, he moved down to free her ankles. She sat and rubbed her wrists to return the feeling to them as he worked the nails out of the other straps.

When he'd finished, he threw the hammer back on the bench. "Feeling all right to walk?"

"I don't know." Rose stared at his face, tried to sense him, and teetered on the edge of an endless void. She wanted to trust him, but it was impossible to gauge his thoughts. Maybe Tristan had lied about his relationship with Niall, but there was no denying the fact that Niall had persuaded her to come here against the advice of her cards.

With a hand on her elbow, he helped her off the table, supporting her as a rush of pins and needles prickled her legs. She bent and rubbed them vigorously, trying to get the muscles to work.

"We must be off." Niall glanced at the door. "I'm thinking Nightshade will not be able to keep Tristan busy much longer." He tightened his grip on her arm. "If walking's difficult, I'll carry you."

Sparks flashed along her nerves at the thought of being carried in his arms. Although knowing Niall, he'd probably throw her over his shoulder like a sack of potatoes. Rose shook his hand away and braced her legs. "I wouldn't want to slow you down." She would rather crawl than have him think she was a helpless female.

Niall led her to the door and checked both ways. "Follow me. Quiet now in case we're overheard."

After pointing to the right, he melted silently into the darkness of the musty corridor.

Rose hesitated. Panic fluttered in her throat as the narrow, dark space closed in around her. *Not now, please.* She concentrated on the pulsing ache in her legs to keep her focus. Placing one foot in front of the other, she moved hand over hand along the cold, damp wall.

A tiny flashlight burst to life a short distance away in Niall's hand, illuminating him as if he were the only thing that existed in the darkness. Rose grabbed the back of his jacket and curled her fingers into the leather. He glanced over his shoulder and arched a brow. She blinked up at him and willed him on. Willed herself outside in the open air. He nodded and led her along a maze of dark corridors carved out of the granite bedrock beneath the house. After what seemed like an eternity, the distant roar of waves echoed and she smelled fresh air.

Halting, Niall pushed her against the wall and placed a finger to his lips. He crept forward and peered around a bend in the corridor. She stared at him, at the tiny light in his hand, heart pounding, fighting back her nightmare of being left alone in the dark, small space. When he beckoned, she dashed forward and gulped the cool, salty air.

Niall raised an arm to stop her at the lip of the cave. Sixty feet below, waves pounded the rock face. The heady rush of freedom burned through her veins, and she turned her face up. She'd never been so relieved to see stars before in her life.

"We should be safe now. 'Tis this way." He pointed up a flight of narrow steps carved in the cliff face, placed his hand on her back, and nudged her forward. "We must keep moving, lass."

Acutely aware of the sheer drop to her right, Rose trailed her hand up the rock face for support. Her heart thumped in time with her footsteps as she mounted the stairs. The stairway emerged from behind a boulder on the grassy clifftop among drifts of gorse bushes. Niall hurried her forward under cover of the stunted woodland to where his motorbike was parked among the trees.

"Here." He held out his helmet to her.

"My car's still out in front of the manor."

"Don't go worrying yourself about that. Leave me the keys. I'll fetch it back."

Light-headed with the sense of freedom, she found her car suddenly wasn't important.

Rose took the helmet and turned it in her hands. She didn't want to enclose her head, not when she'd just escaped from the tunnel into fresh air. "What are you going to wear?"

"I'll be fine without, lass. I'd rather you were protected."

As he was trying to be noble, she could hardly argue with him. Awkwardly, she pulled the helmet on. For a moment, Niall's woodsy fragrance filled her senses and distracted her from the suffocating darkness. Then a bubble of panic rose in her chest. She fumbled to push up the visor. Firm fingers pushed hers aside and the visor lifted. Rose gulped the fresh air like a drowning woman breaking the water's surface.

"I hate this." She struggled to pull it off.

"Hey, lass. Hey, now." Niall moved before her, gently gripped her hands, and pushed them down. "You'd be daft to escape your father only to put yourself at risk now."

"I'm claustrophobic."

"Look at me, Rose Tremain," he whispered.

She stared into his eyes, which were glittering between thick, dark lashes like starlight on sapphires.

"Now, isn't that better?" His presence surrounded her, a warm blanket of reassurance. For a moment she ceased to exist alone. She reached out with her mind, and the thread of her consciousness wove with his to form something new and separate. His thumbs brushed her wrists, the touch returning her to her body. She blinked slowly. Was he using fairy magic on her like Michael used glamour?

"Come now. We must be on our way." Niall released her hands and mounted his bike. "Before you lower the visor, climb up behind me and hold on."

Rose stared at the small patch of seat behind him and swallowed. They were going to be squeezed together. She swung her leg over, found the footrests, and gripped the side of his jacket with one hand while she flipped down the visor.

The little spurt of panic she felt was lost in the roar of the engine. She dug her fingers into Niall's jacket and tried to maintain a space between them.

Before she was prepared, the bike surged forward. For a horrible instant she thought she would be left on her butt in the grass. Grabbing Niall, she glued herself to his back and tried to ignore the sensual tingle as her body vibrated against his.

She held on to the solid security of him, leaned the side of her head against his back, and, for the first time in her life, totally gave up control to someone else. Through the mirrored visor, Rose watched the shadows of hedges, banks, and trees flash past as Niall maneuvered through the Cornish lanes.

By the time they reached the Elephant's Nest, her arms ached from holding him so tightly, and intimate parts of her ached for other reasons. She dismounted unsteadily and pulled off the helmet as he shut down the engine. She had no idea whether she should trust him, no idea whether he was attracted to her, or if Tristan had been right and Niall thought he was too good for her. But after rubbing her breasts against his back for fifteen minutes, she was ready to find out.

"Niall, thank you. I don't know what I'd have—"

"Take yourself upstairs and grab your case." He kicked down the stand on his bike. " 'Tis best you leave Cornwall immediately. There's no telling what Tristan will do when he discovers you're gone."

His cold, practical tone doused her tingling warmth.

Had the kind words and the connection she'd felt been nothing more than his way of calming her?

Facing the estuary, she took a slow breath of the salty air whispering in with the tide. Tristan was right: Niall couldn't wait to get rid of her. *Stupid, stupid.* How many times did she have to learn the same lesson? Okay, she wouldn't embarrass herself by telling him how she felt, but she wasn't leaving without finding out more about Tristan.

She swiveled back to face him and jammed her hands in her jacket pockets. "Do you know why Tristan wants the Magic Knot paintings?"

Niall shook his head as he balanced the helmet on the bike seat. "Forget about the paintings, Rose. We must get you out of harm's way."

"If he's willing to hurt us both to get his hands on those paintings, I'm not just going to forget about them." She followed Niall as he strode toward the pub. "I've had strange visions of the tarot people. I'm sure there's something I'm missing here."

He paused at the door and, for a second, she thought he was about to tell her something. Then his expression blanked. "One thing's for sure, lass. If the druid wants the paintings, he'll not give up easily. Take yourself back to London and move the portraits before Tristan can send someone to steal them. Go get your bag. Me brother will take you to the station."

Disappointment flashed through her. "Why Michael and not you?"

"I have other business to attend to."

He fetched her room key, tossed it to her, then disappeared into the kitchen.

She stood in reception and stared at the old-fashioned key in her hand, so different from the usual plastic hotel key cards. The shiny metal key with its curly top symbolized the world she'd discovered here, old-fashioned, but fascinating. Did she want the plastic key-card life, or the other kind? If she lost a key card, someone would just program another for her. If she lost the metal key, she'd be locked out forever.

Rose scrubbed her hand over her face. If Niall had wanted her, she'd be willing to take the risk, but . . . for now, she'd return to London and have a good look at the paintings. Maybe they'd give her a clue to Tristan's motives. She ran up the stairs, fetched her bag, and dumped it in the hallway.

A few moments later Michael strolled out of the kitchen wearing black leather pants, a gold silk shirt, and a gigolo's smile. "Darlin' Rose. 'Tis me honor to chauffeur you to the station." He dangled a key ring in the shape of a leprechaun and shook his car keys. "Now tell me, lass, will you be giving me the chance to park on the way so I can demonstrate the art of the perfect kiss?" He winked as Niall pushed through the door behind him. "Just so you'll be knowing what the best is like, for comparison's sake, of course."

Niall shoved him in the back, and Michael's smile sparkled with mischief. "Cut the blarney, Mick, and take the lass out to your car." Niall gave his brother a fierce look. "You'll not be stopping until you reach Plymouth or I'll skin you alive, so help me." Niall opened the front door, glanced around warily, then strode over to the Porsche and put her case in the trunk. An owl hooted in the woods, and he spun around into a crouch.

Michael took Rose's elbow, strolled past Niall with a sideways glance, and opened the passenger door for her. "Trust me brother to make a drama out of a crisis." He patted the car lovingly. "Hop in, darlin' and I'll show you what me baby can do."

Rose rested a hand on the car door, her chest tight with conflicting emotions, and watched Niall flex his long, sexy fingers, ready to draw his knives. His hands were the first thing that had attracted her to him. She swallowed and dropped into the cold leather car seat.

Michael slammed her door, circled the car, and hopped in beside her. "Belt up," he said with a suggestive waggle of his eyebrows. "Prepare for the sweetest ride of your life."

Why couldn't Niall be more like Michael? No, what was she thinking? She didn't want Niall to behave like his brother—well, maybe a little bit. The bit where he flirted with her—as long as he meant it. *Oh, darn!* Rose squeezed her eyes closed for a second, then lowered her window. Her heart raced, stumbled, then nearly stopped as Niall came up beside the car.

"What are you going to do now?" she asked in a strangled voice.

"Pay a visit." He fiddled with his cuffs. "Does Michael have your address in the visitors' book?"

She nodded, hope quickening inside her. He did want to see her again.

"I'll collect your car when I can and send it up to London on a low loader."

The hope died stillborn, her nerves stripped raw.

Niall's lips twitched. Nearly a smile. "Farewell, Rose Tremain."

He turned to walk away. Panic clenched inside her. She'd never see him again. She searched for their connection and sensed it, faint and distant, like an echo.

"Niall."

He paused, then turned slowly. "Aye, lass."

She needed to touch him one more time. She beckoned him. He glanced down, hesitating. The moment of reluctance before he moved toward the car crushed her heart. But this was her last chance to touch him, even if she made a fool of herself.

Michael started the Porsche and gunned the engine, its muted roar buzzing in her eardrums.

"Thanks for playing the knight in shining armor," Rose said.

Niall cupped his hand around his ear and bent down.

She grabbed the collar of his flight jacket, pulled him close, breathed in the smell of his hair, floated for a second. "Thank you for rescuing me."

Nodding, he gave her a perfunctory smile. "No problem."

He tried to pull away. Rose's fingers clenched in his sheepskin collar. His eyes met hers, held for a beat, then dropped to her mouth.

A heavy neediness filled her belly. She did have hopes in that direction, as her father had put it— unattainable, ridiculous hopes, but what the hell? She was about to leave and never see him again.

Before common sense could kick in, she slid her fingers over the soft hair on his nape and pressed her lips to his.

Warm and smooth, his lips slid her into another world. Heat rolled through her body, singed the edges of her mind. When he pulled away, she released him, shocked by the intensity of such a chaste kiss.

Niall stepped back and looked down. He held the side of his fist to his lips as Michael gunned the engine and shot out of the parking lot. Rose grabbed a shuddering breath, swiveled, and peered through the car's small rear window. Niall still had his hand against his mouth. Was he rubbing away the touch of her lips? Her heart thumped hollowly as she remembered her father's words. *Our beautiful Tuatha Dé Danaan is so proud, he even turned down his own queen. He wouldn't be interested in you . . . you've missed out on the fairy beauty.*

Niall was choosy. He wouldn't be likely to choose her.

"I'm hoping you have one of those for me when we get to Plymouth," Michael said, grinning at her.

How different Niall was from his brother, who obviously fancied anything that moved. But there was a certain refreshing honesty about Michael. You knew where you stood with him.

Rose sank into her seat with a sigh as the car bumped along beside the estuary. *Life goes on.* The new pain ran along familiar tracks laid many years earlier. Her mother never valued her academic achievements because she thought all that counted was beauty. Then she proved her point by seducing Tom, the boy Rose loved. The lesson still hurt. But she'd recovered, pursued her career. She looked down at her fingers. They dissolved into a pale blur through her tears. She had picked herself up before. She would do it again.

As she wiped her eyes, Michael stamped on his brakes. Rose gasped as the seat belt snapped tight across her chest. The car stopped and, through the windshield, she saw the dark figure of Nightshade illuminated in the headlights.

"Aw, crap!" Michael glanced in his rearview mirror and slammed the car into reverse. "Where's me knifewielding brother when I want him?" The gearbox whined as Michael careened backward. Rose hung on to her seat and prayed as the car jolted along the track, the estuary bank dangerously close. Nightshade pursued them about six feet off the ground, staying just within the arc of the headlights.

When Michael pulled to a halt by the pub, Niall ran out the front door.

"Don't move." Michael jumped out, locking the doors behind him.

The two brothers approached Nightshade and words were exchanged. Flutters of hot and cold raced across her skin as Niall came to her side of the car and the door locks popped open.

She hadn't expected to see him again after her rash kiss. Her pain and tiredness morphed into embarrassment, then irritation. She stared at her hands when he opened the door and cleared his throat. "Rose."

"I can't seem to get away, can I?"

"Nightshade wants to talk to you before you leave. He won't take no for an answer."

She stared warily through the windshield at the nightstalker. He might have been reluctant to help Tristan capture her, but he was the one who'd carried her down to the horrible underground room. On the other hand, if anyone could tell her why Tristan wanted the Magic Knot paintings, it would be Nightshade. "Okay. I'd better speak to him. But don't leave me alone with him."

Niall nodded curtly and stepped aside for her to climb out of the car.

" 'Tis best we get out of sight," Niall said. "Follow me." He led them inside to the small office where Rose had struggled to make sense of Michael's accounts.

Niall indicated the wobbly office chair. She sat and swiveled around to face the room. When all four of them crowded inside, Niall closed the door, leaned back against it, and crossed his arms. Michael slouched against the filing cabinet and Nightshade paced back and forth. She felt as though she were drowning in testosterone.

A strained silence filled the room. Rose steeled herself and leaned forward. "Okay, Nightshade, you've got ten minutes, and then I'm leaving."

He halted, glanced at her, and ran a hand across his face. "Rosenwyn, you must forgive me."

"You've got a nerve. You held me down while Tristan tied me onto that bloody table."

"I knew he wouldn't really hurt you."

"Well, thanks for telling me. I was scared out of my wits."

"Stay with me, please. I promise I'll look after you."

Rose shook her head. "You've got to be kidding. I'll be a lot safer in London." And she'd do her best to forget about Tristan and Nightshade. And eventually even Niall.

"My queen, I beseech you, stay." Nightshade dropped to his knees. "I don't want to be alone anymore." He grasped her hands and kissed them.

"My queen"? Was that an endearment? Nonplussed, she looked to Niall for assistance, but he stared down at his feet. She turned to Michael, but even he evaded her eyes and shifted uncomfortably. A prescient calm settled around her, heralding a storm she couldn't yet see.

She pulled her hands out of Nightshade's grip and tried to ease her chair away from him. "What do you mean by *queen*?"

He leaned closer, his expression earnest, his long hair brushing her knees. "Your grandfather was my king and your mother a princess. They're both gone, so you're now the pisky queen."

Time stopped. Her head felt light. Suddenly the irrational way her mother always behaved made horrible sense. When her mother sold a painting, she and Rose would feast on chocolate and champagne until the money was gone. Rose had to steal money from her mother and hide it to buy food when art sales were poor.

She jumped up, illogically angry with all three men for her years of suffering and confusion. "If you expect me to stay here after what's happened, you're mad. I don't trust you, Nightshade." She looked at the other two and added, "I don't trust any of you. Niall handed me over to Tristan."

Niall glanced up, accusation in his eyes.

"I know, I know. You rescued me. But you got me in that mess in the first place. And Michael . . ."

He raised mournful blue eyes like a child being reprimanded, and her anger faded. How could she be cross with Michael when all he'd done was flirt outrageously? "If you hadn't made such a mess of your business, I'd never have come here in the first place."

His expression morphed into a grin, brightening the room. Rose shook her head. She had a soft spot for him despite everything.

She stared at the desk she'd tidied and polished three days earlier. Only three days ago. What had happened to her? She must get back to London before the life she'd worked so carefully to build became just a memory.

She raked her fingers through her hair. "I wanted to find my father to discover who I am. But I wish I hadn't. I just want to go back to London."

Nightshade's shoulders dropped. "You're my only hope. I can't go on as I am."

"Why me?" What was she supposed to do with a

depressed winged man? She could hardly tell him to go out and make new friends. She glanced at Niall for help, but he stared at a spot on the wall and didn't acknowledge her. Heat fluttered into her cheeks. That was the second time he'd ignored her. Maybe he was embarrassed about the kiss. She turned to Michael. An unlit cigarette hung between his lips. He raised his eyebrows and shrugged at her questioning look.

"You've got Michael and Niall," she said tentatively.

Nightshade sprang to his feet. "They don't want anything to do with me."

So Niall thought he was too good for Nightshade as well. He seemed to think he was better than everyone, by the sound of it.

"I'm more than happy to be friendly," Michael said. Everyone in the room stared at him.

Nightshade stilled. "I'm looking for a close friend, bard. A very close friend."

Tension thrummed against Rose's skin as Nightshade and Michael eyed each other.

Michael pulled the cigarette from his mouth and looked at it. "Truth be told, I've always wondered what a nightstalker's bite feels like." He glanced up from beneath his thick, dark lashes. "Ciar once told me 'tis better than an orgasm."

Nightshade took a step toward Michael. "It'll be my pleasure to demonstrate."

Niall jumped between them. "Great Danu. Control yourselves."

The air reverberated with Nightshade's growl.

With a look of disgust, Niall glanced over his shoulder at his brother. "If you must go doing this, take your tryst somewhere private."

Only Rose's grip on the back of her chair kept her

steady. The thought of watching Nightshade bite Michael set her pulse racing with a churning mixture of emotions she didn't want to examine too closely.

Nightshade backed off. "Another time, bard."

"Aye." Michael grinned. " 'Tis looking forward to it I am."

Nightshade pivoted elegantly, once more the proud warrior, and faced Rose. "Isn't there anything I can do to persuade you to stay?"

"What you can do is tell me why Tristan wants the Magic Knot paintings so badly. Does he want to sell them?"

"Of all the questions you could ask, you have to choose that. I don't want to lie to you—"

"Then don't."

Nightshade hung his head for a moment. "You'd better sit down."

She widened her stance and crossed her arms. She was fed up with sitting while the men looked down on her. "I can hear just fine as I am."

"The people depicted in your mother's paintings are our people, Rosenwyn. The Cornish troop. You and I are the last." He raised his gaze, and pain glittered razor sharp in his eyes.

"The last . . . meaning—"

"They're not alive."

"I remember them," she whispered to herself. No wonder she felt so closely linked to the characters on the cards. Was it their spirits that spoke to her when she touched the pictures?

"How could they all have died? What happened?"

Nightshade looked away, frowned, and looked back. "They're not exactly dead. Each of your mother's pictures binds the physical form of a pisky."

Rose heard his words, but they made no sense. "Say that again."

"The piskies' bodies are imprisoned in the paintings."

"The piskies' bodies are . . . what?" Rose shook her head. "Mom wouldn't have done such a thing." Weak-kneed, she reached back for the arm of the chair and eased down into the seat. What had her mother told her about the paintings and the tarot cards? She'd loved the cards, used them every day of her life. Talked to them, and yes, with a crawling sense of dread, Rose remembered hearing her mom ask them over and over for forgiveness.

"It was not your mother's doing." Nightshade touched her arm, and she shook him off impatiently.

"How the hell? I don't understand. People can't be imprisoned in pictures. How can bodies be made flat . . . ?" Her protests trailed off as she realized how stupid it was to argue the logistics of trapping people in paintings when it must be magic. Her heart beat hollowly as she faced the possibility that Nightshade's words were true.

"Blame Tristan." Nightshade crouched beside her, flicking out his wings for balance. "Your mother was as much a victim as her subjects. Tristan separated their minds, bodies, and spirits and then bound their bodies in the paintings. Their minds and spirits are held in globes of enchanted glass."

Rose's eyes glazed. Memories of the tarot people fluttered through her head like butterflies, beautiful and difficult to pin down. "Why? Why would anyone want to hurt them?" She turned to Nightshade and saw tears swimming in his eyes.

"He was bitter, Rosenwyn. I gather he was a sickly

child, and he blamed the piskies for cursing him with ill health. His father didn't help. As chief druid and mentor to the Cornish troop, he spent most of his time with them. Tristan felt neglected."

"Then why does he want the paintings returned to Cornwall?"

Nightshade shrugged helplessly. "He's obsessed with revenge. Although their bodies are separated from their minds and spirits and trapped in the pictures, the body has its own awareness. To a limited extent they can still see and hear what happens around them."

"God, no!" Rose slapped a hand over her mouth and pictured the dark, airless vault where the paintings were stored. Terror fluttered at the edge of her mind. "I must get them out of that place. Mom can't have known, surely. . . . It's horrible."

Nightshade slid his arms around her. She allowed him to pull her against the comforting warmth of his chest. The fragrance of sweet almond oil tickled her nose. When she looked to Niall for his reaction, his disapproving gaze bored into her. He certainly wouldn't be interested in her now that he knew what her parents had done.

More memories of Nightshade filtered back. He'd been her friend when she was a child. Someone she could rely on. She gazed into his eyes. "What did I call you when I was a little girl?"

"Jacca. Few used that name. Only you and your mother and one or two others who saw me as a friend rather than the nightstalker."

"Jacca." The name triggered a rush of remembered affection. "I must bring the paintings out of storage and try to free the piskies."

"It's more complicated than just freeing their bodies

from the paintings. You also need to free their minds and spirits and bind all three parts back together."

New determination hardened inside her. She had a responsibility to the people depicted on the tarot cards who had guided her and been there for her when she had no one else to turn to. She couldn't leave them trapped in the portraits. "Do you know how to reunite those three parts?"

Jacca shook his head. "That's druid magic." He glanced over his shoulder at Niall. "What about you, Irish? You have experience of earth magic, which is similar."

"I understand how the bond between body, mind, and spirit was broken, but nothing more."

"How?" Rose looked from Niall to Jacca and back.

"The Magic Knot, Rosenwyn." Jacca pulled the three linked stone rings from his pocket and unhooked the clip from his belt. "The tarot cards your mother had printed from the paintings were named after the stones."

So the stones were called a Magic Knot. How could she have gone thirty-two years without knowing?

"Surely you realized?"

Ashamed of her ignorance, she didn't reply. Would her mother have told her if she'd shown more interest in the paintings and the tarot cards? She'd eschewed all her mother's odd habits to try to fit in with the children at school. What else had she missed?

Nightshade cradled his earthy brown stones in his hand and brushed a thumb across them. "One represents body, one mind, and the other spirit. Tristan broke apart each pisky's Magic Knot to trap the parts separately."

Rose grasped her own stones through her shirt, the shock of how vulnerable they were stealing her breath.

"Just by touching another's stones, you forge a bond with that person that can never be broken. Lovers exchange Magic Knots. It's the greatest form of trust. You literally give your body, mind, and spirit into the safekeeping of the one you love." He held his stones toward her. "Touch mine if you wish, Rosenwyn. I offer myself to you."

Rose stared at Jacca's stones, but in her mind, she saw another set cradled in a wooden box on a bed of black velvet. She'd touched Niall's Magic Knot and forged a connection with him that could never be broken. No wonder she could sense him. And he must be able to sense her.

Automatically, she raised her eyes and met Niall's. No reaction showed on his face. Not even an acknowledgment that he'd heard what Nightshade had told her. Whatever type of link she had forged with Niall, there was no doubt he didn't want it. She remembered the kiss she'd given him and curled her toes with embarrassment.

"Rosenwyn," Jacca prompted softly.

She glanced down at the stones on his palm and smiled apologetically. "I'm not ready for this yet."

He closed his hand. "Of course. I'm sorry to rush you."

Michael ambled forward and leaned his hip against the desk. "If the piskies' knots are broken, how is it possible to reunite body, mind, and spirit? Surely they'll be trapped in between forever."

Rose looked up at him, heartened by his interest. "If there's a way, I'll find it."

Michael flicked a glance at Niall and lit his cigarette. "Surely me brother, the font of all knowledge, has an answer to this one. He usually thinks he knows everything."

Rose, Jacca, and Michael all looked expectantly at Niall. He frowned and straightened his cuffs. "I've no wish to get involved. I've decided to return to Ireland."

"Grand," Michael crowed, clapping his hands and jigging around the room. "Life is sweet, to be sure."

"I'll be going alone," Niall said, deadpan.

"Oh, no, my fine fellow, you won't." Michael pranced over and hung an arm around Niall's shoulders. "You'll not be leaving me behind. No way." Michael sucked on his cigarette and blew a smoke ring. "Hey, lass, that'll be the answer to your problem. Come with us. I'll wager Ciar knows how to reunite your people."

"I'm thinking 'tis best Rose *not* meet Ciar," Niall said.

"Who's Ciar?" Rose asked.

"The most powerful fairy queen in Ireland." Michael grinned.

Tristan had told Rose that Niall had turned down his queen's advances. So why was he going back? Curiosity mingled with jealousy. "Sounds like I should meet her then."

"I'll be your bodyguard." Jacca puffed out his chest.

"No," Niall said emphatically. "Ciar is not to be trusted."

"Why not?" Michael said. "Rose is a queen. Even Ciar will honor the protocols for visiting royalty if Rose goes prepared. I'm thinking if we follow the rules, it will be safe."

"It sounds like our best bet." Rose eyed Niall, even more determined to go, since Niall obviously didn't want her to meet Ciar. "In the morning I'll give instructions for the paintings to be moved so they're safe until I get back. Then I'm free. I'd planned to stay in Cornwall for a week, and I've had only three days so far."

Niall stepped forward and pinned Rose with a look. "You don't know her, lass. You cannot just turn up and ask advice. 'Tis not that simple. There will be conditions. She'll play games."

Grinning mischievously, Michael waggled his eyebrows. "I love court games."

Niall gave him a withering look.

Jacca stepped up beside Rose and placed his hand on her shoulder. "You'll be safe. I'll protect you."

With a grim look, Niall glanced from Rose to Jacca and back again. "Don't go being so sure, nightstalker. Ciar is capable of horrors Tristan has not even dreamed of."

Chapter Nine

None of them would listen to him. Niall gritted his teeth as he felt control of the situation slip from his grip. He grabbed Michael's arm, pulled open the office door, and shoved his brother into the hall. "I be wanting a private word."

Niall made sure the office door closed firmly behind him. Michael lounged against the reception desk and fiddled with his cigarette.

"Tristan threatened to hurt Ana. I need you to keep an eye on her."

Michael pouted. "You look after the wee one then. I'll take Rose to Ireland."

"Pull in your lip, and for once think about someone but yourself. 'Tis only one reason I have for going back. To offer meself to Ciar and put an end to this vendetta. Once she's appeased, Ana should be safe. But the wee lass must be protected from Tristan until I return."

Michael gaped at him. "Why on God's green earth would you come back here?" He flicked a derisive glance around the hall. "Once you make up with Ciar, you can stay in Ireland."

142

"Court is not for the likes of me, as you well know. And Ana's happy here. I'll not go uprooting our poor sister again and make her return to a place where leprechauns are treated little better than slaves. You lived so long in the rarified atmosphere of our father's world among the Tuatha Dè Danaan you've forgotten how Ciar treats the leprechauns in her domain."

The office door cracked open, and Nightshade poked his head out. "You don't need to worry about Tristan getting at your sister. He can't leave the manor because he's addicted to feeding on the piskies' trapped spiritual energy."

"You been eavesdropping?" Niall demanded.

Nightshade touched his ear. "Superior hearing, Irish."

With a sigh, Niall wondered how good Rose's ears were. "Will Tristan die if he can't feed on them?"

Nightshade frowned. "I don't know."

Niall walked to the window and tapped his fist against the frame. "Even if the druid can't harm Ana physically, 'tis possible he'll attack her with magic."

"Surely we can leave Ana for a few days," Michael said. "We just need to set a temporary protective ward around the cottage. I know she won't like it as she cannot go outside, but so long as she keeps her wee self in the house, she'll be safe."

Ana hated Niall's making a fuss over her. He did not want to leave her alone, but if she stayed inside her cottage, she should be safe. He sighed. "Very well. Michael can come to Ireland." He lowered his voice and glanced at Nightshade. "But I'll not be taking Rose. 'Tis too dangerous."

"Don't talk about me as though I'm not here," Rose

said from inside the office. "I must come to find out how to free the piskies."

The door opened wider, and she appeared next to Nightshade. Niall winced. Had she heard everything he'd said? It was probably safe for her to know about Ana, but he did not want her to know about his disagreement with Ciar and start asking questions.

"So much for a private word." He pointed at the office door, and they all filed back inside. When Rose took the chair again, Nightshade sat on the desk at her side and rested a hand on her shoulder as though he owned her. The unfairness of her attitude knotted Niall's gut. He had tried to protect her when they'd visited the manor, and rescued her when Tristan took her captive, yet she looked at him with disdain. While the nightstalker who'd betrayed her and her people and helped Tristan capture her was suddenly her new best friend. To make matters worse, Nightshade had revealed the significance of the Magic Knots. The calculating glance she'd given Niall after that revelation clearly showed that she understood she had some control over him via his stones.

Rose crossed her arms, green eyes blazing with determination. "Don't even think of leaving me behind."

"There's no need to put yourself in more danger," he said. "Let me find out if there's a way to reunite the piskies."

She narrowed her eyes. "Why don't you want me to come?"

" 'Tis dangerous for you, lass. Ciar is unpredictable." And he would die rather than have her witness what Ciar would do to him.

"You don't want me to meet this Ciar, do you?"

Wasn't that what he'd just said?

"I can hold my own, Niall. I've taken a course on dealing with difficult people."

He barely clamped down on the urge to laugh. "You have no idea how difficult a self-obsessed two-thousand-year-old fairy queen can be."

She blinked at him in surprise for a few seconds, then seemed to gather her wits.

"You won't put me off that easily. I've dealt with a whole range of people in my job, most of whom didn't want to cooperate with me. I can look after myself."

"Like you did at the manor?"

"That's not fair. Tristan's a madman. Anyway, as I recall, you didn't earn any gold stars either."

He glanced at his boots and clenched his jaw. She had a point. But he was not about to concede it. "You're used to humans who play by human rules. Ciar is one of the ancient Tuatha Dé Danaan. Years ago she was worshipped as a goddess. She makes up the rules to suit herself."

"I'm half-fairy, for goodness' sake. If I'm ever going to understand what that means, I need to visit with other fairies, get familiar with the culture." Rose glanced at his brother. "Michael said there were protocols for visiting"—she touched her hair self-consciously—"royalty, which would protect me."

"There certainly are," Michael piped up in an annoyingly helpful voice. "I remember when King Esras visited. Ciar hated him, but she could do nothing to him because he was a king."

"He also had ten bodyguards, a druid priest, and five shades protecting him," Niall added.

Michael shrugged. "He survived."

"Barely." Niall had the feeling that whatever he said, Rose wouldn't take any notice. It was almost as though she wanted to defy him. When he'd taught her to consult the tree deva, and she'd read the tarot for him, he'd thought she liked him. And then there'd been the good-bye kiss. If he closed his eyes, he could still feel the sweet press of her lips. Not that he was foolish enough to believe the gesture was anything more than her way of thanking him for the rescue.

Obviously, he couldn't persuade Rose to see sense, so he looked at Nightshade. The stalker met his gaze with understanding. He recognized the danger Ciar posed, even if Rose and Michael didn't. "She mustn't come to Ireland," Niall said to Nightshade.

Rose shot out of her seat and stomped toward Niall, her pale cheeks blooming a pretty pink. "Since when did Jacca become my keeper?"

Something inside Niall snapped at the sound of her pet name for the nightstalker. "I was bloody well wondering that meself."

She frowned at him for a moment, then shook her head. "I want to ask Queen Ciar if there's a way to free the Cornish troop. If you're so against my coming with you, Michael and Jacca will take me."

Niall's jaw tensed until it ached. Damned Michael and *Jacca* should be nominated for sainthood. He breathed slowly, hanging on to his control by a thread. "I'll be the one to take you, if you insist. You may not believe me, lass, but you'll need all the protection you can get. The stalker and I will act as your bodyguards." He held up a finger and wagged it in her face. "But . . . you will do exactly what I tell you at all times—if you want to survive."

She gave his finger a disparaging glance. "Don't be so melodramatic. Ciar can't be that bad."

"She's worse." Queen Ciar was possessive and jealous. She didn't really want Niall, but she didn't want anyone else to have him either. To protect Rose, he must keep their bond well hidden. If the Queen of Nightmares ever discovered what Rose meant to him, they'd both suffer.

Rose walked with Michael along the rutted track next to the estuary as they made their way toward the woodland cottage belonging to Niall and Michael's sister.

In the beam of her flashlight, she watched Niall stride away in front of them. She flushed, embarrassed and irritated. Since she'd persuaded him to take her to Ireland a few hours earlier, he'd virtually ignored her.

"Niall doesn't want me around, does he?"

Michael slanted her a sideways glance. "I'm thinking you like me brother?"

Rose considered denial, but if she wanted to pump Michael for information about Niall, she had to tell him why she was interested. She nodded and bit her lip.

"He's sweet on you too, lass, and he's fighting it like the plague."

"Wonderful." Rose shook her head incredulously. "Just now I thought the fact that he didn't like me was all I had to worry about. Now you tell me he does like me, but he considers it a fatal disease. Thank you so much for making me feel better."

Michael grunted a laugh and ruffled her hair. " 'Tis not that bad. He's just frightened."

"Frightened?" Rose halted and stared at Niall's flashlight bobbing among the trees. Somehow the idea of his being frightened of anything didn't seem possible.

"Me brother's locked down this tight." Michael raised a clenched fist. "He doesn't let anyone in. Not even meself."

She couldn't believe Niall was simply a man scared of emotions. "Don't tell me—he had his heart broken and now he won't commit."

"You're on the right lines, but it was no lass who hurt him. 'Twas our father, Troy."

"Troy?" The name had an epic ring to it.

"When we were six, Troy came down to the cave beneath Wicklow House, where we lived with Ma and Ana. Fetched me up to live with him at court. Niall was left behind." Michael paused and adjusted the sacking around the bundle of iron stakes he carried. He stared silently at the ground for a few seconds and shook his head. "Was always a mystery to me why. 'Twas Niall he should have chosen. As a wee lad, me brother crept up and watched Troy practice every day, rain or shine." Michael glanced at her. "Troy is the queen's bodyguard. Niall worshiped the ground he walked on. Wanted to be like him. Me, I was never interested in fighting." Michael laughed. "I'm the original coward. The only pain I like is when I'm naked and sweaty and 'tis mixed with sex."

Rose tried to picture Niall as a little boy with dark curls and a cheeky grin. She could imagine Michael easily, but Niall was the sort of man who gave the impression that he'd never been young and carefree. "Are you sure your mother and father didn't make some sort of arrangement so that they each had one of you?"

Michael laughed hollowly. "Hardly. Ma didn't want us great hulking lads in her little cave. We may be half-blood leprechaun, but our only resemblance to Ma and Ana is our hair color. If not for Ana, Ma would have turned Niall out."

Rose's throat tightened as she imagined how Niall must have felt when his father took Michael and left him behind. How could a parent choose one twin and reject the other?

"Did Niall resent you for what happened?"

"Naw." Michael stared into the darkness. "It would be better if he had." For the first time since she'd met him, she saw pain on his face. "Niall blames himself."

"Michael." Niall's shout echoed between the tree trunks. "What in the Furies are you up to? I be needing the stakes."

"Come on." Michael puffed a misty breath in the cold air and grinned at her. "Or he'll think I've pressed you up against a tree for a quickie." He waggled his eyebrows. "Not a bad idea, now I come to think of it."

Rose managed a small smile in return. "I'm afraid I like my sex somewhere warm and comfortable."

" 'Tis funny you should say that, lass. I have this lovely big bed—"

"Michael." Rose slapped his arm. "You have a one-track mind."

"Oh, enough of the flattery, darlin'." He sobered and glanced in the direction Niall's voice had come from. "Don't mind me wicked ways, lass. 'Tis only joking I am. I like me pretty face too much to risk Niall's rear-ranging it. When he gets attached he's a mite protective. He guards Ana with the ferocity of a hellhound."

Rose quashed the flutter of envy in her chest. What would it be like to have a man care for her that much?

They turned up a narrow woodland path and followed it for a hundred yards until they emerged into a clearing. She recognized the small thatched cottage in the center from Niall's screen saver. That meant the brown-skinned child in the picture had to be Ana.

She scanned the clearing with her flashlight and caught Niall in the beam, kneeling, his arms around someone small. The figure ducked her head against his shoulder. "Douse that bloody light," he bellowed. "It hurts her eyes."

Michael leaned close and whispered, "Sorry, lass, should have warned you. Keep the light down now. We'll work by the moon."

Rose retreated to the edge of the clearing and leaned against a tree. She'd planned to help them place the ward around the house, but Niall was so hostile at the moment, it seemed best to keep out of his way. Michael must be wrong about Niall liking her. He'd probably just picked up the link she'd forged with Niall when she touched his stones, and misread it.

The two men knocked the iron stakes into the ground at intervals around the house, so each stake was in sight of the ones on either side. Once the ring was complete, no fairy could pass through. Then with the addition of a line of salt around the house, the druid's magic would also be kept at bay until they returned.

After a few minutes, Ana's small form emerged from the shadows on the opposite side of the clearing and came purposefully across the garden toward Rose.

"Ana," Niall called softly. "Stay here by me."

The small woman flapped a hand at him and kept walking.

"Rose won't eat her," Michael said.

Niall grunted. A weight of sadness settled inside Rose. He didn't even want her to meet his sister.

Ana stopped in front of Rose and looked up. Moonlight glowed on her brown curls and illuminated her wrinkled, leathery skin.

"Greetings to you, Rose Tremain."

Rose smiled, unsure what to say. Because of her size, she wanted to treat Ana like a child, but she obviously wasn't. "Hello . . . Ana. I'm sorry. Is your second name O'Connor?"

The tiny woman gripped Rose's hand and pulled. "Come down here, lass, and let me take a look at you." She angled her head and scrutinized Rose's face with her large brown eyes. "Aye." She nodded slowly. "You'll do for me darling boy."

"Um . . ." Rose cleared her throat. "I think maybe we've got our wires crossed."

"Nonsense. 'Tis there plain as the nose on me face. Give Niall a chance. He's taken some knocks along the road."

"But I don't think—"

"Aye, you do. You own part of him. Be patient . . . please." Tears filled her eyes, glittering in the moonlight. "He'll take a while to trust you before he gives of himself willingly, but the lad deserves to be loved."

What should she say? Before she could decide, Ana squeezed her hand, turned, and trotted back to her front door.

Ana's tears left a tinge of guilt in Rose, as though she'd hurt Niall, yet he was the one being unfriendly. She released her breath. Both Michael and Ana had told her Niall liked her. They must know him better than anyone else. Maybe she would give him a chance. But he'd have to come halfway to meet her. She wouldn't make assumptions again and end up feeling foolish as she had after she kissed him.

Nightshade hesitated in the hall outside the kitchen when he arrived back at Trevelion Manor. Silence filled the room, but he knew from the smell of processed food that Tristan was inside. He flexed his muscles, composed his expression, then burst through the door.

"Niall has Rose! I saw her through a window at the Elephant's Nest."

Tristan looked up, his pupils black pinpricks of anger. "Damn that interfering, righteous son of a bitch. Why couldn't he forget her and do as I asked? I should never have involved him." Tristan threw his fork down into the TV dinner before him. "He'll pay for crossing me. Bring him here."

Nightshade held his breath and waited for Tristan to realize he'd asked the impossible. When Tristan didn't rescind the command, Nightshade said, "If I try to bring him by force, chances are we'll both end up dead."

Tristan rubbed his lips. "Bring me the sister then. The leprechaun. He'll come to retrieve her."

Nightshade had expected this strategy and planned his answer. "They've warded her house with iron and salt. I can't get at her unless she comes out."

Tristan stood, marched across to the sink, and dumped his meal in the trash. "The Tuatha Dé Danaan are prouder than the bloody piskies. I won't let him trample me as if I'm dirt beneath his feet."

How could Tristan's view of life be so warped that he believed he was the one being trampled? Nightshade watched the druid pace back and forth. Now was the time to set his plan in action. "Niall and Michael are taking Rose to Ireland."

Tristan jerked around and glared at him. "Why?"

Nightshade shrugged and snapped his wings against his back. "I couldn't hear everything they said. I think she wants advice on how to rescue the piskies."

"Damn, damn." Tristan stamped his foot and stared

at the ground. "Why would Niall agree to go back to Ireland now? He's absented himself from the Irish court for nearly five years." Tristan turned a questioning glance on Nightshade. "Surely he isn't willing to suffer Ciar's wrath for my daughter's sake?"

Nightshade shrugged. "I've no idea." For once, he told the truth. He didn't understand Niall's motive for returning to Ireland, and it troubled him.

"You must follow them. Find out what they plan."

Nightshade hid his smile. He could have suggested following them to Ireland himself, but it was so much better if Tristan believed the idea to be his. "Ireland's a long way."

"Break the journey in Wales. You'll fly that distance with no problem. Nightstalkers have been known to fly hundreds of miles in a day."

Nightshade exaggerated the haughty carriage of his head. "I'll make the flight to Ireland in one jump easily." And he would. Especially as he'd be flying in the private plane Niall had chartered. "I'll have a few hours' rest, then leave." He was due at the Elephant's Nest to meet them first thing in the morning.

Life was so satisfying when events unfolded as he planned.

Tristan headed toward the door and paused. "First opportunity you get, kill Niall. He's become a pain in the neck. When he's out of the way, bring my daughter here to me."

Damn. Nightshade stilled as he listened to Tristan's footsteps retreat down the hallway. However annoying the Irish half-breed was, he didn't want to kill him. Rosenwyn would not be impressed if he did that, nor Michael. And Nightshade had high hopes of forming a blood bond with the bard. Michael's blood was tainted with alcohol and tobacco, but his skin smelled sweet, and he was easy on the eye. The thought of sinking his teeth into Michael's beautiful neck made Nightshade's pulse throb in tender parts of his body.

For now, he would accompany Niall, Rosenwyn, and Michael to Ireland and keep his options open. He didn't want Rosenwyn to succeed in her bid to release the Cornish troop. But he respected her motives. Ailla had possessed the Magic Knot paintings for years and made no attempt to restore them to life. Rosenwyn had only just discovered the true nature of the paintings and already she was making plans to free the piskies.

Rosenwyn deserved his loyalty and support. He just wasn't sure he was strong enough to pay the price.

Chapter Ten

Two days later, Rose peered out the back window of the rental car as dusk fell over the Wicklow Mountains of southern Ireland, turning the moorland purple. Niall stopped their SUV beside huge metal gates embellished with gold leaves and set in a seven-foot wall.

"This here's the main entrance to Wicklow House," Niall announced, "home of the Daoine Sidhe, descendants of the Greek gods who set foot on the Emerald Isle one Beltane thousands of years ago."

"You told me you were Tuatha Dé Danaan." Rose frowned. With their arrival at the Irish fairy court imminent, all the strange names and words the men had taught her in the last two days were jumbled together in her head, and she couldn't get them straight.

" 'Tis another term used for our race, lass. Theoretically, we are descended from the Tuatha Dé Danaan, though very few of us are considered worthy of the name."

Rose held up her hand to stop his explanation. "Keep it simple for me. What do I call the Irish fairies?"

"Daoine Sidhe," Niall replied.

"Or Sheagh Sidhe," Michael said. "And don't go

forgetting what we told you about the elements. We're all of the earth, so our powers are grounded, but you'll see air elementals who can become invisible and walk unseen, and the queen is a fire elemental."

"Enough." Rose rubbed her eyes, then remembered her eye shadow and looked at the smear of gold on her hand. She wasn't used to a lot of makeup. No doubt the gold powder would be smudged all over her face by the time she made her grand entrance.

Nightshade patted her shoulder reassuringly. He knelt in the back of the SUV like a giant dog with his arms resting on the seat beside her, so he had room for his wings. Niall had tried five rental car companies before he found an SUV with privacy glass. "Don't fret, Rosenwyn. You have equal status to Ciar, my sweet. Believe in yourself. Act the part. Never show weakness."

"Ciar's been a queen for two thousand years. I've just about managed two days. It takes a little getting used to, you know." Feeling like a kid on her first day of school, she glanced down at the lovely dress Niall had persuaded her to buy in Dublin: green silk with a scattering of transparent sequins across the front glittering like water droplets on a leaf. It was the type of dress her mother would have loved, the type of dress Rose eschewed in favor of plain business suits. She'd spent years molding her professional image; now everything she believed about herself was being turned on its head. She rolled her eyes to heaven. Someone up there had moved the goalposts on her, big-time, and the closer she got to meeting Ciar, the less sure Rose was that she herself could carry off the role of queen.

Rose sighed. "Okay. If we're going in, let's do it. How do we open these gates?"

"We shan't be entering here," Niall said. "It'll be impossible to find the house."

"I thought you lived here for years before you moved to Cornwall?"

"Aye, but the house is invisible and the entrances move." Niall glanced over his shoulder and arched an eyebrow as if daring her to question him.

Rose raised her hands in acceptance. "Whatever you say." She was tired of challenging him on every detail she didn't understand. In the last few days, she'd learned that some things defied rational explanation.

"I assume that now we've come all this way, we can get inside?"

Niall put the car into gear and continued along the road running parallel to the wall. "We'll be entering through the forest to the west of the estate. I'm on good terms with Lesidhe, who guards the trees."

Rose flipped her brain into neutral. She didn't want to know who Lesidhe was, or why he needed to guard the trees. Nightshade's hair brushed her neck as the car swung right and bumped along a rutted lane. Closing her eyes, she rested her cheek against his shoulder. The sweet scent of almond oil on his skin soothed her as it had when she was a child.

"Take the lass through the important rules again," Niall told Michael.

Rose groaned but opened her eyes and met Michael's cheeky grin.

Michael held up his hand and ticked the points off on his fingers. "Don't go saying Ciar's name unless she invites you to."

"I've got to call her something. I can't just say, 'Hey, you.' "

"Best say as little as possible," Niall said. "But if

you must address the queen, I've told you before, use 'Fearsome Goddess' or 'Queen of Nightmares.' "

"I thought you were kidding me about the names, but you're serious, aren't you?" Rose rolled her eyes. " 'Excuse me, Queen of Nightmares, will you pass the salt?' Give me a break."

"Rose," Niall said, an edge to his voice. "Listen well and do what we say. I assure you 'tis what she'll expect. We're trying to keep you out of trouble. I hope you remember I warned you not to come."

She was certain Michael and Ana were wrong in thinking Niall liked her. Since they'd arrived in Ireland, he'd made it abundantly obvious he didn't want her there. Michael, on the other hand, had been sweet and helpful. She turned back to Michael and smiled. "Continue with the lesson. I'm all ears."

"Don't go touching her unless you're invited. Never let her set foot on your shadow. She might steal it." He winked. "And last but not least, darlin', don't make her angry."

"Yeah. I'd better be careful on that last one. I seem to be good at making people angry." Rose met Niall's stony expression in the rearview mirror.

"That be all the important things. Remember, if you get her to promise she'll tell you how to free your people, the advice will be trustworthy. She won't go breaking a promise."

The SUV bumped to a halt in a gateway beside a copse of stunted trees draped with lichen.

"This is our way in." Niall cut the engine.

Rose looked out at the soggy ground. "You told me I needed to dress up, and now you're going to drag me through that lot to reach the house?"

"Needs must," he said, and climbed out of the car.

"Stir your stumps. We don't want to be caught outside when dark falls."

Rose slid out and wrapped her thin waterproof coat around her shoulders. The heels of her green pumps sank into the mud. "This is ridiculous. Can't we find the front door and ring the bell or something?" Rose pulled her cell phone from her pocket and held it out. "Call Ciar. Let her know we're coming so she can make the house visible or whatever she does."

Niall glared at her. "Do not go saying her name again."

"Oh, come on—"

" 'Tis serious I am, Rose."

"She can't hear me out here."

"The queen has ears everywhere. And that's a waste of time." He nodded toward the phone in her hand. "She knew we were here the second we placed foot on Irish soil. She'll be expecting us. I know me queen, and she'll have left us some surprises. For that reason, we take the back door."

"I guess from your tone of voice you mean the unexpected-tax-bill type of surprise rather than the you've-won-the-lottery sort."

Niall unlatched the gate and held it wide for them. "Never you mind, lass. When 'tis time to start worrying, you'll know."

Rose stomped through the gate. Niall had made a big fuss about her clothes, but the only concession he'd made to the occasion was to swap his usual mud-brown shirt for a blue one.

Michael, on the other hand, was decked out in black leather pants and a silky red pullover that fit as though they'd been poured on. Jacca had stuck with black jeans, and she wondered if he ever wore anything else.

When they walked through Dublin airport, he'd worn a long coat, dark glasses, and a gray silk fedora, so he resembled a fifties gangster—if you ignored the slight bump on his back from his wings.

Jacca took her arm and helped her negotiate the wet ground. Once they entered the woodland, the track became firmer. They followed a narrow path between the trees for about fifteen minutes.

Dark clouds loomed over the mountaintops, bringing premature night. Jacca took a flashlight from his pocket and snapped it on so she could see the path.

Niall paused at the front, and they grouped behind him. He glanced at the sky and swore beneath his breath. "We could have done with another half hour's light."

Michael glanced down at her and pulled an exaggerated sad face. "Don't go taking any notice of Mr. Doom-and-gloom. 'Tis fine we'll be."

Holding a hand out, Michael linked his fingers with hers, then guided her down a slippery incline toward the river.

"Nearly there," Niall announced.

"To the house?" Rose asked.

"No." He glanced at her over his shoulder. "To the cave where Lesidhe resides."

Niall stopped at the bottom of the hill and raised a hand. "Hang on here. I'll be back in a tick." He ducked beneath a branch and climbed the slope into the trees.

Rose shuddered at the nip in the air and pressed against the warmth of Michael's back. Between the stunted trees, she saw Niall stop before a heap of boulders. "Surely no one lives there?"

Michael put his finger to his lips. "Watch," he whispered.

Niall crouched, and Rose heard the low drone of his voice as he chanted some foreign words. After about thirty seconds, green mist streamed out of the cave like steam from a kettle. The mist formed a column and solidified into a tall, slender man with green skin.

He exchanged a few words with Niall, then drifted wraithlike between the stunted trunks toward them, and emerged onto the path.

He inclined his head toward Michael. "*Seanchai.* 'Tis a pleasure to see you return, keeper of ancient tales. The troop has been without a storyteller since you left." His gaze flitted over her briefly as though she were of no consequence, then rested on Jacca. "Nightstalker. A visitor to entertain the Fearsome Goddess."

Niall had walked up behind the green fairy and hooked his thumbs in his pockets while he watched the exchange. "Where's the gap in the mist, Lesidhe?"

The creature ran his hand down his body. He appeared to be clothed in leaves, or they might have been part of him, like scales.

"You must take the path around the lake to the topiary. 'Tis the east door open today. The dark man will see you in if his mood be sweet." He turned his strange translucent green eyes onto Rose, and her skin prickled beneath his scrutiny. "I'm thinking he'll not allow access to the human."

Rose opened her mouth to tell him she was half fairy, then noticed Niall's fierce expression.

"We'll cross that bridge when we get to it." Niall bowed to the green man, pulled a small moss-colored stone from his pocket, and held it out. "May the Lord of the Wildwood bless you."

The creature's eyes widened. He grasped the stone from Niall's palm as though it were a gold nugget. "My thanks to you, friend of the trees." Then he fractured into tiny green drops and dissolved before her eyes.

Rose gaped at the space where the man had stood, then glanced at the others for their reaction. None of them even appeared surprised.

"The topiary gate's not too bad," Michael said.

"Not too bad," Niall agreed, and ran a hand over his face. "Unless there have been changes since we left."

"Uh-huh." Michael glanced at Rose and gave her a tentative smile. "You're not frightened of animals, darlin', are you?"

"It depends what sort."

Jacca's hand squeezed her shoulder. "Rosenwyn will be safe with me. You find the door, Irish, and get us in."

Niall's eyes focused on Jacca's hand gripping her shoulder and hardened to blue ice. He turned and strode on along the path. Michael took her hand and helped her keep her footing as they hurried after him.

"When you asked if I liked animals, you didn't just mean animal-shaped bushes, did you?"

"Rose, darlin', remember what we've been telling you. Expect the unexpected."

Rose shivered. That was what she was afraid of.

They walked for another ten minutes and emerged onto lawns bordering a lake dominated by a fountain jetting water thirty feet into the air.

Niall pointed across the lake toward a group of dark animal shapes silhouetted against the fiery streaks of the setting sun. "The topiary. We'll skirt the south of the lake." He glanced at Rose. "Keep an eye out for boggy patches."

"My whole life's turned into a boggy patch," she mumbled.

"Would you like me to carry you?" Jacca asked from behind.

"Thanks for the offer, but—"

"The lass is perfectly capable of walking on her own two feet." Niall's imperious tone irritated her. She'd been about to refuse Jacca's offer herself.

"It would help if we didn't have to dash along as though we're in a race."

"There be no time to dawdle." Niall marched on without looking around. "Our pace is slower than expected. The light's nearly gone."

Rose was fed up with Niall's implied criticism of her every move. "If it was important to get here in the light, why did you wait until so late to arrive?"

" 'Tis only at times of change that we'll get access: dawn, when night fades to day, or dusk, when the night sweeps down from the mountain and swallows the light." He glanced back at her, frustration shimmering in his eyes. "Or, at the rate we be walking, midnight when one tick o' the clock jumps the crack between days. Given the choice, I normally would not be abroad at midnight. Too many dangers waiting to wriggle out of the crack in between and catch the unwary."

"So I've held us up and doomed us all to certain death." She shook her head. "And I thought Michael was supposed to be the storyteller."

As her shoes squelched into the boggy ground, reality started to penetrate her carefully constructed illusion of control. Someone hadn't just moved the goalposts. This was a whole different ball game. And she didn't know how to play.

When they arrived at the perimeter of the topiary, Niall shone the beam of his miniflashlight up at the huge, leafy creatures. They towered above the narrow path, sinister and intimidating.

Niall gripped Michael's shoulder. "Don't wait for us; go straight through to the east door and call the dark man. If he asks what we be wanting, keep your request simple—an audience with the queen." Niall patted Michael on the back of the head. "Take care, Mick."

Then Niall turned to Jacca. "Nightshade at the rear. Keep Rose in sight at all times. I'll mind her front. If anything happens, stalker, don't pick her up and fly over the top. The queen will view that as cheating. She won't go letting us in if we don't play her game."

"What's likely to happen?" Rose asked, her pulse suddenly loud in her ears.

Niall fiddled with his cuffs and glanced at her. "Maybe nothing. Stay alert. Stay close to me, and if there be trouble, do what I say without arguing."

The clouds slid apart, revealing a silver claw-shaped moon. Niall twitched his wrists, and a crystal blade glittered in each hand.

"Flashlights off. We'll not make it easy for them. Come on."

Michael jogged away in front of them. Niall proceeded more cautiously along the narrow gravel path into the topiary, and Rose followed. When she passed between the first two towering animal bushes, the temperature plummeted. She shivered as her breath drifted away in foggy clouds.

"Why's it so cold?"

Niall swung around and placed a finger to his lips.

Jacca grasped her shoulders and pressed his lips to her ear. "Magic."

Rose took a fortifying breath, and followed on

Niall's heels, staring down the dark avenues separating the groups of bushes.

For a few minutes, nothing happened. Apart from the crunch of her shoes and the sound of her breath, all was silent. Niall and Jacca walked without making a sound.

Suddenly, a white minitornado spun out from the shadow of a towering bush creature. Rose gasped as ice crystals jabbed needle-sharp, piercing her exposed skin. She scrubbed at her face but they clung like icy ticks burrowing into her flesh.

"Niall!"

He jumped in front of her, blocking the shower. The icy needles hissed against him and dissolved harmlessly. Jacca sheltered her back as Niall cupped her face in his palms. She closed her eyes and sighed as the warmth of his hands melted away the pain.

Niall eased open her coat, pressing his palms against her bare throat and shoulders. The gentleness of his touch relaxed every muscle in her body. Her skin hummed beneath his fingers. She caught the woodsy fragrance of him on the damp air. Tender emotions she thought smothered by his hostility welled up stronger than ever. She screwed her eyes tight, frightened she would lose control if she looked into his face.

For the first time since she'd persuaded him to bring her to Ireland, she extended her senses and flowed along the mental thread that joined them. Inside, he quivered against her tentative contact, raw and edgy as a trapped animal. She clutched at the front of his jacket and held on tight. What did he expect to happen that had him so rattled?

He brushed the drips of water off her cheeks with his thumbs. "Are you all right, lass?"

She nodded. How could something as simple as tiny scraps of ice be so shocking? Niall had warned her of danger, and Michael had taught her rules, but until that moment the reality that she might be hurt hadn't sunk in. "I didn't believe you until now," she whispered.

Niall's hand stilled against her cheek. "Open your eyes, lass." When she looked up at him, he ran his thumb along her cheekbone and his eyes softened. "I won't go letting anything bad happen to you, Rose Tremain; that I promise."

Her heart fluttered and then jolted with surprise when Jacca touched her back.

"That attack was intended for Rosenwyn alone," Jacca said. "Your queen knows she's here."

"Aye, and she wants me to get the message that she disapproves."

The two men looked at each other over her head. "Be watchful," Niall said. "We be only halfway through."

"I thought it was you she had a problem with, Irish?"

Niall stepped back, took a breath, and faced forward. "Aye. But she'll let me arrive in one piece. Our disagreement is personal."

A burn of jealousy made Rose curl her fists in her pockets. She wanted to know exactly what Niall and Ciar's personal disagreement was about.

As they walked on, Niall prowled ahead, tense and ready. For the first time she realized how much trouble she'd caused him by coming, and wondered if she should have allowed him to obtain the information on freeing the piskies. Too late to change her mind now.

After another few minutes, Niall cocked his head, raised a hand, and stopped. She closed the gap between them and laid her hand on his back. Until the incident with the ice, he hadn't invited physical contact like Michael and Jacca had. That shared danger had broken the invisible wall between them.

Rose heard a grating sound followed by a tearing, dragging noise, like a huge brush sweeping the gravel. Dread streaked through her. She swiveled her head quickly, trying to identify the direction of the sound. "Should we run?"

"No good." Niall circled, his expression tense. "I can't make out where 'tis coming from." He pulled her down beside a bush. "Stay quiet and don't move." He gripped her shoulders, the silent demand in his eyes reinforcing his words. Then he stood. "Stalker, watch out for her. I'll be back."

Fear rose in her throat as Niall twirled his daggers and slipped soundlessly into the darkness.

Jacca positioned himself in front of her so all she could see was the back of his long coat. For a few seconds the confinement comforted her; then it became annoying because she wanted to watch for Niall. "Psst."

Jacca glanced down at her.

"Give me some space."

He stepped forward just as a violent scuffling sounded to her right. Every muscle in her body locked rigid as she scanned the dark bushes. In the faint moonlight she caught movement, and then Niall grunted.

Jacca shrugged off his coat, dropped it, and braced his wings, the muscles in his back and arms bunching like steel hawsers beneath the skin.

Rose picked up his coat and pulled the warm, almond-scented leather around her shoulders, an extra layer against the bone-numbing chill.

More grunts and flashes of movement came from the bushes. What if Niall were wrong and Ciar did plan to hurt him out here? Anger, frustration, and fear twisted knots in her gut at her own powerlessness. She stared into the darkness and, concentrating all her attention on Niall, tried to sense him.

Something tickled her neck. She brushed the irritation away absently and kept feeling for Niall. The tickle came again, a flutter against her skin like delicate wings. Rose froze, her attention one hundred percent back in her body. A firm touch caressed her neck. Rose screamed, the sound out of her mouth before she had time to consider the wisdom of pinpointing her location to every creature for a mile around.

Jumping forward, she thumped into Jacca's back, the soft, leathery feel of his wings against her face shocking the breath from her. He staggered, turned, and swung her behind him.

She peered around him, her heart thumping like a drum in her ears.

"What was it?" he demanded.

"Something touched me." She scanned the area of the bush she'd been crouched beneath, desperately looking for movement.

The sound of Niall's fighting had stopped. A heavy silence hummed in her ears.

Jacca stared into the night. She followed his gaze and saw a patch of darkness detach itself from the deep shadows. She tried to focus her eyes. It disappeared.

"Did I imagine that?" She stared around wildly. "Where's it gone?"

"It's a shade. Watch out of the corner of your eye."

She turned her head and scanned the shadows with her peripheral vision. The shadowy shape of a man drifted toward them.

Jacca shoved her back and stepped forward. "Get

down and stay out of the way." He took up a fighting stance, and faded from sight like the shade.

Slapping a hand over her thumping heart, Rose backed up and tried to see them out of the corner of her eye. Faster than she could follow, the shadows of Jacca and the shade fought. Grunts and the sickening smack of fists hitting flesh and bone filled the night.

They spun like mad dancers. Rose retreated and pressed herself into the bushes as they moved closer. Panic fluttered in her belly. She couldn't get out of the way. Pain exploded in her jaw, knocking her off her feet. After landing on her butt with a stinging thud, she skidded on the gravel. When she came to a rest, her head throbbed, and her world spun. After a few seconds, she wiped the shocked tears from her eyes and examined her injuries. Luckily Jacca's leather coat had tangled around her body, protecting her skin from the gravel path.

A hand touched her shoulder, and at the same instant, the reassurance of Niall's presence slid into her mind, smooth as silk. He crouched and gathered her within the protective vee of his thighs. "Hey, lass." He checked her elbows and knees. Ran a hand over the back of her head. "Are you hurt anywhere?"

Rose rested her head on his chest, swallowing the tightness in her throat. "I don't think so." The scarred leather of his flight jacket was ridiculously comforting. "What about you?"

"I shall live."

She glanced up at his face in the moonlight and picked out dark, bloody scratches on his skin and leaves in his hair.

"There will be no more bushes taking to their feet this night. I've scattered the charms that were set."

Niall's fingers gently smoothed her hair. His breath warmed the top of her ear; then his lips brushed her temple. Rose closed her eyes, trembled inside, hardly daring to breathe for fear of spooking him. If being in danger brought them closer, she was willing to put up with the pain and fear.

"When we make it inside, lass . . ." Niall hesitated, then looked away. His chest heaved. "I must keep me distance from you. 'Twill be dangerous if the queen senses something between us."

"Why?"

Niall tensed and drew back a fraction. " 'Tis not something to discuss now. If we get home . . . later."

Rose clung to his jacket as he tried to stand. "Is there something between you and the queen?"

His lips thinned. "Naw, lass. 'Tis not the time."

Erratic movement nearby demanded her attention, and she tensed, ready to escape. A patch of shadow wavered, then solidified into Jacca.

He strutted forward, pretending to polish his fingernails on his chest. "Amateur. I sent him scuttling back to his queen in tatters. That'll teach them to send a shade against a nightstalker."

Niall helped Rose to her feet and dusted the gravel off the coat.

"You're full of surprises," she said to Jacca, a little wary of him again. "What else don't I know about you?"

"Why do you think I'm called Nightshade? That is my gift. None can beat me in shadow form."

"Niall, over here." Michael's voice came from their right, not far away.

"Grand." Niall shot Rose a rare smile of relief.

"Me brother always was good at finding his way into places he's not meant to be."

He gripped her hand and pulled her against his side. "Let's get out of here."

Rose jogged to keep up with him, and her bottom ached from the fall. Within twenty yards she saw light blinking between the bushes at the end of the path.

When they passed out of the topiary, the temperature climbed as they left the magic behind.

Michael stood, hands on hips, unscathed and completely out of place in his scarlet pullover and leather pants against the backdrop of cloud-topped mountains. "I've found the dark man." He glanced toward a tall figure holding an oil lamp whose face was lost in the shadow of his deep hood.

Rose looked around for the house and caught a glimpse of a huge Palladian mansion out of the corner of her eye. The building was like the shade: visible only in her peripheral vision.

"Did you ask permission for an audience with the queen?" Niall asked his brother.

"Aye. No problem. 'Tis all agreed."

"Great." Rose smiled at Michael. She wasn't sure what she'd face inside, but it had to be better than outside. At least something was going according to plan.

"Sounds too easy." Niall walked across to the sinister hooded figure and inclined his head. "What be the conditions of entry, guardian?"

"You must go before the Fearsome Goddess skyclad," the man whispered in a voice that brought to mind the sound of wind whistling across desolate moorland.

Niall's jaw hardened. Jacca groaned. Michael grinned.

"I don't recall your teaching me that word." As usual, Rose was the only one who didn't understand. "Don't tell me that after wasting a day shopping for this dress—which cost an arm and a leg, by the way—I should have worn something else."

"No, Rose," Niall bit out.

"No what? I shouldn't have worn something else?"

Niall's blue eyes burned in the flickering light of the oil lamp. He raked his gaze down her body, leaving her skin tingling in his wake. "Skyclad means we go naked."

Niall watched Rose's jaw drop. Surprise, then annoyance flashed across her face. "This is outrageous."

" 'Tis not as strange as you might think," Niall said. "Nakedness is viewed a little differently by the Good People."

"You don't look too eager to strip off."

"The queen knew it would not be to me taste, which is why she's made the condition."

"Don't be shy," Michael said, strolling across to Rose. "You have a beautiful body."

Rose put her hands on her hips and looked at him. "I think you're missing the point here."

Michael caressed her face and murmured something in her ear. She put her hand over her mouth, but Niall could see she was smiling. Anger whipped through him. This was one woman Michael had better keep his hands off of, or there would be trouble.

Niall turned away to cool his head. However hard he tried, he couldn't get Rose out of his mind. He admired her sense of duty, her inner strength and determination. She hardly knew the Cornish troop but was willing to put herself at risk to set right her parents' wrongs and bring the piskies back to life. She might not have Ciar's power, but she had noble qualities Ciar would never possess.

Michael pulled off his red sweater. "Come on, darlin', we'll get undressed together."

Niall strode forward and pushed his brother away from Rose. "Oh, no, you don't, laddie." Nobody was going to see Rose naked, especially not Michael and Nightshade. And he wasn't willing to demean himself by stripping in public. "This condition is the queen's opening gambit. I've a few tricks up me own sleeve yet."

Niall pulled a small package wrapped in gold silk from his pocket and unfolded the fabric. The ancient Greek medallion, acquired from a contact in Dublin the previous day at a cost of nearly one hundred thousand pounds, gleamed in the moonlight.

The dark man's eyes flickered like marsh gas beneath his hood as Niall held out the bribe. Ciar wouldn't pass up a trinket from her ancient homeland. "I hold in me hand a gift for the Queen of Nightmares. We shall enter her demesne clothed as we are."

After a few moments' silence, the dark man said, "One must enter skyclad."

Niall had expected that comeback. The queen couldn't be seen to capitulate completely and lose face. He had only one option. "Michael. You up for this?"

His brother grinned.

Niall sighed, full of conflicting emotions. He really didn't want Michael parading around naked in front of Rose.

"You know me, boyo." Michael unfastened his leather pants. "I came prepared, so I did." He kicked off the pants and posed, arms bent like a strongman, in only a black leather G-string.

"Grand." Niall struggled to keep the grimace off his face. Part of him hated his brother's lack of restraint, while another part envied it.

Rose stared at Michael, lips pursed and eyebrows raised. Niall had thought she might be embarrassed, but she looked anything but.

He twisted away, muscles rigid, ready to pound a few rocks to dust. Rose caught his arm. Reluctantly he halted, eyes fixed on the mansion, determined not to look at her. After a few seconds he relented and glanced down. A wicked smile danced on her lips as she nodded toward Michael. "I can imagine you'd look pretty good in that outfit."

It took a few seconds for Niall's befuddled brain to process her words. Heat gathered in his belly and tightened his groin. He grunted and pulled away. If Ciar sensed his bond with Rose, it would put her in danger, and above all else, he must protect her. "Come on. We must get inside."

Michael strolled past them, an eager grin on his face. The house shimmered into view, and he stepped over the threshold of the east door.

Nightshade approached. "I'll watch her back, Irish."

When they reached the doorway, Rose nearly stepped on the wooden threshold. Niall jerked her back, his heart missing a beat. "Never, ever set foot on a join where one place becomes another."

She turned wide eyes up to him. "Shit, Niall. You scared the living daylights out of me."

"'Tis possible to fall through the crack in between, lass." A simple precaution every fairy child knew, yet Rose did not. Fear ground like broken glass in his gut. She was so vulnerable. She needed watching all the time. He should never have given in to her demand and brought her. Once Ciar got hold of him, he wouldn't be able to keep her safe.

He glanced over his shoulder at Nightshade as Rose jumped the threshold into the house. The stalker's silver eyes held understanding.

"Whatever happens to me, you look out for the lass. Get her home in one piece."

Nightshade nodded in silent assent.

They walked down the spacious marble hallway toward the great hall, where the troop would be settling in for the evening entertainment—tonight he'd probably become part of it. He clenched his fists, felt the reassuring pinch of his wrist sheaths, and pushed aside the knowledge that his knives would soon be taken from him. He would not let fear strip his courage.

Rose watched Michael's naked back. Niall welcomed the hot rush of jealousy her look caused and let it fire his anger, readying him to face his nemesis.

The drumming and piping of traditional Irish music lilted gaily into the silence as they approached the double doors of the great hall. Michael made a sign in the air and the doors silently opened.

The rise and fall of conversation stuttered, then died. The music faltered, the last beats on the bodhran drum discordant in the uneasy silence. Every face in the room turned their way. When Nightshade entered, a murmur of surprise ran through the crowd. Niall had hoped the stalker would be a talking point to detract attention from Rose. Something was working to plan.

The crowds parted and Ciar approached, her delicate body dwarfed by those around her. She stopped ten yards away. Michael dashed forward, dropped to his knees, and kissed her feet. Sweet as a child, she smiled and ran a tiny hand across his hair.

"Good evening to you, *Seanchai*." She looked genuinely pleased to see him. Maybe Niall had been wrong in thinking she would hurt his brother.

Michael backed away to be swallowed by an enthusiastic crowd of welcoming friends. Ciar tilted her face up at Niall as he and Rose approached. The tiny queen's air of wounded innocence shot flashes of warning up and down his spine.

"By what right do you bring this human into my demesne, scald crow?"

Niall ignored the insulting name and fought to keep the satisfaction from his face as he extended his hand and played his trump card. " 'Tis my pleasure to present Rosenwyn Tremain, the Cornish pisky queen."

Ciar's mask of control slipped. The wrinkled hag beneath the glamour scowled up at him for a few seconds before the beautiful fairy face shimmered back into place. If she'd known Rose's identity earlier, she'd have denied them entry to the house. Now custom dictated that she must welcome Rose and offer her hospitality befitting royalty. Niall had done as he'd promised: gained Rose entry and given her a temporary advantage. He would pay for his audacity shortly, but it was worth it to show Ciar he wouldn't go down without a fight.

Chapter Eleven

Rose stared in awe at the tiny woman before her. She had expected a statuesque queen. Ciar was little more than four feet tall, and petite as well. But she made up for her lack of height by her amazing appearance.

Her hair danced—a mass of golden flame—around her delicate face. Her skin glowed as if lit from within. Jewels glittered at her throat, fingers, and ears. She wore layer upon layer of diaphanous metallic fabric that appeared to smolder with heat.

Rose stared at her, slack jawed. Then it dawned on her that the effect was probably a glamour. Mentally Rose stepped back and tried to detach herself from her emotions. The fire faded from Ciar. Her dress no longer smoldered. A cascade of red-gold hair, only marginally less spectacular than the flames, flowed around her shoulders. Her delicate features should have been pretty, but they now appeared pinched and spiteful.

When Niall introduced Rose as queen of the piskies, she wasn't sure what she expected Ciar to do, but she didn't expect to be ignored.

Ciar made no comment about Rose, looking past

her toward Jacca and raising a delicate eyebrow. "I'm impressed, Niall. This magnificent creature alone is worth the price of your entry."

She passed Niall and Rose with steps as dainty as a ballerina's. Rose tensed when Ciar stopped before Jacca, scanned him critically, and skimmed her fingers across his chest. Her face level with his ribs, she resembled a child petting a monster.

Jacca eyed her warily, his stance rigid.

"Another proud one." Ciar shot a malevolent glance at Niall. "Like attracts like, so they say. Don't tell me he's yours, scald crow?" When Niall didn't answer, she glanced around the room and focused on Michael, who was downing the contents of a silver goblet. "Or maybe he's blood-bonded with the *Seanchai*?"

The arrogant woman had purposely cut Rose. Anger throbbed, growing with each passing second. Over the last two days the men had drummed into her that she was a queen and Ciar's equal. Rose was fed up with being ignored because of her human half, first by Lesidhe and now the queen.

Facing Ciar, Rose slapped her hands on her hips. To hell with the "don't talk to her unless she speaks to you" instruction. Her professional success came from taking action, and she'd learned in school that nobody respected a wimp.

"He's mine," Rose announced in the don't-mess-with-me voice she normally reserved for difficult clients.

The crowd around them caught a collective breath. Out of the corner of her eye Rose saw Niall's warning look. She ignored it. He'd purposely sprung her identity on Ciar for maximum impact, and Rose had the impression that the woman didn't like surprises. Well, Rose didn't like surprises either, and in the last few days she'd had enough to last a lifetime.

Ciar turned her head toward Rose, eyes narrowed. "Did I hear something?"

"If you've got a problem with your hearing, I'll repeat it for you," Rose said innocently. "He's mine. Part of the Cornish troop. My bodyguard."

Ciar looked Rose up and down, eyes burning slits of gold. "Well, human, you'll need more than one bodyguard here. How—"

"I have." Rose jabbed a thumb at Niall. "Bodyguard number two, present and correct."

Ciar advanced on Rose, her nose scrunched up, her mouth an ugly pucker. "Niall belongs to me." She invaded Rose's space, bringing with her a sickly sweet smell of decay.

"Gently, now." A compelling masculine voice floated out low and musical, charming and intimidating at the same time. Ciar's expression relaxed, and Rose's anger seeped away. Stepping back, she gazed around for the speaker. The crowd parted respectfully, opening a way for the owner of the voice.

Her first impression was of colors, jewel bright. Hair the color of spun gold trailed across ruby velvet. Eyes blue as sapphires, skin the pale perfection of a pearl. His appearance stunned her. Michael, Niall, and many of the fairies gathered around had a beauty that could pass as human. This man's ethereal perfection could only be preternatural. He placed a hand on Ciar's shoulder like a father gentling a child. "Do not distress yourself, my queen."

Was he the king? Strange there'd been no mention of

him. The man gave Rose a brief, intrigued glance, then turned to Niall. "You choose to come back and make trouble, I see," he said, regret heavy in his words.

The air sizzled with emotion as the two men locked eyes. Unspoken accusations shot between them.

"You gave me no choice," Niall ground out, his skin pale, cheeks flushed with anger.

The man held Niall's gaze for a few seconds longer, then blinked slowly as if the contact pained him and transferred his attention to Jacca. Niall's jaw muscles knotted, and Rose heard his teeth grind. Whoever this man was, bad blood existed between him and Niall.

"Troy!" Michael's joyful shout echoed around the room. He dodged through the crowd like a kid in a playground, threw himself at the man, knocking him back a pace, and gave him a bear hug. "I'm back."

"I'd never have guessed, Michael." The man's eyes sparkled with pleasure for a moment before he disentangled himself gently from Michael's embrace.

Troy. Oh, my God. Rose pressed a hand to her mouth. This was Michael and Niall's father. If she looked past the otherworldly gloss and golden hair, the resemblance was apparent. His enigmatic expression matched Niall's, his easy charm reminiscent of Michael.

He returned his all-knowing gaze to Rose and gave her a courtly nod.

"It appears you have an eminent visitor, my queen," Troy said to Ciar. "Have you offered your guest refreshment?"

Ciar huffed and wrinkled her nose. "She's only human."

Troy extended his hand toward Rose. She flushed as

his eyes met hers with subtle demand. "May I touch you, pisky Queen?"

Niall's alarm sliced through her mind, breaking Troy's spell. Rose blinked to clear her head. How could she refuse the request without causing offense? She shrugged helplessly. "I suppose so."

Troy pressed two fingers against her wrist as if taking her pulse, and his eyelids drifted down. Mist filled her mind, soft as thistle down on a warm summer breeze. Rose sighed. Too soon he withdrew his hand and smiled. "Thank you, noble Queen." He turned to Ciar and touched her hair. "Although the fairy characteristics are deeply hidden, her blood sings with the music of the Good People."

Ciar scowled. "Huh!" She pivoted toward Niall and extended her hand. "If I must be imposed upon, I want recompense."

Niall pulled a small package from his pocket and held it out. She gave him a self-satisfied smile, unfolded the silk wrapping, and held the gold medallion up to the light. "An original?"

"Of course. Only the best for my queen." Niall uttered the correct words, but the steel in his voice cut the air.

Troy leveled a warning look at him, and the skin on the back of Rose's neck crawled as the two men eyed each other. She sensed that, given half a chance, they'd tear each other apart. Was this why Niall had wanted to return? To settle old scores?

Troy instructed someone to provide Rose with food and drink, then guided Ciar across the white marble floor toward a dais beside the velvet-draped windows at the end of the room. As Ciar mounted the platform, everyone in the room paused and dropped to one knee while she plopped down onto an ornate gold throne; then the chatter in the room resumed.

Rose eyed Troy as he positioned himself behind Ciar's throne. "What's your father to the queen?" she asked Niall.

"Her bodyguard, her champion. Offend Ciar, and 'tis likely you get to fight Troy."

That tallied with what Michael had told her. But Rose was sure Troy had more power than Niall was letting on. She felt as though he'd mesmerized her with his voice, and Ciar had calmed down when he spoke.

"It was not a good idea to let Troy touch you, lass. If he sensed our bond, they may use the fact against you. You must have guessed I'm not too popular here."

"I didn't feel him in my mind," she replied defensively. She glanced down and smoothed her dress. It would be embarrassing if Troy had read her thoughts. They contained fantasies about Niall that she certainly didn't want his father to know about.

Niall beckoned to Jacca while the curious crowd surrounded them like spectators at a zoo. "Take Rose to a safe corner, and keep the lass out of trouble."

He glanced at Rose. " 'Tis too late now to be worrying what Troy sensed. Don't talk to Ciar again until I've finished me business with her." He stared at his boots. " 'Tis possible I won't be returning to England with you."

"Niall—"

"Listen, Rose Tremain." He squeezed her hand, for once a shimmer of emotion in his eyes. "I wish things could have unfolded differently." He cast a fierce look at the watching crowd, and they backed away. "Promise me one thing. If I'm not able to return, when you reestablish the Cornish troop, will you allow Ana to live among them?"

"Why wouldn't you come back?" Rose reached out to him with her mind and sensed an endless abyss of darkness. They'd never spoken of their link, but they'd both used the connection. "You're shutting me out."

Pain grazed his face. "I've withdrawn, 'tis all. I want to spare you, lass."

"Spare me what?"

Niall shook his head and glanced at Jacca. "Keep her busy for a while. You understand me meaning?"

Jacca nodded and draped his arm around Rose's shoulders as Niall pushed through the crowd toward the dais.

Foreboding clutched her gut. "Tell me what's going on."

Before Jacca could answer, a young man bowed before them. "As Troy instructed, a feast has been laid out for the pisky queen in the jeweled parlor. Would you be so good as to follow me?"

"Come, Rosenwyn." Jacca turned her toward the door. "Maybe Michael will join us."

Rose shrugged away his arm. "Don't treat me like an idiot." She rubbed her temples and tried to clear her mind. Since Troy had touched her, she felt as though her brain were full of cotton wool. "Tell me what Niall's doing."

Jacca let his hair fall across his face and shrugged.

Michael sauntered up, a cigarette in one hand and a silver goblet in the other. When he stopped and grinned, he swayed unsteadily. "You're looking grand tonight, darlin'."

"Snap out of it, Michael. I want some answers."

Rose pointed toward the dais. "What's your brother doing?"

Michael followed the direction of her finger, and they watched Niall drop to one knee before the queen.

Troy stiffened at Niall's approach and adjusted his stance, hands ready at his sides in a posture she'd seen Niall assume when he expected trouble. She'd be willing to bet the wide velvet cuffs of Troy's jacket concealed weapons.

Niall exchanged words with Ciar. Rose strained unsuccessfully to hear over the hum of conversation. Ciar smirked and glanced in Rose's direction, her gold eyes flaring in triumph. Whatever was going on, Ciar was too damn happy about it. Rose glanced at Jacca and Michael. "I'm going closer so I can hear what they're saying."

"No, Rosenwyn," Jacca said.

Rose strode forward and halted a short distance from the dais, remaining among the crowd so Niall wouldn't see her.

Niall bowed his head to Ciar. The fairy queen smiled, sharp as broken glass, and rested her hand on his head. Flames licked around her fingers, and the tendons in Niall's neck stood out. Hot flashes of fear shot up Rose's spine, and her scalp burned in sympathy. Surely if the fire were an illusion it wouldn't hurt him, but it looked so real.

Rose twisted her hands together, mentally reached toward Niall, and hit a solid wall of darkness. This time he was definitely shutting her out. Desperate to know what Ciar was so pleased about, Rose glanced from the queen to Troy. Niall's father was no longer braced for a fight. He gripped the back of his queen's chair, knuckles white. His eyes were fixed on Niall.

Niall didn't move, didn't utter a sound. After a few minutes, Ciar huffed and snatched her hand back. "You're no fun, scald crow." She glanced behind her and beckoned to two guards stationed in the corners of the room. "Take Niall to my chamber and lash him to the bedposts."

Michael wandered up. He sighed, and the mask of drunken fool fell away. Rose stared at the lines of tension around his mouth and wondered how much of his behavior was an act. "May the spirits of the old gods give Niall strength."

"Why's she having him tied up in her room?" The question sounded naive, but she really hoped Ciar wasn't planning what she suspected.

The glitter of pain in Michael's eyes as he watched the guards approach Niall sent shivers through her. "Even for me, submitting to Ciar is trying. For me brother . . ." He shook his head.

Ciar looked up; her triumphant gaze arrowed through the crowd and fixed on Rose. "The scald crow will sing me a pretty song when I place my hands on more delicate parts of his anatomy."

Anger swelled inside Rose until her muscles vibrated at the thought of that horrible little woman touching Niall . . . hurting him. "Why the hell's he letting her do this?" she snapped.

Michael pressed his lips together, and for a second his fierce expression made him resemble Niall. "This here's what he came back for. If he doesn't submit to the queen, she'll keep threatening to hurt Ana. Tristan used to cast spells to hide the wee lass, but he won't help us again."

The truth sucker punched Rose. She pressed a fist to her belly. "I should have known Niall was involved with my father only because he had no choice. This is my fault, isn't it?"

Jacca touched her shoulder. "Easy, Rosenwyn. This is Niall's choice. Come away. He didn't want you to watch."

The two guards grabbed Niall's arms, pulled them behind his back, and looped silver chains around his body.

Niall's choice? Impossible. He always wanted to be in control. She remembered the Justice card she'd pulled for him. He was the dispenser of justice, not the victim. He must hate this. Rose hated it. A thread of fire burned through her body like a fuse stuck in dynamite. Mentally she pushed outward, followed the sizzling wire toward Niall, smashed through the barrier he'd erected to keep her out of his mind, and fell into the churning nausea and pain of his humiliation.

With a surge of determination that nearly turned her inside out, she willed him to stand. For a second he resisted her encouragement; then he yanked his arms from the guards' grip. Silver chain whipped through the air as he sprang to his feet. A fiery thread of pure energy bound them at a level deeper than thought, deeper than intention, where instinct ruled like a primeval beast.

At that moment, Rose knew Ana was right: Rose held a part of Niall. He belonged to her. She would never let Ciar have him, even if she had to fight the woman.

Rose elbowed through the curious crowd, Jacca on her heels. He grabbed at her dress but she pulled away, ignoring the ripping sound. She jumped up on the dais beside Niall, glared at the startled guards, who backed away hastily, and slapped a possessive hand on Niall's arm. "Maybe you didn't understand me earlier," she said, raising her eyebrows at Ciar. "Niall comes under my jurisdiction now. Five years in Cornwall makes him an honorary pisky."

A stunned silence swept around the room until the hall was filled with absolute quiet. Ciar gazed at Rose, her blazing eyes spitting angry sparks. "You . . . can't . . . stop me." She seemed to have trouble getting the words out. People obviously didn't challenge her often.

Rose shook her head. "He's mine." To emphasize her point, she stepped between Niall and Ciar.

"No, lass," he whispered, and pulled on her arm to move her back. She resisted.

Something Michael had said about protection surfaced in her brain. "We're bound in body, mind, and spirit. Harm mine; harm me."

Ciar blinked repeatedly. Her fire faded. Her forehead creased like crumpled paper. For a second Rose glimpsed a wrinkled old hag, her body withered and decrepit, her rheumy eyes smoky with malevolence. After a moment of gut-twisting horror, Rose leaped back and bumped into the solid reassurance of Niall. He grasped her waist to steady her.

How the ancient queen still lived in that state was beyond imagination. Skin on bone. A living skeleton. She must wear layer upon layer of glamour to maintain her normal appearance. No wonder she was known as the Queen of Nightmares.

Ciar's glamour floated back, gradually altering her appearance until she looked young again, but her features remained twisted and bitter. She started to rise. Troy gripped her shoulder, and she sank back obediently.

Troy scrutinized Rose and Niall with an intensity that seemed to press against her skin. Understanding flashed in Troy's eyes. He inclined his head toward Rose. "Touché."

Lifting Ciar's hand, he brushed his lips across her knuckles. "There are complications with protocol, Fearsome Goddess. Unfortunately, you must reconsider your plans. Perhaps the pisky queen will suggest another entertainment for you." His eyes focused on something behind Rose. "Maybe the nightstalker will amuse you?"

"I don't want to be bitten." Ciar pouted like a sulky child.

"Maybe you'd like to watch him bite. It's something we don't often see."

Ciar brightened and straightened in her seat. "That would be an acceptable alternative, I suppose."

Rose opened her mouth, intending to refuse, when Jacca stepped up beside her and squeezed her arm. He bowed to Ciar, spread his wings, and snapped them dramatically, causing the crowd to jump back. "It would be an honor to entertain you, Fearsome Goddess. Whom would you have me bond with?"

While Ciar scanned the crowd for a victim, Rose stared at Troy, mystified at his seeming control over the queen. His intervention had defused the situation and redirected Ciar's attention. Who was really in charge here? Slowly he turned his head. He and Rose studied each other. Creases formed between his eyebrows, and she sensed that he was reassessing her.

Michael swaggered up beside Jacca, grinning at everybody. "Ready, willing, and able. Where do you want me?"

Niall tensed against her back. She remembered him berating Michael, *Have your tryst in private.* It

looked as though Michael was about to have his little
session with Jacca in as public a place as possible.

Ciar jumped up and clapped her hands. "On the
chaise longue." She pointed to a blue-and-gold bro-
cade seat against the wall to her right.

Gathering her thoughts, Rose looked at Michael
and Jacca. "You don't have to do this."

Jacca arched an eyebrow and his lips twitched. "I'm
sure I can force myself to partake of the bard."

Michael grinned hugely and rubbed his bare chest.
"Try and stop me."

Troy appeared beside Rose with a chair. "Sit, pisky
Queen. I suggest the wisest course now is to remain
silent and watchful." As he seated her, his hand
brushed her arm. The room faded. She stood alone on
a desolate rocky peak surrounded by mountain air
clear and cold enough to make her teeth ache.

Rose gasped, and the vibrant colors and noise of
the room returned. What was that? A warning? She
glanced up at Troy and saw him exchange a look with
Niall she didn't understand. Niall moved behind her
chair and placed his hand on her shoulder as Troy had
done with Ciar. Support or restraint? Rose bit her lip.
Either way Niall's touch felt right.

Michael wandered across to the chaise longue and
leaned back, flexing his muscles. Jacca walked toward
him. He paused and scanned the length of Michael's
body like a man admiring his lover. Rose swallowed,
cleared her throat, and patted her mouth. She had
gotten so used to Michael being virtually naked,
she'd forgotten. Seeing him lying on the chaise longue
wearing nothing but the tiny black jockstrap, he suddenly seemed to be showing an awful lot of exposed
flesh.

Looking down, Rose fiddled with the sequins on her dress. She'd imagined the two men would remain standing. But if Michael were lying down, Jacca would have to lie on top of him. Niall squeezed her shoulder, and her heart skittered.

Maybe now was a good time to find the jeweled parlor where her meal was set out. Not that she would be able to eat anything, knowing what was going on in here. She glanced around. Everyone stood in rapt silence, the sparkling array of blue, green, and gold eyes fixed on the chaise longue. Ciar leaned forward in her chair, gnawing her nails like a rat.

Rose glanced at Troy to see his reaction to his son's role in this performance. While everyone else in the room stared at Jacca and Michael, Troy gazed longingly at Niall. Troy's dark pupils glittered, sharp points of pain that stabbed her heart. Why had Troy rejected Niall when he obviously cared about him very much?

Niall's fingers dug into her shoulder. She glanced up at him, assuming he'd noticed her looking at his father, but his furious gaze was riveted on his brother.

With a rush of trepidation, Rose looked toward the chaise longue. Jacca sat beside Michael's hip and ran a hand across Michael's chest. The nightstalker stroked his partner's face, smoothed his hair—a cross between a lover's touch and petting a cat.

Wriggling to get comfortable, Michael closed his eyes. With gentle command, Jacca placed two fingers against Michael's jaw and pushed his head to one side, exposing his neck.

Rose heard Ciar squeal and tried to ignore her own guilty flush of excitement.

Jacca leaned down, dark hair tumbling against Michael's chest. He ran his tongue along Michael's collarbone, onto his neck. The low rumble of Michael's groan slithered through Rose like an erotic stimulant. Part of her wanted to look away, but she was hooked on the rush of illicit pleasure.

Michael reached his arm around Jacca's shoulder and pulled him closer, as the nightstalker's neck muscles corded, a predator about to strike.

Niall's fingers bit into Rose's shoulder again, but she hardly noticed the pain. Transfixed by Jacca's gleaming silver eyes, she imagined the dark mix of fear and pleasure Michael must be feeling as he parted his lips and bit down.

Rose gasped with everyone in the room and clutched the arms of her chair. Michael tensed, his body bowed against Jacca, then released a lingering breath and relaxed.

Continuing to feed, Jacca slid down and lay on the chaise longue. The nightstalker lifted his leg across Michael possessively before spreading his wings so the two of them were hidden.

Ciar let out a frustrated huff. Troy crouched at her side. "He's not blocking you out on purpose, my queen. The nightstalker instinctively protects his partner while he's vulnerable."

"I know, I know." Ciar screwed up her nose and threw her small body back in the throne. "I'd hoped for something more exciting."

"I doubt there will be any sex, Fearsome Goddess," Troy said. "Michael doesn't usually show interest in men. I don't know about the stalker." He lifted an inquiring eyebrow at Rose.

Guiltily dragging herself back from the pleasurable voyeuristic haze, she shrugged. This was definitely one conversation she did not want to be involved in.

After a few minutes, Jacca raised his head and folded his wings. He ran his tongue over the puncture marks in Michael's neck, then lay with him and stroked his face and hair while he recovered.

When Michael opened his eyes and smiled sleepily, Jacca stood, stretched, and ran the back of his hand over his mouth. He gave Rose a dazed smile and wandered toward her. "I think I'm experiencing secondary intoxication from the alcohol in Michael's bloodstream, but the sensation is not unpleasant."

Worried he might keel over, Rose stood and offered him the chair. He shook his head and slapped his chest. "After taking blood, my body sings."

Niall shot a cold, fierce look at Jacca, which sent ripples of warning through Rose. *Please don't let them start fighting now.*

"Keep your prejudice to yourself, Irish," Jacca said. "It was a willing giving on both sides. He gave me blood. I gave him pleasure." He glanced over his shoulder to where Michael lazed on the chaise longue like a sated lover, and grinned. "Maybe you're just jealous."

Troy strolled across to Michael. With one finger he tipped Michael's head to the side and examined the place he'd been bitten. "The mark is healed, lad. Did you enjoy that experience?" Michael grinned up at his father, and Troy shook his head indulgently. " 'Tis good to have you back, son."

Niall glared at Troy and Michael, checked his knives, and turned his back. "I'm going to have a look at the exits." He stomped off, disappearing among the crowd.

Rose stared after him and sighed. What would it

take to repair the relationship between Troy and Niall? She had a feeling Niall would have to come to terms with what had happened between him and his father before he would open up emotionally and give her a chance of reaching him.

She took Jacca's arm and nodded toward Ciar. "Now that a certain person who shall remain nameless is looking happy, I'm going to try asking her advice on freeing the piskies." This was the reason Rose had come. Much as she wanted to get close to Niall, that would have to wait until later.

As they approached, Ciar's eyes passed over Rose and settled on Jacca. She wrinkled her nose and smiled. "You're welcome to stay and entertain us for as long as you like. We rarely get a visit from your kind these days."

Rose felt Troy's eyes on her, and she glanced toward him where he stood behind Ciar's throne. He met her gaze thoughtfully. "I believe you came here for a reason, pisky Queen. Will you share it with us?"

How very obliging of him to give her an opening. But could she trust him? "I need the benefit of your experience." She flicked her gaze from Troy to Ciar, including them both in her request. She hesitated a second. Admitting that her whole troop was trapped and she was queen of nobody and nothing would undermine her position, but she had no option. "The druid who worked with the Cornish court betrayed the piskies when I was a child. He broke the Magic Knot of each individual and trapped their bodies in paintings, and their minds and spirits in enchanted glass globes. I've come here in the hope that you"—she glanced at Ciar and tried for a genuine smile—"in your wisdom, will know how I can rejoin the three facets of each individual to bring the piskies back to life."

Troy scrutinized her with the same unreadable expression Niall often wore. Ciar gaped, eyes wide with outrage. "You allowed such a thing to happen to your own people?"

"Hang on a minute. I was only a little girl when it was done."

"Irrelevant." She slapped her tiny hand on the chair arm. "Your family allowed this atrocity. You're culpable."

Thank heavens Rose hadn't mentioned that it was her father who'd imprisoned the piskies.

"My mother was tricked. I'm trying to save my troop."

"Your troop?" Ciar jumped up and burst into flames.

Rose backed away from the heat. Although the flames were glamour, they were hot. Poor Niall must have suffered agony when Ciar touched his head.

Fire crackled in Ciar's hair and clothes. She pointed at Rose. "You have no troop. You deserve no troop. You are no queen."

Troy's face froze with the pale perfection of marble carved by the hand of God. He touched Ciar's shoulder. "Fearsome Goddess, I suggest—"

"Not this time!" She shrugged away his hand and glared through wicked slits of fire. "Human impostor. I see no evidence of fairy blood. I'll not reveal fairy lore to a human. Get out!"

Desperation filled Rose, pushed out her fear. She couldn't leave without discovering how to free the piskies or the trip to Ireland would have been for nothing.

Jacca moved closer. She sensed him, tense and ready

to protect her. His steady presence gave her focus, kept her calm. There must be a way to reason with the woman. "Queen of Nightmares"—she cringed inwardly as she said the name, but it had to be done—"my mother was a pisky princess and my father human. I'm as much fairy as human."

"If so, your fairy essence is buried beneath the mire of humanity. You come in here and speak to me as no fairy would dare. You understand nothing of our ways."

Rose jammed her fists on her hips. "No, and I never will unless someone helps me learn. I have seventy-two piskies who've spent the last thirty years in limbo. If I don't free them, they'll be there for the next thirty years and the next"—Rose threw out her arm in frustration—"ad infinitum. Is that what you want?"

Ciar tensed to leap forward. Rose cringed. Jacca stepped in front of her. Troy grabbed Ciar's shoulders before she could move, and she hissed a smoky breath.

"Perhaps if the pisky queen were to awaken her inner fairy, it would be more acceptable to share our knowledge with her," he suggested in the same low, musical tone he'd used the first time Rose heard him speak.

Ciar's fire faded. She pouted and plopped down in her seat. "If she can dredge it up from beneath the sludge of her human ignorance."

"I suggest she runs the light with a fairy," Troy said.

"Ready, willing, and *very* able." Michael's voice sounded from the chaise longue. He stood and scratched his chest. "I'm horny as hell after that session with Nightshade."

Warning bells sounded in Rose's head. She leaned closer to Jacca and whispered, "What's 'running the light'?"

"It's a way of channeling spiritual energy."

"How?"

"Usually via sex."

She'd suspected as much. Where was Niall when she needed him? Her heart picked up, and she chewed her lip as she glanced around. Opening her mind, she tried to sense him and found the empty void of his withdrawal. *Damn him*. She grabbed a breath and faced Troy. "Isn't there another way to activate my fairy half?

He gave her a steady look. "Intense suffering can also work. If you're exposed to enough pain, your instinct for self-preservation might activate your fairy powers."

Rose looked at her feet. Sex with someone she didn't love or intense pain. She wasn't keen on casual sex, but she wasn't stupid either. "Okay, that one's a no-brainer."

Michael ambled toward her, his lips tilted in a seductive grin, his eyes sparkling with mischief.

Troy frowned at his approach. "Perhaps, Michael, there may be another. . . ." Troy scanned the room from his raised viewpoint on the dais and focused his attention on the back of the hall.

Rose stood on tiptoe and followed his gaze. Niall sat alone in the far corner twirling one of his crystal knives recklessly between his fingers like a cheerleader with a baton. Thank God he was around. Her heart lurched with relief.

"Niall," Troy called across the room, and everyone fell silent. Niall ignored him, his eyes never straying from his knife.

"Niall," Rose called, hating the crack of desperation in her voice. *You can't do this to me, Niall*, Rose screamed in her mind, reaching for him, finding nothing. Pain clenched in her chest. Surely, after what they'd felt earlier, he wouldn't let another man sleep with her?

Ciar gave Rose a self-satisfied little smile that made her clench her fists and want to scream.

A few males in the surrounding crowd pushed forward, and she noted their eager expressions with alarm. If she was going to sleep with someone, it would at least be a man she knew. If not Niall, that left Jacca or Michael. Much as she liked Jacca, the thought that he might bite freaked her out. And she hated being prejudiced, but sex with a man with wings was just a little too much for her to get her head around.

Michael waggled his eyebrows at her, and she gave him a tentative smile. He might not be Niall, but she liked him, despite . . . no, because of his glaring faults. With Michael, what you saw was what you got. "Congratulations, Michael," she said in a croaky voice. "Looks like I'm tonight's second conquest."

Troy frowned and walked toward them. "The gold guest suite on the upper floor," he said, then whispered something to Michael.

"Understood." Michael nodded to Troy, then curled his arm around her waist. He squeezed gently and eased her against his naked side. "Don't go worrying, darlin'. You're in the hands of an expert."

Rose avoided everyone's eyes, especially the flash of hurt she saw in Jacca's. Her hand fluttered to her throat, her lips. She had to do this, if it was the only way to make Ciar tell her how to free the piskies.

What would it feel like to have her fairy half activated? God, she should have thought about that before she agreed.

The crowd parted before them as Michael guided her toward the door. Rose willed herself not to look for Niall. If he didn't want her, she wouldn't beg.

When they reached the door, she jerked to a halt. "Shit!" She craned her neck around, searching the back of the room. She didn't want to sleep with Michael. She wanted Niall. Where the hell was he? *Damn him!* She wouldn't do this without speaking to him. She reached for him mentally—nothing—then scanned the far corner of the room.

The chair he'd been sitting in lay on its side. Niall had gone.

Chapter Twelve

Niall escaped along the hidden service corridor he'd crept through many times when he'd spied on court activities as a boy. Instead of taking the narrow stairs down to the caves where the leprechauns who served Ciar lived, he pushed open the secret exit behind a picture into the hallway.

Hand gripping the worn oak handle of his blade, he strode toward the east door. Why had he thought returning to the Irish court would solve his problems? He'd achieved nothing. Rose had forced her will on him, used their link to hijack his mind, and ruined his chance of appeasing Ciar. Who knew what the Queen of Nightmares would do now that she couldn't take her wrath out on him? When Ciar forgot the distraction of Nightshade and Michael's tawdry little show, Ana could be in increased danger.

The last sight he'd had of Rose flashed into his mind. He blinked away the image of her cuddled against his brother's side. He spun around, kicked out, shattered a small ebony table, and sent a Waterford crystal vase crashing. Breath heaving, he stared at the splinters of dark wood and shards of glass. Rose was better off without him. If she ran the light with Michael, Ciar was far more likely to reveal the fairy lore to free the piskies.

By remaining in Ireland, Niall would only put his friends at risk. He must return to Cornwall and make sure Ana was safe.

He hated to admit he'd hoped his father might be pleased to see him. After all these years, Niall should have learned to stop banging his head against the wall, hoping to be accepted. He flipped his knife and snatched it from the air, anger tight in his chest. Michael could have Troy—and Rose. Niall didn't need any of them. Ana was the only person who'd never let him down. He wouldn't let her down.

Footsteps sounded in the hall behind him. He increased his pace. Whoever was following could go to the Furies.

When he wrenched open the east door, cool mountain air bathed him like balm on a sore. Snatching a breath, he headed toward the topiary. He flipped his blade with relish. Just let something try to attack him on the way through this time.

"Niall." Troy's voice sliced the damp air.

A subtle coercion to halt tugged at Niall's mind. He shook off the effect and increased his pace. He needed to get as far away from this place—as far away from Rose and Michael—as possible. The harder he tried not to think of them together, the more lurid the images became.

Troy's steps flew lightly up behind him. To most, they would have been silent. Niall knew what to listen for: not the touch of feet to the ground, but the movement of air. At the last moment Niall spun, crouched low and ready, knife in hand. Troy pulled up a mere thrust from the tip of Niall's blade and raised an inquiring eyebrow. "Abandoning your friends so quickly?"

" 'Tis not your place to question *my* morals." Niall backed up a pace, giving himself room to maneuver. "Look to your own." He longed to fight his father, but would prove himself the better man by resisting the desire for revenge.

"The pisky queen wants you. Why let Michael have her?"

" 'Tis bad enough I've put me sister in danger from the nameless one. I'll not condemn Rose to suffer because of me."

Troy raised a hand. Light spun from his fingers, forming a glowing web-dome of privacy around them. He glanced back toward the house, snapped his fingers, and the cocoon sealed, popping Niall's ears.

"I would never let Ciar harm Ana." Troy shook his head sadly. "Surely you knew that."

Anger twisted inside Niall like barbed wire. "How? Not once have you given me reason to believe you'd protect me, or anyone dear to me."

"You surely don't believe I'm that heartless? I promise you, lad, I'll do all I can to keep Ana and Rose safe from Ciar."

"I saw no evidence of this *protection* when Ciar played her childish games in the topiary. Rose could have been hurt."

Troy dismissed Niall's complaint with a flick of his shoulders. "I had no doubt you'd handle the shade and the topiary with ease." Niall thought he heard a hint of pride in his father's voice, but he couldn't believe it.

"I've no interest in your games." The anger drained from Niall, leaving him weary. "I've a duty to Ana. I look after me own." He turned to go.

"Then look after Rose." Troy's voice punched through Niall. "I sensed the bond between you. She's yours by right, not your brother's."

Niall's heart ached at his father's words. He wanted so much, but he dared not take it. "You were me father by right. Rights mean nothing. Let Michael have Rose. I'm sure you'll help him protect her. Me . . ." Niall turned his back on his father. "I don't need anyone."

"Wait, lad."

The soft entreaty in his father's voice was so unusual, Niall halted. He looked over his shoulder. "Haven't you said enough?"

"My duty to the queen has always prevented me from speaking my mind." Troy reached for Niall, but let his hand fall. "Ciar was much stronger when you were a lad. I wanted you with me, but she forbade it. Bade me leave you with your mother."

Pain glazed his father's eyes. Hope and distrust knotted in Niall's chest. "Why did you accept her dictates? You could have bargained—"

"I tried." Troy shook his head. "Believe me, lad, I tried."

Troy glanced over his shoulder at the shimmering outline of the house and raised his hand, whispering a few ancient words to strengthen the protective cocoon.

"Our bloodline has served Ciar for generations. We're directly descended from the ancient ones who stepped onto these shores with her and established the Daoine Sidhe. When you and Michael were born, Ciar looked into the dark mirror to determine which one of you would succeed me as her protector. The image showed you crowned as king. Ciar was convinced you'd destroy her and take her throne. I pleaded for your life. Had I not promised I'd never bring you to court, she'd have slaughtered you as a babe."

Troy reached for Niall again. Numb with shock, Niall let his father lay a cautious hand on his arm. "Even Ciar's will could not keep you down. I'm proud of you, lad."

Each breath burned into and burst painfully out of Niall's lungs. He pushed away Troy's hand, a maelstrom of emotion swirling through him. How could he believe this now, after decades of soul searching to uncover what he'd done wrong? He pressed the heels of his hands against his eyes. It was too painful to think his life might have been different, if only . . .

He allowed anger to burn away his uncertainty. "Too little, too late. You were always the queen's man."

"I still am. I have a duty to her."

"You had a duty to me. Why even make me—a scut, half-blood, never quite good enough? Why lay with Ma at all?"

Troy stared at the ground, his golden hair obscuring his face. "Ciar read the match between your mother and me in the dark mirror. It was ordained."

"It was your choice! Great Danu, Troy. How could you go letting that little hag rule your life?"

Troy shrugged. "Maybe I made mistakes, but I made no mistake in fathering you."

He looked up at Niall, searching his face for response. Shattered inside, Niall reacted the only way he knew how: he locked down his emotions.

"For years the vision of you as king puzzled me. Now I understand. It never had anything to do with the Irish troop. You're destined to rule the piskies with Rose. She is truly yours, Niall. It's ordained."

Niall grated his fingernails through his hair, wishing he could scratch the ache in his brain. "I struggled for acceptance on the periphery of this court, held on by dint of me skill with the blades. Leadership is not for me."

"The very challenges you've faced have molded you into the man for the job. You've the passion and determination, and the bloody-minded contrariness to face the impossible task and not give up. Rose is the hand of reason. She has a foot in both the human and fairy worlds. She'll guide her troop into the twenty-first century. You're the hand of power. You'll fight for their right to exist." Troy cut his hand through the air. "Don't you see? You've fought for the right to exist all your life."

Niall turned away and stared toward the jagged silhouette of the distant mountains. Tiny lit farmstead windows glowed like bright spots of hope in the darkness. The seed of a new identity took root in the depths of his being, fed on his father's words. Could he really be this man his father imagined?

What would it mean if he followed his heart and accepted the bond with Rose? He'd hold the fate of the piskies in his power. It would take strength and dedication to defeat Tristan and bring the piskies back to life. His father sounded confident in him. But could he trust a man who'd never shown any interest in him before?

Troy raised his hand, snapped his fingers, and the shiny cocoon of privacy dissolved. "Go to Rose." The wind flipped Troy's hair over his face and he flicked it away. "Go now before Michael is tempted beyond endurance by the proximity of a bed and a beautiful lass. Self-control has never been his forte."

Niall thought of Rose's slender body, imagined Michael peeling away her green dress, but it was his own hands he saw against her pale skin. "Very well." Tonight he would take the first step toward a new future and claim his woman. Niall jammed his knife into his wrist sheath. For the first time since he was a boy, he nicked the skin and drew blood in his haste. Striding toward the house, his heart pounded against his ribs. His breath jumped. His belly tightened.

"Niall," Troy called.

Pausing at the doorway, Niall glanced back impatiently.

"To run the light you must be upright. Energy from the earth enters the base of the spine and runs up the backbone. Energy from the higher realms enters the top of the head and runs down."

"We need to stand?"

"No. Sit her up on your lap. Running the light takes time." Troy grinned, a wholly masculine smile, man to man. "Her legs won't hold her standing."

Rose halted just inside the tall double doors and listened to the decisive click as Michael closed them behind her. He touched her back gently as she gaped at the gold-encrusted king-size bed and silk sheets. There were mirrors everywhere, reflecting the gold-and-white furniture like the set of a high-class porn film. She felt as nervous as a novice actress about to take her clothes off for the first time.

Wringing her hands, she paced across to the window and stared into the darkness. Her own ghostly reflection stared back at her. Was Niall out there somewhere? She must stop thinking about Niall and face facts. He'd abandoned her when she needed him most.

Michael could be trusted to treat her well. Probably better than well. But every time she looked at Michael's face she saw Niall. This would be a lot easier if they weren't identical twins.

"Getting cold feet?" Michael took her arm and turned her to face him. He cradled her clenched hands and eased them apart, stroking her fingers. "You don't have to go doing this with me."

Rose looked into his Mediterranean blue eyes, remembering the first time she'd seen him and fallen under his spell. She was fond of him now. If not for Niall, running the light with Michael would be a pleasure. The facade of inebriation Michael had worn all evening melted away. His eyes softened with compassion and a hint of melancholy. Niall hid behind a scowl; maybe Michael hid behind his smile.

He brushed the tips of his fingers over her hair. "It would give me great pleasure to make love to you, Rose, that it would." A quick flash of his usual grin lit his face. "There's this fantasy in me mind: you in your dark blue suit and stockings, lying across the desk in me office at the Nest." The grin faded and he cupped her shoulders in his hands. "But I'm not blind. 'Tis not me you want, lass."

"Michael, it's not—"

He pressed a finger to her lips. "Don't go worrying. I'm not offended." He flicked his eyebrows up. "You have to be the only woman who's ever preferred Niall to meself. There had to be one around somewhere. Maybe if me brother gets laid, he'll stop stalking around like he's got a stick up his arse and have some fun. But then again, pigs might fly." He laughed, wandered across to the dresser, and poured himself a drink from a decanter. He slanted her a knowing sideways glance. "Although I have to say, around here 'tis not beyond the bounds of possibility to see a pig with wings. So maybe there's hope for me brother yet."

Rose watched Michael, hope surfacing through her churning emotions. "But Niall's gone."

"Maybe." Michael reached for the cigarettes in his back pocket. When his hand touched bare buttock he grinned sheepishly and glanced down at himself. "Oops, no pockets."

Rose paced to the bed and back to the window. "Look, Michael, I know you're loyal to Niall, but I've got to do this or Ciar isn't going to help me."

"Don't go worrying yourself. Troy's gone after Niall. The stupid arse will be along soon, although in my opinion he doesn't deserve you."

Rose's heart ceased beating altogether. She dragged in a breath and her heart scampered to catch up. "How do you know?"

"Fairies can sense each other, twins more so. Sometimes I feel his emotions. Sometimes I think he feels mine, but he never says."

Rose stumbled to the bed, grasped one of the bedposts, and dropped to the mattress. Her head swam with relief. She looked at Michael and blinked. "He's really coming? You're sure?"

"Would I lie to you, darlin'?" Michael poured a second drink and brought the glass to her. "Have a little laughing juice to loosen up." He stroked her arm as she took the drink. His eyes flicked over her face and settled on her lips as she pressed the glass to them.

The Irish whiskey burned down her throat. Her blood caught fire, scorching through her body. She pressed her hand to her mouth and gasped.

"Hot stuff, isn't it?" He traced her cheekbone with

his knuckle. "I'm wishing I weren't such a good brother. I must be daft to hand a willing lass over to Niall. Maybe I'll just steal one kiss."

"Only if you have a death wish." Niall loomed in the doorway like a soldier storming the building.

Relief surged through Rose, brought her to her feet. Guilt tinged her pleasure as Michael backed away with a reluctant smile. "Lost me chance. Ah, well. Places to go, people to see." He ambled across the room and pressed his half-full glass against Niall's chest. "Tank up, boyo, and enjoy."

Michael left, closing the door. Niall stood stiffly, his camouflage pants and flight jacket out of place in the decadent splendor of the room. His usual mask of indifference slipped. Doubt creased his brow. Confusion flickered in his eyes.

Rose didn't know what to say. She wanted to be angry with him for walking away, but the emotion wouldn't come. Uncertainty crept up as her initial relief faded. Did Niall really want her, or had she forced him into this relationship by touching his Magic Knot? Finally he roused himself and prowled across the room toward her.

Rose's skin hummed, ready, waiting for his touch.

He halted a few feet before her, downed the rest of Michael's whiskey, and tossed the glass aside to land with a muffled crack on the thick carpet.

She shifted awkwardly, aware of her ripped dress, muddy shoes, and smudged makeup. She had no illusions that she was pretty, while even scruffy and scratched, Niall was beautiful. She'd forced him into this. Many times he'd made it clear that he wasn't interested. He'd walked away, for God's sake. Troy had fetched him back. Rose curled her fingers around the bedpost as heat flooded her face. "Don't feel you have to do this," she choked out.

Surprise flashed in his eyes. "Use your senses, lass."

He reached out, pulled her toward him, and pressed his mouth to hers. The hot demand of his need flared in her mind, consuming all doubt. The cool demand of his night-chilled lips opened her mouth to the taste of whiskey, blended with the delicious flavor of man.

Cupping the back of her head, he released her lips. With a sigh he laid his forehead against hers. "Forgive me?"

Compassion, desire, and emotions Rose had never felt before surged up, making her tremble. Every cell in her body screamed to touch him. She put her arms around his neck, pressing against the rigid strength of him.

Trapped between them, her Magic Knot throbbed in time with her heart, echoing her desire. She wanted to complete their bond and prove she trusted him, so he'd let himself trust her. Easing back, she pulled the chain bearing her stones from inside her dress.

He looked down as she cradled the three stone rings, his eyes intense blue slits between thick, dark lashes. "You don't have to go doing this now, Rose."

"I want to." Reaching behind her neck, she released the chain, then dropped into his hand the stones that held the essence of her mind, body, and spirit. The thread of connection between them pulled at her heart, taut and quivering. Every cell in her body reoriented itself.

Niall slipped her chain around his neck and fastened it.

She was no longer alone.

Rose closed her eyes, leaned her head against his

chest, and let go. Her consciousness flowed into him. They were one, somewhere—everywhere. She'd expected boundaries. Niall's borders. Her own. But there were none. The sense of boundlessness stole her breath.

Niall stroked her hair. "You can't take this back. I'll be with you always."

She sensed his presence inside her, a core of masculine strength. For the first time since she'd embarked on her quest, she really believed she could save the piskies, because she didn't have to do it alone. She remembered the first tarot card she'd drawn for Niall and sensed the balance of his nature. "You are Justice," she murmured against his chest. "You'll be the man to save us all."

"If you believe in me."

She looked up into his face, awed at the determination in his eyes.

He touched her cheek, ran a thumb across her lips. "Now 'tis time to awaken your fairy side to keep the Fearsome Goddess happy."

Rose pulled a face. "This has got nothing to do with her. This is for us."

"Aye, lass. Just you and me." Niall dipped his head, feathering his lips across her cheek and over her mouth. Rose closed her eyes as need rippled through her body. He lowered the zipper on the back of her dress, eased the fabric off her shoulders, then pulled away and watched the green silk slither to the floor.

Niall ran a sizzling look over her white cotton bra and panties. She wished she'd thought to invest in something more enticing when she'd bought the dress. It had never occurred to her that anyone would see her underwear on this trip.

He ran a fingertip across the seamless white cup,

making nerves spark beneath her skin, and gave a rare grin. "You're a practical lass, Rose. 'Tis a valuable quality."

She blinked away her little surge of regret. Practical was okay. Right now she'd rather be pretty.

Niall's fingers trailed over her ribs and back toward the closure on her bra. Rose could see she was about to end up naked while Niall was fully dressed. "Uh-uh." She wriggled away and pushed the lapels of his flight jacket over his shoulders. It fell to the ground with a metallic thunk.

She frowned at the sound.

He raised his eyebrows. " 'Tis best to be prepared."

"To open a hardware shop?" It sounded as though he had the contents of a toolbox in each pocket.

Now that his jacket was off, she could see that his shirtsleeves were folded up. She examined the webbing and Velcro wrist sheaths, each holding a crystal-bladed knife. "How very untraditional of you."

He opened the Velcro and dropped the knives and sheaths onto the nightstand. " 'Tis more comfortable and convenient. I told you, lass, I value practicality."

With a relaxed smile, he took her hand and drew her toward the side of the bed. "Unless me sums are wrong, I've removed three pieces of clothing, and you've taken off only one." He hooked one of his sexy long fingers beneath the shoulder strap of her bra and flicked his eyebrows. "I'm thinking 'tis your turn again."

Rose laid her hands on his chest and reveled in the flex of muscle beneath his shirt. Soon she would have her hands on his skin. All her inhibitions fell away as she grinned up at him. His eyes glowed with pleasure. For a moment time seemed to stop. Was it possible to lose oneself in the gap between seconds and feel like this forever?

Niall blinked; her heart stumbled and she snatched a breath. "Weapons don't count," she said, trying to keep a straight face.

"Who says?"

"Me."

With a little grunt, Niall wrapped an arm around her waist and flung her backward onto the bed. Rose squealed as he trapped her legs between his knees and tickled her. "I say we get equal voting rights on this, and 'tis me vote that weapons count."

He grazed his fingertips across the front of her panties. The muscles in Rose's stomach quivered and jumped. An aching clench of need grabbed low in her belly.

"Oh, God," she whispered, and stilled. Suddenly she didn't care who took what off, as long as all the clothes came off and fast.

"I say we both take something off." He nudged the tip of his finger beneath the waistband of her panties. Rose grabbed his wrist, felt his tendons flex beneath the skin. Their eyes met and held for a beat. Rose remembered to breathe.

She pushed up on an elbow, unhooked her bra, and tossed it away without caring where it landed.

Niall stared at her breasts. A flush of arousal crept across his cheeks, and he licked his lips.

"Your turn," Rose said softly.

"Aye." Niall pulled his shirt over his head without unfastening it. Rose bit her lip, hard.

She'd imagined he'd look the same as Michael, but Niall's muscles were precisely defined, his body a living sculpture. With an unsteady hand she traced the bulge of his pecs, his ribs, the ridges of his abs, solid as warm wood beneath her fingertips. Anticipation rippled through her, making her hand tremble against his skin.

When she touched the waistband of his pants, his abs tightened and she heard him swallow. She glanced at his face, but he was looking down at her hand. Rose brushed her fingers across the heavy cotton of his combat pants, and flattened her palm over the ridge of his erection.

Niall closed his eyes. His nostrils flared. In precise, economic movements, he stripped off the rest of his clothes.

Rose lay back and dug her fingers into the satin bedcovers. Heat sizzled beneath her skin as he moved toward her, lean muscles rippling beneath silky skin.

"Move back." Niall knelt next to her, his eyes devouring her body as she slid up the bed. Stretching out beside her, he placed his palm on her belly and splayed his fingers. "You're so smooth."

Running her hands over his shoulders, she molded his muscles in her palms like a sculptor savoring her creation. He kissed her, his body warm and heavy against her side. The swirling well of emotion filled her chest, leaving her light-headed.

With work-calloused hands, Niall rubbed her breasts, cradling them in his palms, first one, then the other, as though he wanted to learn her shape. Rose closed her eyes as his kneading fingers shot silky ribbons of pleasure through her.

"Rose, lass." He waited for her to open her eyes. "Watch me." Then he touched the tip of his tongue to her nipple.

Oh, my God.

Rose flexed against him. Wanting more. Wanting everything. Now.

When he closed his mouth over her breast and sucked, flashes of fire raced across her skin, igniting a flaming core of need low in her belly.

Burying her fingers in his hair, she pulled him closer, moving her thigh against the hot, hard length of his erection. With a small grunt of pleasure, he rubbed against her, the friction sending shocks of desire into her tender places. She pressed her nose to his face, drugging herself with the fragrance of him: green leaves, spicy wood, the tang of mountain air.

The bumps and hollows of his muscles flexed beneath her palm as she fingered his biceps. She ran her hand along the taut strength of his forearm, his ribs, gripped the angle of his hip. He stilled when her fingers drifted onto his belly, hissed in a breath as her hand slid lower. Wrapping her fingers around his hard, silky shaft, she explored the sensitive parts of him until he gasped and pulled away.

Niall raised his head, hair tousled, cheeks flushed, pupils huge and dark. "I want you naked."

With shaky legs, Rose lifted her hips. He stripped her panties and tossed them away.

Niall sprawled over her, heavy, hard, hot, pressing her into the soft embrace of the mattress. Her Magic Knot around his neck throbbed between them. With the rough hunger of dwindling control, he found her mouth, demanded her body, and she gave him her soul. Rose clutched at his back, wrapped her legs around his waist, lost herself in the sensual press of him against her delicate flesh.

"Not this way," he mumbled, and raised his head. He slid to the side, exposing her to his gaze, and grazed his palm down her body to the join of her legs. He touched her with exploring fingers, watching her face as he found his way inside.

Rose closed her eyes, trembling on the edge of losing herself as he stroked.

He pressed his mouth against her ear. The wet tip of his tongue circled, and then he whispered, "Must be sitting up."

She opened her eyes and watched him trail his hand up her body to rest over her heart. "Why?"

" 'Tis the way it works, lass." He pulled her into a sitting position, then balanced the pillows behind him and sat, his back against the ornate gold headboard. "Come here."

With gentle command, he steadied and guided her as she lowered herself onto his lap. Hands on his shoulders, she gazed, breathless with wonder, at the eager intent on his face. He nipped his lip between his teeth and stared at her body as though she were a priceless treasure.

The fact that he trusted her enough to accept her Magic Knot and reveal his emotions brought tears to her eyes. He was normally so guarded. She would never hurt him, never make him regret this. Rose framed his beautiful face in her hands and pressed her lips against his forehead, his eyes, his nose, breathing him in, languishing in the heat undulating around them like a warm sea.

Her career, her professional image, the acceptance of her colleagues—none of it mattered anymore. Niall mattered. He'd help her make her future with the piskies. Confirmation of who she was and the acceptance she'd searched for all her life shone from his eyes.

Gripping her hips, he pulled her closer. The hot length of his erection pulsed against her belly. Heat exploded through her. Rose gasped before pressing her mouth to his.

"*A ghrá.*" Niall's endearment whispered in her mind, wound silken threads around her heart. At his bidding, she let her weight carry her down on him. Colors exploded behind her eyelids as he slid inside. Holding her hips, he urged her down, pushing deep. Pleasure rippled up through her, sighing from her lips.

Rose pressed her cheek to his, shuddering as waves of sensual heat overtook her. Niall touched his mouth against her ear. "Move, my love. Move."

She watched the pleasure on his face as he lifted her, then let her slide back down. The flash of blue between his dark lashes glowed inhumanly bright, the light of a million stars trapped in sapphires. He moved within her, physically and with the boundless caress of the infinite. Deep memories stirred within the fabric of her being, unfolding toward the light.

"Niall." His name rolled over her tongue, dark and rich. Had she known he was the one from the first moment she saw him? "Niall," she whispered against his lips, sharing the delicious sound.

They devoured each other with long, breathless kisses feeding mind, body, and spirit. Blissful peace ran deep and quiet beneath the sparkling ripples of pleasure that shook her body. She'd waited all her life for this. She trusted him. He wouldn't let her down.

When the ache of delight grew too much to bear, Niall held her still and rubbed his lips over her face. "Steady, lass. Take your time."

He stared into her eyes, his gaze so deep and intense it mesmerized her. Slowly he lifted her, then let her slide back on him. Rose gripped his arms, his muscles granite hard as he took her weight. He rubbed the side of his nose against hers, nibbled her lips. Love consumed her, gave her the strength to forget what she'd been and become what she must.

Nothing in her life had prepared her for these feelings. Ecstasy pulsed in rhythm with her heart. Was this her inner fairy waking up?

"Now." Niall urged her faster. Her thighs trembled as pleasure bloomed, a hot surge from her belly, streaking along her limbs, singeing the edges of her mind, consuming her. Niall put his face against her neck, held her down, grunted softly.

Rose pressed her lips into his hair, stilled, breathed him, tasted him, felt him around her, inside her. All was perfect in the world, and she never wanted to move again.

Niall sucked in a ragged breath against her skin. A tiny frisson of disquiet skittered through her. Warily she reached toward him mentally, and brushed cold ripples of pain. The breath locked in her throat. As cautiously as if she were handling a panicked animal, she cradled his head, stroking his hair. Slowly increasing her connection, she let warmth and love flow into him. "Are you all right, my love?"

His eyes remained closed, lashes scrunched into dark semicircles against his skin. Disquiet grew into jagged spikes of fear. "Niall," she whispered. "Talk to me."

Finally he raised his head. The cool distance in his eyes twisted her heart.

She shook her head. "Don't do this to me now. What just happened between us was fantastic." She cupped her Magic Knot where it hung around his neck. "I trusted you."

"You shouldn't." Niall lifted her off him as though she weighed nothing. He slid from the bed, retrieved his clothes, and dressed.

Confused tears swam into Rose's eyes, and she banished them with anger. "What the hell's the matter with you? At least explain what I did wrong. You owe me that much."

Niall unfastened her Magic Knot from his neck and placed it on the nightstand. " 'Tis not you. I'm to blame."

"And that's all you've got to say, is it?" So angry she thought her brain would explode, Rose snatched up the sheet, yanked it over her nakedness, and stood on the bed glaring down at him. "Did you ever intend this to be serious or were you just after a quick shag?"

He froze in the middle of pulling on his jacket and stared at her, wide-eyed. "Of course me intentions were serious."

"Then what the hell's changed?"

"I was misled, Rose." His jaw knotted. "I'm not the one for you." He flicked his wrists, practicing dropping his knives into his hands and flipping them point out.

Rose's breath came fast and shallow. Fury burned in her head, making her cheeks flame and her vision blur. She'd never wanted to hit anyone before in her life, but she wanted to slap Niall and knock some sense into his stupid, stubborn head. "That's a load of crap, and you know it."

He stared at her, his eyes razor-sharp slits of blue. "Do you not realize what happened?"

"What sort of question is that? Of course I do. We had great sex. I enjoyed it. You enjoyed it. It was special, Niall. And don't you dare try to tell me it wasn't."

He shook his head. "It didn't work."

Rose smacked her hand on her thigh, ready to scream with frustration. "It worked pretty damn well for me. What the hell were you expecting?"

"It did not work, Rose," he said with exaggerated patience. "We failed to run the light. If you want to keep Ciar happy, you need to find another man." He strode toward the door and wrenched it open. "'Tis obvious I'm not up to the job."

Chapter Thirteen

Niall slammed the bedroom door behind him and strode away from his chance of a happy future. He heard the door yanked open again, but he didn't pause to look back. The hurt and accusation in Rose's eyes had ripped at his heart. If he stayed to placate her, he might weaken. Anger roiled through him at the unfairness of life. He could not risk letting it fade or the despair lurking in the shadows of his mind would consume him.

"Niall," Rose shouted after him. Her tone demanded he come back now or never return. As if he had a choice. Didn't she realize he'd failed her?

"I'm no good to you," he tossed over his shoulder. "I'll be sending Michael or Nightshade."

As he rounded the corner at the end of the corridor, she shouted, "Lover to pimp in one evening. Good going, Niall."

Once out of sight he jerked to a halt, his breath coming in fast, tight gasps. *Bloody Troy*. Why had he believed his father's lies? Niall slammed his fist into the wall, sending a spider's web of cracks across the plaster. Pain shot up his arm. Grimacing, he shook his throbbing hand. He needed to regain control.

Niall ran down the wide stairs, along the corridor, and yanked open the east door. He turned his face up to the chill night air and drew in three deep breaths. The cleansing energy of his element, earth, flowed up his legs and gave him strength to do what must be done.

Although he wanted nothing more than to return to Cornwall, Troy had been right about one thing: Niall shouldn't abandon the others. Especially Rose. Now that he'd touched her Magic Knot, he was fully bonded to her. If he couldn't raise enough energy to run the light, he wasn't worthy of her, but he would protect her, as he'd promised.

With eyes closed, he opened himself to her and gritted his teeth at the twisting whip of vivid emotions beating at him: confusion, anger, love. Niall's eyes flashed open and his breath caught. The link between them was more than the binding of the stones. She loved him—and he'd let her down. He didn't deserve love.

Rose must bring her fairy half to life. Not only would Ciar refuse to reveal any fairy lore otherwise; she might even decide Rose was human and punish her for the deception. Niall couldn't take that risk. He had to send another man to Rose to make up for his failure.

Michael was the obvious choice. But it seemed likely that, as he was of the same blood as Niall, he might also have trouble running the light with Rose.

That left Nightshade.

Niall pressed the heels of his hands to his eyes and yelled, a primal burst of anger and pain that left his throat raw. His muscles trembled as he fought to banish the image of the nightstalker's dark body against Rose's pale skin. Fisting his hands, he stared into the night. He *would* conquer this weakness and put Rose's needs first if it killed him.

Niall straightened, stilled, controlled his breath, and composed himself. Whatever happened, he would maintain his dignity. It was all he'd ever had.

For the third time that evening he yanked open the east door and strode inside. After he'd sent Nightshade to Rose, he'd have a quiet father-son chat with Troy, and find out what in the Furies he was playing at. Niall flexed his wrists and felt the reassuring grip of his wrist sheaths. There was nothing like a blade in each hand when you had something important to say.

Anger possessed Rose like a malevolent spirit. She stomped around the bedroom, snatching up her clothes. *Bloody Niall.* What was his problem? She'd never hated a man and wanted him so much at the same time. Something inside her had definitely changed when they made love. Before anger had burned it away, she'd been filled with a dreamy tingling. Maybe her fairy half had started to activate but needed more energy to be completed. They could have tried again. If only he'd asked how she felt before he ran away.

There was no doubt that Niall had had a tough time as a kid. Well, her childhood hadn't been a cakewalk either, but she didn't behave like a martyr. She was getting a bit tired of his whipped-dog routine every time something didn't go his way.

She yanked on her underwear, then forced herself to stop, calm down, take care as she stepped into her dress. Any more rips in the delicate fabric and she'd look like a scarecrow.

After slipping on her shoes, she turned toward the door and paused. She glanced at the decanter on the dresser. If she'd ever needed a drink, it was now. She strode across, sloshed some whiskey into a glass, and downed it in three rapid swallows. Her throat exploded with fire and she coughed.

Despite the awful taste, a welcome warmth crept up from her belly, numbing the pain in her head, smoothing the edges of her anger into a manageable shape.

If Niall thought he could climb out of her bed and send another man to service her as though she were a broodmare, he had another think coming. And Ciar didn't like her being half human. Well, hard luck. The ugly little hag would have to get used to it. Rose was fed up with the lot of them. She'd come for information and she was going to get it. Demand answers in the same way she did when she conducted an investigation. Then, when *she* was happy, she'd leave.

Rose marched down the magnificent staircase. When she threw open the double doors into the great hall, she stiffened her spine before striding forward. The bustle and noise in the room faded. People stepped aside to let her pass. The crowd around Ciar's throne melted back.

A man with long hair gleaming like polished oak knelt before the Irish queen, kissing her feet and calves. Rose stopped behind him and gave the tiny queen a don't-mess-with-me look. "I've done what you wanted. Now, are you going to tell me how to save my people or am I wasting my time?"

Ciar narrowed her eyes and wrinkled her nose. "You don't look any different to me, human." She bobbed a foot, kicking the man. "Liam, touch her. Tell me what you sense."

The man turned apologetic green eyes on Rose. He brushed his fingers around her ankle. Frowning, he cast Rose a sideways glance. "I'm not sure, Queen of Nightmares."

"Is she fairy?"

The man stared at his hand. Poor guy, what could he say? Stuck between two queens, one of whom wouldn't like his answer. Rose wanted to touch his bowed head, reassure him.

"She is fairy, but it's shrouded," he whispered.

Ciar flashed a vicious grin full of small, sharp teeth. "You haven't changed. Maybe you can't." She jumped up. With the extra height of the dais, she stood face-to-face with Rose. "Maybe you aren't really fairy at all and you're tricking us. It's been known for humans to masquerade as one of the Good People."

"I can assure you my mother was one hundred percent fairy." This announcement would have shocked Rose to her foundations a few weeks ago, but now it had a reassuring ring.

"There's an easy way to prove your claim. An ancient test." Ciar pinned Rose with a gaze that jabbed icy needles down her spine. "Humans have used it for centuries when they suspect we've taken one of their babies and replaced it with a changeling." She sneered. "As if we'd want their feeble, ugly spawn."

A frigid lump of foreboding solidified in Rose's stomach. She glanced around the room for Troy. Now would be a good time for him to show up and put his queen back on her leash. There wasn't a friendly face in sight. Michael was probably holed up for the night in one of the bedrooms with a woman, and Jacca? Who knew what a nightstalker did in the dark. Stalked around, she supposed. They probably both thought she was safely tucked away with Niall.

Warily, she turned back to Ciar. "Not a problem. I always ace tests."

Ciar gave her spiteful little pinched-face grin. Tongues of gold and blue flame licked across her skin; fiery snakes slithered through her hair. Rose raised a hand to shield her eyes and stepped back, gagging on the foul smell of scorched fabric and charred flesh. The man at Ciar's feet leaped away to a safe distance. Deep inside Rose trembled, her confidence shaken.

"Fire," Ciar crooned like a lover. "My element." She stroked her skin, gathered a ball of blue flame into her palm, and held it up. "Those, like Troy, whose element is air are unharmed by it. Fairies such as the piskies and leprechauns who are of the earth feel the pain of its touch, but none of the Good People suffer injury. Pass through my fire unscathed, and I'll reveal the fairy lore you seek. If not"—she uncurled her fingers and flames burst from their tips—"you'll burn."

"Hold." At the shout Rose swung around, relief flooding through her at what she thought was Niall's voice. With surprise, she watched Michael push through the inquisitive crowd, Jacca on his heels.

Jacca stopped at Rose's side while Michael went forward and dropped to his knees before Ciar. "I entreat you, Fearsome Goddess. Surely the test of fire isn't necessary."

Ciar reached out, her hand dripping flames, and gripped the naked skin of Michael's shoulder. He hunched and whimpered like an animal in pain. Shock darkened the edges of Rose's vision. Before she could do anything to help Michael, Ciar released him.

"You see? No injury."

The Irish queen was right: Michael's shoulder was unmarked.

"You did feel pain, though, didn't you *Seanchai*?" She reached a flickering finger toward Michael's face, and he cowered away, his expression pale and taut.

"You bitch," Rose whispered, her gut tight with a mix of anger and fear.

Ciar raised a tiny foot and pushed Michael aside. "The pain will serve as a warning to this earth elemental to mind his own business in the future."

He scrambled to his feet and slunk back to Rose. "Where in the Furies is Niall?"

"Don't know."

Michael rubbed his shoulder and screwed up his eyes. "Shit."

Jacca leaned toward her, his silver eyes mirroring the dancing golden flames. "Niall was here a few minutes ago. He asked me to go to your room."

A fresh stab of pain spiked Rose's heart. Although Niall had told her he'd send another man, she'd hoped he wouldn't go through with it.

"What in the Furies has gotten into the idiot?" Michael asked, and turned to Rose.

"Not now." She couldn't think about what had happened with Niall, or she wouldn't be strong enough to deal with Ciar.

The Irish queen walked into the center of the room trailing a cloak of red and gold flame. The crowd swam back like a school of fish around a shark. "Give me a circle." Everyone retreated to the edge of the room, dragging the furniture along to leave a clear space. Ciar raised her arms at her sides like a dancer and tiptoed around, forming a ten-foot-diameter circle of fire in her wake. She halted, leaving a gap large enough to pass through. "Come here, pisky Queen, and prove you're more than a human fraud."

Rose stared at the tongues of flame leaping from the marble floor and wet her parched lips. Her whole body throbbed with her heart. Would she burn? Or would her fairy blood protect her? Even if she weren't injured, it would hurt.

"Don't go," Jacca said, and started to move in front of her.

"I'm half fairy. Theoretically, I should be okay."

He frowned. "You're human as well."

"And it hurts like crap," Michael added.

They both cared about her. Probably more than anyone other than her mother had ever cared. *Except for Niall.* She was certain he cared, despite his behavior. The connection between them when they'd made love had been . . . bliss. Rose reached out a tentative psychic touch and sensed something cold, hard, and impenetrable. He was close. Would he come if she needed him? Rose blinked back tears and laid a hand on Michael's arm. "Thanks for speaking up for me. You were very brave."

Michael grimaced. "If I'd known she'd go hurting me, I'd have kept me trap shut."

She squeezed his arm, met the glint of concern in his eyes, and made herself smile. "You're brave, believe me. And I appreciate it more than you'll ever know."

Michael covered her hand with his. "I'd say let's make a run for it, but 'tis not an option."

"I'll make it an option," Jacca said.

Rose scanned the packed hall. She glimpsed the

vicious anticipation on Ciar's face and knew Michael was right: if she didn't pass this test, Ciar wouldn't let any of them go.

Fear quivered inside her as she stared into Jacca's silver eyes. "Promise you'll try to free the troop for me if I can't."

He blinked as if it hurt, then took a deep breath and straightened his shoulders. "You can count on me."

Her gaze fluttered to the ring of fire, then back to Michael. She tried to give him a smile, but it felt tight, like a grimace. "I'm going to pass this test, but just in case . . ." Tears tightened her throat and she swallowed them back. "Just in case something goes wrong, tell Niall I love him."

Before either of the men could say more, Rose walked forward, head high, placing one foot in front of the other by sheer force of will. She clenched her teeth to still her trembling lips and entered the ring of fire. As soon as she was inside, Ciar took three more dainty steps, sealing the flaming circle.

Wheeling around, Rose searched for a spot where the flames were weaker, but the blaze was even. She'd heard of people walking over hot coals unscathed. If she jumped through the fire quickly, it couldn't be too bad.

She clenched and released her fists, psyching herself up. *Come on, woman. Courage.* Through the shimmering heat of the fire, Michael's and Jacca's encouraging smiles looked like a mirage.

"Hurry up and I'll reward you with a kiss," Michael shouted. He beckoned her, frantically waving his arms. Where was Niall? If he were on the other side calling her, she'd be through in a heartbeat.

God. Stop wasting time. She slapped her thighs, chewing her lip. She could do this. Rose took a step toward the flames. Then another. She drew a calming breath, filling her lungs with the hot air. As she approached the blazing wall, the heat grew nearly unbearable. *Ignore it. Do it quickly. Jump.* Rose leaned on her back foot as if preparing for a high jump. Out of the corner of her eye, she saw Ciar raise her hands. The flames roared, doubling in intensity.

The bitch. Rose scooted back to the middle of the circle and shielded her face. The bitter stench of burning hair filled her nose. A searing knot of terror pulsed in her chest, sizzling around her icy heart. She'd believed she'd come through this alive, but now the fire was too hot to jump through.

She was a coward. She'd let all her people down. "Niall." She screamed his name, hoping he was near. They'd parted so angrily, but that didn't matter anymore. She wanted him. More than anything else in the world, she just wanted him.

The heat stung her exposed skin. Sinking to her knees, she covered her head with her hands. With a crackling burst, the fire became even more ferocious, sucking the oxygen out of the circle. Her eyes watered; her lips dried and cracked. Unless she got out, she would be cooked alive.

Why hadn't she gone back to London when she had the chance? Left the fairy stuff to fairies? She was just an accountant.

No, she was more than human, but her human half was going to be her downfall. Not because she'd burn, but because she'd hung on to her humanity and denied her true identity. Rose pressed her palms against her eyes and wobbled onto her feet.

Niall. She screamed his name in her head. *Don't give up on me. I love you.* If she'd really believed in herself, running the light with Niall would have worked. She took a step toward the fire. She wouldn't give Ciar the satisfaction of watching her die like an animal, curled up, petrified of the fire. She must escape and give herself the chance to live the life she'd really been born to.

Rose faced the roaring flames and braced herself to run.

Niall leaped onto the massive round walnut table in the dining room and dropped into a fighting stance. Gripping a blade in each hand, he watched Troy raise a weary brow, shake his head, and jump up to face him. Niall attempted to follow his precombat routine, quiet his mind, ready his body, but agonizing images of Nightshade touching Rose blocked everything else. A red haze circled his vision, screamed in his brain. *Revenge.*

"You don't want to fight me," Troy said, his voice low, compelling.

"You've no idea what I want, *Father*." Niall flipped the blades, slashing them through the air.

Five years ago, Ciar had set Troy on him for insulting her. Niall had nearly beaten him. This time he would. Hate scraped his brain, honed razor sharp by his father's lies and scheming. Troy had hurt Niall many times, but this time he'd done the unforgivable— set Niall up to hurt Rose.

Troy's skin glowed with the pearlescent cast of an air elemental, but he still bled red and bruised purple. Niall ached to bring his father down, rub his beautiful pureblood face in the muck.

"I told you the truth about your future with the

pisky queen," Troy said, his tone infuriatingly calm and reasonable.

"You wouldn't know the truth if it bit you on the arse."

Troy raised his eyebrows. "Fighting will get us nowhere. We need to talk."

Niall pivoted, tracking his father's movements. "Why so keen to start talking to me now? You've never bothered before."

"Didn't you listen to what I said to you earlier?"

"Aye, you spin a good yarn. Michael must have learned to tell tall tales from you."

Troy shot Niall a wounded look.

"Oh, for sure, I'm wrong. I'm always wrong." Anger exploded in Niall's head, blasting through him, leaving a trail of despair.

He lunged, slicing the point of his blade across his father's thigh. A scarlet line seeped along the cut in the gold fabric.

Troy reached beneath his jacket, drew Death's Kiss, his short sword, and pointed the deadly black blade at Niall's chest. "Don't make me hurt you, lad."

"That's a joke." Niall laughed, the sound a hollow bark in the empty room. "You're just afraid I'll win. Last time—"

"Last time," Troy snapped, "I could have killed you. I chose to let you go into exile."

"Crap!"

"This is ridiculous." Troy stepped back and re-sheathed his sword. He raised his palms. "I'm unarmed. Finish this if you will."

Seething, Niall held his quivering muscles in check. This must be another trap.

The instant he blinked, Troy leaped. Niall's back slammed down on the table. His head cracked against the wood. Light and pain flashed behind his eyelids. Anger splintered into confusion. His father pinned him, twisting Niall's wrists until his blades clattered to the table. With a knee pressed against Niall's groin, Troy leaned close. The tender concern that would never be voiced between them shone in his blue eyes. Out loud, he said, "Never . . . ever . . . drop your guard. Not if you want to live. Did you learn nothing from the times you watched me train, lad?"

Shock, cold as ice water in the face, made Niall gawp at his father. The man knew he'd watched him practice?

"Close your mouth before you catch a fly." Troy loosened his grip and moved back. "I always knew where you were, how you were doing."

Niall scrambled up and shook his shoulders, trying to regain some dignity; he shook his head, trying to sort out his jumbled emotions. "You've no idea where I've spent the last five years."

"The Elephant's Nest Public House in Cornwall. Ideal for Michael, not quite your thing, I would guess. Your sister lives close by in a cottage you had specially built for her."

A jolt of fear and confusion kicked the last of Niall's composure to hell. He stared at his boots, raking his fingernails over his head. "Why did you not send someone to capture Ana? Ciar threatened—"

"Ciar doesn't know where Ana is." Troy was silent until Niall looked up; then he continued. "*I* know."

Niall stared into his father's eyes. "If this is a trick to make me trust you . . ."

Troy strolled to the end of the table, turned, and

flipped back his hair. "Believe what I told you earlier, Niall. Rose is for you. Your destiny is with her in Cornwall."

"But I couldn't run the light with her."

"There'll be a reason. Maybe your mixed blood." Troy narrowed his eyes and swore beneath his breath.

"What is it?"

"I wondered why the Nameless One didn't intervene when I came to find you. She must have known you'd fail." Troy's delicate nostrils flared. "Go to Rose, lad. Try again."

Desolation pressed in on Niall. " 'Tis too late. I've sent the stalker to run the light with her."

Troy laughed, a lilting peal of genuine mirth. Niall's misery was joined by irritation. Was his pain so entertaining? He took a threatening step forward. Troy stayed Niall with a raised palm and shook his head. "If you believe the lass will let you dictate her bed partners, you have much to learn about women."

"But she needs to run the light."

"No, she needs to find out how to release her people." Troy walked forward and placed a hand on Niall's shoulder. "She's bonded with you, lad. You misjudge her if you think she'll forsake you so easily. If you want her to trust you, first you must trust her judgment."

"She forged the bond with me unintentionally."

Troy shrugged. "It's as the dark mirror foretold. Her human half may not understand, but her fairy half acted on instinct. Otherwise, the link would not be so strongly wrought."

Niall stared into his father's eyes, gauging the truth of his words. The reasoning made sense. Guilt and fear tightened his chest. What if the stalker had taken Niall's request as a command and given Rose no choice?

Troy grasped Niall's arm as he turned to go. "Best fetch her and leave, lad. You need not face the Queen of Nightmares again. I summoned *The Book of Longings* from in-between while you were upstairs and persuaded it to reveal the fairy lore you need in exchange for knowledge of my deepest longing. To reanimate the piskies, all you need to do is retie their Magic Knots. This is done with the blood of the queen."

"Rose's blood?"

"Yes. But deep blood, mind. Use leprechaun earth magic to enchant a blade so that it leaves no wound."

Niall's gut clenched at the thought of stabbing Rose to bloody the blade. "If I'm to be king, can I not use me own blood?"

"It will only work with pisky blood." Troy raised his eyes heavenward. "Damn me for an oaf! That must be why you couldn't run the light with her. You do not carry pisky blood."

"Nightshade is the only pisky left."

"You were right then. To activate her fairy half, she'd have to bed the stalker." Troy slapped Niall on the back. "Lucky she no longer needs to do it in a hurry. With exposure to her people, over time it'll happen naturally."

Niall rubbed his face. Emotions mixed and roiled inside him. He'd hurt Rose badly by walking out. How could he make it up to her?

For the first time since he'd sent Nightshade to her, he opened his mind, tentatively reaching out to let her sense his feelings before he faced her and asked for forgiveness.

Terror streaked along their link. Searing heat roared over his body. "Great Danu!" Niall clenched his eyes, gritting his teeth against the pain.

"What is it?" Troy gripped Niall's shoulders and shook him.

"Rose!" Fiery snakes of fear coiled through him. "She's burning."

Troy leaped from the table and landed beside the door. "Fire can mean only one thing." Niall pushed back the mind-consuming dread as they sprinted along the hallway side by side.

As they approached the great hall, the strange metallic smell of Ciar's fire wafted into the corridor on pale fingers of smoke.

At Troy's command, the crowd parted before him, and he surged forward, Niall on his heels. He recognized Rose's hunched form trapped within a circle of raging fire. Despite the furnace temperature, icy claws of fear gripped him.

Troy slowed as he approached Ciar and raised a restraining arm in front of Niall. He ignored the signal and sprinted on toward the flames. There was no time to sweet-talk Ciar into releasing Rose. Her pain and terror screamed in his brain. He had to get her out now.

Niall readied himself as he neared the wall of flame and jumped. He closed his eyes, tensed against the moment of agony when the searing air above the blaze would have flayed a human. He landed in the circle, skidded to a halt, and fell to his knees. Alerted by the acrid tang of singed fabric, he slapped out the flames that ate at his pants. Rose crawled to him. He enclosed her within his arms, turning his back to the closest flames to protect her.

She burrowed against his chest. "I'm sorry. I'm sorry."

" 'Tis my fault. All my fault." Niall pulled off his jacket, wrapped the sheepskin around her to shield her from the heat, and pressed his lips to her crispy hair. Half fairy or not, she burned like a human.

How had he let this happen? The heat made his eyes tear up.

To get her to safety, he must carry her over the top of the fire. He stared around the circle, gauging the height of the flames. They had faded slightly since he'd jumped in, but it was going to be tough to clear them carrying Rose. He glanced toward Ciar and saw Troy bent close, entreating her.

"Rose." He lifted her chin, made her look at him. "Climb on me back. I must carry you out."

"But the flames . . ."

"I'll jump over them, lass." He cupped her cheeks in his hands. She gazed at him, glassy-eyed with shock, her face scarlet and puffy. Fear oozed from her, filled his mind. His chest tightened. Why had he walked out on her and let her face Ciar alone and unchanged?

The air swirled. Smoke raced around the circle of flame. Niall looked up to see Nightshade hovering above them.

"Pass her to me, Irish."

Rose looked up, blinked, and let her head fall back against Niall's chest. He gripped her shoulders and squeezed. "Come on, lass. Stay awake." She raised her head, wide-eyed, confused. "Nightshade's going to carry you back to England. You'll be fine."

"What about the fairy lore to free the piskies?"

How could she think about that now? "Don't go worrying, lass. I know."

She frowned and rubbed her eyes. "I can't leave you here." Rose aimed a kiss at Niall's mouth, missed, and bumped her lips on his chin. "I love you."

Joy, guilt, and pain twisted around his heart. Niall

breathed through his mouth to ease the rush of emotion. "Wherever you land on the other side of the Irish Sea, you wait for me. I'll find you. I promise."

Niall grasped her hips and hoisted her toward Nightshade. She gasped, clutching at Niall's shoulders.

"Rosenwyn," Nightshade called. "Reach up to me."

When Rose didn't respond, the stalker dipped lower and caught her beneath her arms. Niall released her, quaking with relief and a tinge of uncertainty as Nightshade took her weight, balanced her in his arms, and flew up to the ceiling.

Niall cupped his hands around his mouth. "Get her out of Ireland."

Ciar's furious banshee screech ripped the air. The wall of flame dropped and sputtered to nothing as her attention focused upward.

With spitting gold eyes, Ciar raised a hand and in quick succession blasted four streams of whooshing fire at the stalker. He ducked and dived, narrowly avoiding the flames. Burning paint bubbled in black streaks across the ceiling. The dark red velvet curtains burst into blazing columns. People shouted, those whose element was earth scrambling toward the door.

All her energy focused on her attack, Ciar dropped her glamour. The withered hag grimaced, revealing brown teeth. She raised a skeletal arm, ready for another blast.

No way could the stalker keep avoiding the flames. Niall had to help Nightshade escape. Dodging flakes of burning paint raining from the ceiling, Niall approached Ciar. Would his father intervene? Troy stood motionless beside her, his face tight with shock. He glanced at Niall, then, with a shake of his head, melted into the air and disappeared.

Although Ciar was one of the ancient ones, she didn't deserve respect. Since his birth she'd made his life a misery. He'd defied her, run from her, but now she'd done the unpardonable—harmed Rose. He seized Ciar's skeletal body. Flames licked around his hands. He clenched his teeth against the pain, raised her above his head, and hurled her at the nearest window. She crashed through, glass exploding in a deadly rain of splinters across the floor.

As soon as the glass stopped falling, Nightshade flew out. Niall stared after them, his heart pounding as the stalker and his precious burden were swallowed by the night.

Gradually, Niall became aware of the unnatural silence. Out of the corner of his eye he saw the hardy fairies who'd stayed to watch shrink back against the wall. With a flick of his wrists he dropped a blade into each palm. Ciar might be down; her bodyguard was not.

For the first time in Niall's life, his father had sided with him against the queen. But Troy couldn't stand by and neglect his duty for long. Light-headed with wonder, Niall swiveled around and searched the room. Surrounded by a pearlescent glow, Troy stepped from the smoke-shrouded air, and touched his fingers to his forehead in a gesture of respect. Niall stood tall and replied with the same gesture, one warrior to another.

Michael walked up beside Niall and held out a hand. "Give me one of those daggers." Frowning, Niall flipped over a blade and presented the handle to Michael.

Troy walked toward them and shook his head. "Michael, lad, what on earth do you intend to do with that?"

Michael gave a wry grin. "I've not got a clue, but

I've realized me brother has the right of this argument. I'm thinking I'll have to go back to Cornwall with him."

Troy grinned. For a few seconds he looked the image of Michael. "You'll have your part to play in the pisky court, lad. You two had better make yourselves scarce before Ciar comes to."

He drew his short black sword and took a fighting stance. "Looks like you'll get your fight with me after all, Niall. The queen must believe I attempted to detain you." Troy glanced at Michael. "Keep out of the way for a few minutes, lad. I don't want you hurt by accident."

Troy firmed his grip on his sword. His mouth flattened to a grim line as he faced Niall. "Looked like your lass might be badly burned. The surest way to cure her is to activate her fairy half."

Dread clutched Niall's chest, locking smoky air in his lungs.

"She'll have to run the light with the stalker."

Chapter Fourteen

Jacca cradled Rosenwyn against his chest and flew with the chill wind toward the southeast coast of Ireland.

He looked down and tried to see her face, but her head was wrapped in the sheepskin collar of Niall's jacket. Although his wing muscles ached from the extra weight, sharp spurs of remorse urged him on. He'd promised to protect Rosenwyn. Why had he allowed her to step within the fiery ring? He should have had the strength to defy Ciar alone, not waited for Niall to take a stand before he acted.

She wriggled in his arms.

"Easy," he said.

"Niall and Michael," she croaked. "We can't leave them."

"The Irish brothers will be fine." He had no doubt Niall would make sure they both got back to Cornwall safely. He had always respected Niall's fighting skills. In Ireland, he'd witnessed strength in the man that was humbling. Niall faltered, but eventually he faced his demons and won.

Nightshade rose higher to clear the top of a mountain. As he descended on the other side, salty air whipped his hair across his face. The sparkling, dark expanse of the Irish Sea lay before him like a sea of stars.

Rosenwyn shivered in his arms. The shock of the burning and then the chill of the night air must be taking their toll. He needed to check her condition, and he wanted to rest before striking out across the water.

Descending, he landed on a deserted stretch of scrubby grassland topping the cliffs above the sea.

With a sigh of relief, he let his wings fold. The muscles in his shoulders and back pulsed with a dull ache as he relaxed.

Nightshade crouched on the damp grass, sat Rosenwyn on his knee, and gently eased the sheepskin collar away from her face. He hadn't thought she was too badly burned, but in the cool light of the moon her skin was the color of raw meat. For a moment fear stripped his strength. The cold sea breeze spiked his bare chest, penetrated his bones. What would happen to him if she didn't recover? He couldn't bear to return to his old life with Tristan.

Her teeth chattered. She snuggled deeper into Niall's jacket and hugged herself. "You must go back . . . help . . . Niall."

Nightshade gathered her into his arms and laid his cheek on her hair. Here he was thinking of himself, and Rosenwyn was worried about everyone except herself. She was much stronger than her mother. Far more deserving of his support and respect. He'd thought he loved Ailla once, but he'd only worshiped her beauty. That was not what made a good queen.

Although the piskies might punish him when they

were released, he must help Rosenwyn free them. Make amends for his betrayal.

Rosenwyn pressed her hand to her mouth and sobbed. "Should have . . . walked . . . through . . . the fire."

"No, no." Nightshade stroked her hair. "It doesn't matter."

"It does," she sobbed.

"Shh." He hugged her tighter, unsure what to say. If only her fairy half had activated, she wouldn't have burned. Niall had said he couldn't run the light with Rosenwyn, but he didn't explain why.

"We must make a move," Jacca whispered.

She gazed up at him, bleary eyed.

"I'll take the shortest route and head for Wales."

"Aren't you cold?" She blinked at his bare chest.

He flicked out his wings with a snap. "A coat cramps my style."

When he set her on her feet, she stood like a child as he fastened the zipper up to her chin. "Ready?" He picked her up and she clutched at him. "Don't hang on, sweet one. You'll impede my wings."

Rosenwyn laid her cheek against his chest and closed her eyes. As the blustery wind whipped needle points of sea spray against his skin, he glanced down at the woman in his arms. Tenderness swelled from his heart, warming his body. She trusted him with her life, just as she had when she was a little girl. Last time he'd let her down. This time he would protect her or die in the attempt.

Rose jolted awake, blinked, and realized she was still in Jacca's arms. They'd landed in a field beside the sea. He went down on his knees and, with a groan, deposited her on the damp grass. Her bare legs were so cold she couldn't feel them, which was probably a blessing, as the warmer bits of her were in agony.

Wincing, Rose rubbed her eyes and looked at Jacca in the moonlight. His face was in shadow, but she made out the tremor in his muscles as he tried to close his wings.

Poor guy must be exhausted. Ignoring the screaming sting of her skin, she struggled to her feet, legs clumsy with lack of feeling. "How long were we in the air?"

He shook his head as she tried to help him up. "Give me a moment."

Tentatively, Rose placed her fingers on his trembling shoulders and massaged. When he sighed with appreciation, she rubbed lower, worked the taut, quivering muscles where his wings joined his back.

He held still for a few minutes until the tension eased. "You've missed your vocation. That was wonderful."

Jacca got to his feet, rolled his shoulders, and settled his wings against his back. "We need to find shelter and get some rest. Look"—he pointed to the right— "—there's a cottage in darkness. Perhaps the place is empty."

Rose squinted at the faint outline of a building and glanced at the luminous numbers on her watch. "It's probably in darkness because it's two in the morning."

"If we're lucky, it's an empty tourist cottage." With a hand on her back, he guided her over a narrow strip of road to the building. As they approached the gate, he released her. "Wait for me here."

Rose watched him melt into the shadows and shivered inside Niall's thick jacket. She pulled up the collar and sniffed. Beneath the clinging stench of smoke, his woodsy fragrance lingered. For a moment she remembered being surrounded by his scent, the feel of his skin, tasting him, being one with him. "Niall," she whispered into the darkness, "I need you." Rose closed her eyes, relaxed, and felt for him. He swamped her mind suddenly and completely, as though he'd stepped inside her. Rose gasped, staggered, and clutched at the gatepost for support.

As quick as he'd come, he was gone, leaving a pulse of reassurance. He was safe and on his way to find her. Rose blinked, a touch light-headed, but relieved.

The muffled smash of stealthily broken glass cut into her calm and she grimaced. In the last few days she'd gone from respectable professional to desperado on the run, breaking and entering.

The darkness beside her thickened, took form, and Jacca appeared. Rose pressed a hand over her heart. "Don't do that near me again."

"Why not? The ability to become a shade is highly valued among the Good People."

"It freaks me out." She pressed her fingers to her throbbing temples. She still had so much to learn, but right now she just wanted good old-fashioned human comforts: painkillers, coffee, and a warm bed.

Jacca wrapped an arm around her and led her to the open front door. "We're in luck. This must be a holiday cottage left empty in the winter."

She clicked the light switch but nothing happened. "Can we turn on the electricity and find a heater? I'm freezing." The temperature was no warmer inside than out.

"I'll look. Make yourself comfortable." He faded into the darkness. Rose felt her way along the hall until she found an open door. Faint slivers of moonlight between the window-blind slats illuminated a basic kitchen. Her stomach rumbled at the mere possibility of food.

Starting at one end of the room, she ignored the pounding in her head as she bent down and methodically checked the cupboards and drawers for anything edible. She found three tea bags and a lot of mouse droppings in a chewed cardboard box, a supersize box of salt, and a sticky bottle of sauce. Her stomach churned at the sour smell of mice. On a wave of nausea she dropped into a chair and rested her aching head against the cool Formica table.

Every square inch of her skin burned as though it were still exposed to the fire. Since she'd woken, the pain had increased with each passing second. Tears swam into her eyes. She fought to keep them from falling. She must be strong until Niall arrived; then he'd know what to do.

With a metallic hum the fridge came to life, and the microwave oven started flashing, SET CLOCK. *Well-done, Jacca.* When Rose snapped on the light switch, the room burst into white Formica brilliance.

Shiny pain spiked her eyes before she shielded her face.

Jacca loomed in the doorway, his skin blacker than black in contrast. "Anything to eat?"

She shook her head, and her brain screamed at the movement.

He glanced around, then strode over to the cupboards and randomly opened a few doors. Rose quashed her irritation that he didn't believe her. Maybe she had missed something in the dark.

He sighed and slammed a cupboard door. "Never

mind. Come into the sitting room—there's an electric fire."

When Rose moved, the pain where the jacket abraded her arms and neck made her head spin. Darkness chased away the light around the periphery of her vision. She swayed.

Jacca was beside her in an instant. "Rosenwyn."

She fumbled at the coat zipper. "Get it off."

With a frown, he unfastened Niall's jacket, eased it off her shoulders, and dumped it on the table. The cool air relieved the soreness, and she became aware of another sensation. "Where's the bathroom?"

"End of the corridor." He surveyed her through narrowed eyes. "Can you manage?"

"When I need you to help me pee, I'll really be in a bad way." Rose clamped her teeth against the pain as she walked down the hallway. The faint odor of mold and soap scum led her to the bathroom door. She stared at the stained green toilet. A far cry from her own carefully decorated flat in London.

Fresh tears surged into her eyes. Clean and neat was how she liked her home and her life, and nothing was ever going to be clean and neat again. What she wanted was a hospital bed with smooth white sheets and nurses pumping morphine into her until everything went away.

When she finished, she sent up a quick prayer for painkillers to whatever god she should talk to now that she was pisky, and opened the bathroom cabinet. A curled bar of soap lay in a puddle of dried scum.

The small window above the toilet rattled. Rose glanced up and caught the flash of movement outside. Her breath lodged in her throat. When the rattling became a regular tapping against the glass, she backed up, eyes glued to the window, and reached blindly behind her for the door handle. Black mist streamed from the outlet, swirled into a column, then resolved into the form of a man.

"Jacca!" Rose wrenched open the door and sprinted along the corridor. "Shade in the bathroom," she said in a gasp as she pushed past him into the sitting room. She glanced around wildly, checking that the windows were closed and looking for holes where a shade could get in.

"Damnation, I thought Ciar would send shades, but not this fast. Let's hope our visitor's a lone scout." Jacca scanned the room. With the tips of his fingers, he plucked an ornamental horseshoe off the mantel above the fire and tossed it on the sofa. He shook his hand and nodded at the horseshoe. "A weapon for you. Iron is inimical to fairies. When they're in shade form the metal can sever the bond they have with their body."

After Jacca ran from the room, Rose picked up the horseshoe gingerly. Trembling, she clutched the back of the sofa for support and flicked her gaze between the door and the window. A few minutes passed; then black mist drifted out of the old chimney behind the electric fire and started to take form.

With a firm grip on her strange weapon, Rose stepped forward and swiped the horseshoe through the shadowy figure. It shattered into inky droplets, spun into a minitornado, then shot back up the chimney. Rose's heart raced so fast she could hardly breathe. Collapsing on the sofa, she stared at the horseshoe with new respect. Maybe the lucky horseshoe superstition had a basis in truth.

Jacca burst through the door with the shaker of salt from the kitchen in his hand. "Still in one piece?"

Rose nodded.

"Only one shade, I think," he said, sprinkling salt around the edge of the room. "We can't proof the whole house, but we can keep the blighter out of this room." He poured generous amounts near the window, door, and fireplace, then levered off the lid with a fingernail to extract the last few grains.

Although Niall and Michael had used a ring of salt around Ana's house to keep out malevolent fairies and her father's spells, she still wasn't convinced it would work. "You've got a backup plan, haven't you?"

Jacca dropped the plastic container beside the door and walked over to her. "They won't pass over the salt. We'll stay here until light, then try to get back to Cornwall." He sighed. "I can't fly in daylight. We'll have to find a vehicle and you can drive us."

"Niall's coming." When she quieted her mind, she could feel him in the distance, a safe harbor in a storm. "Let's wait." Rose sank back against the cushions, careful not to let the fabric rub her sore skin. "I'm not up to driving, anyway." Now the immediate threat was over, her brain felt as though it were being poked with red-hot wires. She put her hand over her eyes. "I feel awful."

The sofa dipped as Jacca sat beside her. He laid a gentle hand on her back. "You need the immunity of your fairy powers. I know Niall came to you. What went wrong?"

She remembered the hurt in Jacca's eyes when she hadn't chosen him to run the light. Having to discuss it with him was awkward. "We tried." She waited a few head throbs for him to respond, her ears buzzing in the silent room. When he said nothing, she continued. "It didn't work."

"I can see that."

"I think it's my fault." Rose avoided his curious gaze. "I didn't let go of my human side when we . . . you know."

Jacca shook his head. "I think I know what might have happened."

He suddenly had all her attention. "Niall blamed himself. Do you think he was right?"

"Indirectly, he could be."

Fear shivered through her. Did that mean there was some fairy reason why she and Niall shouldn't be together?

Jacca took her hand, cradling it in his. "I had a long time to think on the journey. I believe Ciar intended you to fail by allowing you to choose Michael or Niall. You are both of different mixed blood. To be successful, my guess is you need a pureblood pisky."

Rose stared into Jacca's eyes as the implication of his words penetrated her aching brain. "So you're saying"—Rose licked her lips—"you're saying that to activate my pisky half, I must sleep with you?"

Jacca blinked slowly and held her gaze.

Rose stared at her slim pink hand lost between his dark fingers and remembered Niall's long fingers, so gentle on her skin. "There has to be another way."

"Not that I know of."

She pulled back her hand and clenched it with the other in her lap. "I'll stay human. I can still be the queen."

"Look at yourself, Rosenwyn." He indicated the scarlet skin of her arm. "If you'd activated your fairy side you wouldn't have been burned. Your link with Niall would also be stronger."

Rose glanced at him questioningly.

"I sense him in you, Rosenwyn. You owe it to him to make the bond as close as it can be."

"That just about takes the biscuit." Rose laughed incredulously. "Sleeping with you will bring me closer to Niall. I don't think so." She stood shakily and walked to the fire to get some distance from him.

"Niall asked me to come to you himself."

"But he might have changed his—"

A shrieking sound from the chimney made her jump back and fall on the sofa.

"What the hell?"

"At least we know the salt's working."

"Scared me half to death." Rose squeezed her eyes closed.

"Run the light with me and your injuries will heal immediately."

Rose stared at her red skin. The heat from the electric fire made the pain worse, but didn't reach her icy core. Whatever Jacca said, if she slept with him, Niall would never get over it. He'd jumped into the circle of flame for her and shielded her body from the fire. She loved him, and in his own way he loved her.

Rose curled up on the lumpy sofa. "I'm going to wait for Niall."

When she closed her eyes, light flashed behind her eyelids, then faded. Cold crept through her limbs, spreading heavy and dark into her mind. Locked deep inside, her survival instinct cried, trying to make her take notice. But she was so tired. All she wanted was oblivion.

Niall drummed his fingers on his leather armrest and stared out the aircraft window as the lights of the Dublin airport faded into the distance. "Grand going," he whispered. He was on his way back to Rose. Her pain grated in his mind like an off-key note, his head throbbing in sympathy.

With Michael's sweet-talking and a generous amount of cash, Niall had rerouted his charter to Bristol. As soon as they set down, he planned to find a rental car and drive to the west coast of Wales. Three hours, maybe four, and he'd be with her.

He closed his eyes for a moment, reaching out to check her. His chest tightened. She was weaker.

Michael snored, mouth open, sleeping like a baby. Full of surprises, his brother. Who'd have guessed he'd take Niall's side and return to Cornwall?

Niall tried to relax. An hour of sleep would be a good idea, if he could rest with Rose in his head.

Rose!

He bolted upright, sending a cup of apple juice flying. Suddenly he couldn't feel her. Psychically he cast around for their link. No barrier, no presence. Nothing.

Fear gripped his heart with icy claws. It was as if she'd ceased to exist.

At just after nine in the morning, Niall accelerated his rental car along the motorway past Cardiff. He kept his mind open, searching for Rose. As he neared the coast, he felt Nightshade and tracked him. The longer he went with no sense of Rose, the more difficult it was to resist the waves of desolation pounding at his mind. But he wouldn't give up. Not until he knew for certain.

Weaving the car along the narrow roads toward the coast, he found himself circling the area, unable to pin down Nightshade's location. The fugitives would be near the cliffs, probably in a sparsely populated area. In desperation, Niall parked in a muddy field, left the car, and hiked, crossing fields and leaping hedges.

Off in the distance, the front door of an isolated cottage opened. An unmistakable black form filled the doorway. Niall ran until he was close enough to be heard, then grabbed a breath and shouted, "How's Rose?"

The stalker came forward and opened the gate, his face grave. "I can't wake her. She's been asleep for hours."

At least she was alive. Relief sparked along Niall's nerves, firing him with energy. He raced through the doorway, burst into the room where she lay on a tattered green sofa, and dropped to his knees beside her.

She lay motionless beneath a tan blanket and his flight jacket, her face scarlet and swollen. Niall pressed his palm against her burning forehead. Closing his eyes, he extended his touch into her mind. With a burst of relief heady as a shot of finest Irish malt, he slid along the delicate thread of connection between them. He skimmed around the taut boundary of her consciousness. Drawn in tightly, she had instinctively focused her strength inward to survive and recover.

Niall's relief faded to fear as he sensed the shallowness of her breath, her thready pulse. Rest alone would not mend her. She needed some form of human medical care fast.

Or she needed to activate her fairy half.

"What shall we do?" Nightshade asked from the doorway.

Niall stared at him, imagining Rose's slim, naked body pressed against the muscular bulk of the stalker. Much as he hated the idea, he would make any sacrifice to save Rose. But she was in no condition to run the light with the stalker now.

Niall looked down at the shallow rise and fall of her chest. "We'll have to get the lass to a hospital."

Nightshade snorted. "Impossible."

"There's no other way. To all intents and purposes, she's human. If we let them treat her, she'll recover."

"Eventually," Nightshade added scathingly. "After she's suffered."

Niall jumped up. "Do you have a better idea?"

"Let me run the light with her."

"Not with the lass sick."

Nightshade approached and halted just out of reach. "There's a chance my bite will have the same effect as sex."

"Aye. And you'll be blood-bonded to *my* woman!" Jaw clenched, Niall rode the wave of jealousy that surged through him. When his turmoil subsided, he pressed his temples. He must put Rose first, whatever it cost him.

"If you're in her mind when I bite, the blood bond won't form."

"And what if you're wrong?"

"You're fully bound to her, Irish. Her link with you is strong enough to prevent another bond from forming."

Niall gazed at the brown carpet. "Looks like I'm out of choices." He glanced at Rose and sighed. "Are you wanting me on the sofa with her?"

Nightshade scanned him from head to toe. His nostrils flared. "The sofa is good."

After easing Rose's limp body onto his lap, he sank back into the couch, his back against the armrest. She moaned and mumbled his name.

He pulled her closer, touching his lips to her ear. "Rose, me love. I be here with you now." Loosening the boundaries of his mind, he extended his awareness, enveloping her with his strength. He hated to feel her weak and suffering. This must work.

The ancient sofa creaked in protest as Nightshade knelt beside them. Niall had become so used to the stalker's almond scent he normally didn't notice it. Now the sweet fragrance swamped his senses. Nightshade leaned close, staring into Niall's eyes. "You'll feel it when I bite her."

Niall shifted Rose on his lap, positioning her between him and Nightshade. "Just pretend I'm not here."

Nightshade licked his lips, and the glistening white points of his fangs appeared.

Great Danu! Have I lost me mind?

With effort, Niall clamped down on his instinct to push Nightshade away. He focused on Rose, on her pain grating in his mind. "Don't you go taking too much of her blood."

Nightshade inclined his head in agreement. "I have her best interests at heart. She's my queen."

Niall considered Nightshade's expression, judged his words true, and relaxed a notch. "It goes without saying, I'll have to kill you if you bite me."

With a flick of his eyebrows, Nightshade grinned, exposing hooked fangs. "I have a taste for O'Connor blood, but I'll endeavor to restrain myself."

Tilting Rose's head to the side, Niall exposed her neck. "Don't go touching her."

"That's going to be difficult if you want me to bite her."

"I'm meaning don't go putting your hands on her."

"In Ireland you sent me to her bed. Now I mustn't even lay a hand on her?"

Niall stared at the glowing electric fire. He remembered Rose's anger when he'd told her he would send another man to run the light. "I had no right to go making that decision for her. We won't be taking liberties while she's unconscious."

"Very well. You have my word." Placing one hand on the sofa's back and the other on the arm, Nightshade corralled Niall and Rose between his arms. Muscles trembling with the instinct to escape, Niall leaned back as the stalker bent over Rose's throat.

Long, cool hair slithered across Niall's neck. Ignoring the stalker, he concentrated on Rose, praying this would activate her fairy half. He focused on the warm weight of her against his thighs, chest, and groin. With a sigh he sank into her mind, slowed the tripping beat of her heart, drew her breath in and out steadily, softened the clench of nausea pinching her gut.

"Ready?" Nightshade whispered.

"Get it over with."

"Your wish is my command . . . Niall."

Sweet, sharp pain radiated through Niall's head and neck. He hung on to his connection with Rose, pushed deeper, boosted her endurance. The pain resolved into tiny points of ecstasy in his neck—no, Rose's neck—then spiraled along his nerves in a dark dance of sensation in which pain and pleasure became one.

Niall's muscles spasmed. The back of his head thumped against the sofa. His groans mingled with soft gasps from Rose. He fought to stay detached as primitive longings lured him deeper. Dark lust pulsed in his heart, inside Rose, outside her. Pleasure tasted hot, thick, metallic.

Light flowed into her belly, his belly, gathered in a spinning ball, hummed along veins, chased away doubts. Went supernova. Niall's body arched. Rose groaned, and her bottom ground into his groin. Pleasure exploded in flashes of dark and light that seared the sense from him.

A long way off on the edge of awareness, Nightshade sniggered softly.

The world was dark, silent, unbearably sweet. Niall floated in the dreamy aftermath of pleasure. There was somewhere he should be. If only he could remember.

"Niall?"

The soft entreaty in the voice snagged him, pulled him up through diaphanous layers until he felt breath fill his lungs. He became aware of a warm weight on his lap. His eyes snapped open, and Rose stared back at him, an enigmatic smile on her face.

"Rose. Shit! Sorry. It worked." Relief washed through him, mixed with wonder as he stared at her smooth, pale skin and glowing green eyes. "You're looking . . ."

"Beautiful," Nightshade finished for him.

Niall turned at the sound of the stalker's voice. His vision wavered, as if the room were full of water. Nightshade grinned with predatory satisfaction that shot warning bolts up Niall's spine.

"Well, well, Irish. Who would have guessed you're so . . . sensitive?"

Niall shook his head to clear the fluff out of his brain. "What in the Furies are you talking about?"

Rose framed his face between her hands and feathered his lips with hers. His recent pleasure echoed through him.

"Thank you, my love. I knew you'd come for me." She grinned, a mischievous sparkle in her eyes. Pressing her cheek against his, she whispered into his ear, "We won't tell anyone you came for Nightshade as well."

The truth sucker punched him. He squeezed his eyes closed. When Michael found out, Niall would never live this down.

Chapter Fifteen

As Niall maneuvered the rental car through the narrow Cornish lanes, Rose flipped down her sun visor and stared at herself in the mirror for the hundredth time. Not only were her burns healed, but she looked amazing. Her features were finer, her skin smooth and glowing. She'd always wondered why she didn't resemble her mother. With her fairy half activated, she did. If Ailla could see her now, she wouldn't call her plain anymore.

What would her work colleagues think? She'd have to tell them she'd had an extreme makeover— administered by a bloodsucking fairy. She smiled and snapped the visor up. Okay, maybe not. Her smile fell away. She shivered with a strange mix of emotions. Maybe she wouldn't see her old colleagues again. Everything had changed so fast.

She glanced over her shoulder at Jacca lying under a blanket on the backseat. He grinned and blew on the tips of his fingers as if he'd burned them. *You're hot,* he mouthed silently.

The smile flitted back to her lips. At least Jacca appreciated the change in her appearance. She cast a sideways glance at Niall's stoic expression. Maybe she shouldn't have teased him about losing control. Niall was lucky to have found release. Since Nightshade's bite she'd been primed and ready. If she'd been alone with Niall, she'd have made him pull the car over and jumped him long ago.

When they arrived at the Elephant's Nest half an hour later, Jacca left to report to Tristan.

Rose followed Niall in through the bar. The same fair-haired woman who'd been serving the night Rose first arrived stared at her with no recognition. She really was a different person from the accountant who'd walked in a week ago.

There was no going back. Ever.

For a moment the realization froze her in place. Then a little thrill of excitement crawled into her belly. She didn't want to go back. This new life was her future. Niall—she breathed through her mouth to control her swell of emotion—Niall was her future. And she'd damn well break through his protective shell and make him understand.

"Is Michael back?" Niall asked.

The woman grinned. "Few minutes ago. He got a taxi from the station."

They mounted the steps toward the kitchen. Michael's presence glowed on the other side of the door like the promise of a warm fire in winter. With her new fairy senses, she could feel any fairy who came close, and each had his own energy signature.

Pausing with her hand on the door, she glanced at Niall. The feel of him melted into her, permeating every cell of her body. She sensed confusion. The burn of desire tempered by wariness. She touched his arm. "Now that Jacca's gone, please talk to me."

He shook his head. "I need to clean up."

Without thinking, Rose dropped her gaze to the stain at his crotch. The shadowy barrier he used to keep her out of his mind fell back into place.

"Niall, I didn't mean—"

"Later." He pulled away, turned, and walked off down the hall.

Rose sighed and shoved open the kitchen door. Michael stood in his usual spot against the counter with a cigarette in his hand. He grinned at her and waggled his eyebrows. "Wowee, Rose, darlin'."

She couldn't help smiling at him as he stubbed out his cigarette and advanced on her.

He grasped her hips and shimmied closer. "You're looking scrumptious." He pulled a face. "What a foolish fellow I am for passing you on to me brother. D'you think there's a chance I can change your mind?"

Sudden tears filled her eyes. He always made her feel good about herself. She wrapped her arms around him and hugged fiercely.

He yelped. "Mind me bruises. Fighting for your safety, I was, and not a word of a lie."

"I believe you." She kissed his cheek and stared into his eyes until his smiling facade slipped. "Thank you, Michael. Thank you for being there for me when I needed you."

"It was nothing." He glanced away, faint color in his cheeks.

"Yes, it was. You could have taken advantage of me, and you didn't."

Michael stood a little taller. "Well, sometimes I like to show me brother I'm not the waster he believes." His tone was lighthearted, but there was a sharp edge of pain beneath the words. In his own way he was as complex and guarded as Niall.

"I thought you wanted to stay in Ireland."

He sighed and touched her cheek wistfully. "Naw, lass. I've moved on. I can never go back to being one of Ciar's pets. I want more from me life now." He pressed his lips to her forehead and grinned. "Maybe some of Niall's stubborn pride has gone and rubbed off on me. Think I'll blame me brother. Always makes me feel better." Michael laughed and, as usual, Rose couldn't stop herself from joining in with the contagious sound.

"This is cozy." The sharpness of Niall's voice cut off her laughter. She glanced at the door. He had changed his clothes, but obviously not his attitude.

"You sharing the details of our jaunt with Michael?" He hid behind a menacing expression, but hurt hollowed his voice.

Did he really believe she'd make fun of him the first chance she got? She wished she'd never teased him about the incident with Jacca. She should have realized he'd blow it up all out of proportion.

He turned away and fury whipped through her. "Don't be so bloody certain everyone's out to hurt you. And take that 'I'm above this silly emotional crap' look off your face." Rose stormed forward, grabbed the back of his jacket, and yanked him to a halt. "I love you. Don't shut me out."

With a cough, Michael grabbed his cigarettes from the counter. "Time to make meself scarce, I think."

Niall tried to pull away. "I have to go check on Ana."

Pausing as he pushed past Niall in the doorway, Michael gave him a serious look. "You can't go running away forever. Let me check on Ana for you."

Tightening her grip on Niall's jacket, Rose tugged

him back a step as Michael let the door slam. "Tell Ana I'll be seeing her later," Niall shouted after him.

When Rose grasped Niall's arm, he allowed her to turn him around. He stared down, his expression rigid with control.

The angry knot inside her loosened, and she ached for him. He must have been hurt so much to be this defensive. "Talk to me, Niall," she said gently. "How do you feel?"

He shrugged, short and sharp. "Furious."

"Why?"

He stared past her, his internal battle raging in his eyes. "You're meant to be mine, but it took the stalker's bite to turn you. I couldn't and I . . ." He glanced down. "I made a fool of meself."

You're meant to be mine soaked into her, sweet as honey. "You admit we should be together?"

He cast her a brief glance. "That's beside the point. I failed you."

"Crappy logic, Niall. I failed you as well. Ciar set us up to fail."

Niall swung away and paced to the window. He stared at the trees. "I shouldn't have agreed to take you to Ireland. I knew the risks well enough."

Rose walked up behind him. "I didn't give you a choice. I make my own decisions. Always have. Always will." She laid her hand in the center of his back. "So you see, tough guy, however much you want to blame yourself, I won't let you." She ran her fingers up his spine and played with the short hair against his nape. "Let it go. Move on. Forget about what happened with Jacca."

He glanced at her over his shoulder, and she raised her eyebrows. "Gonna turn around and talk to me?"

Facing her, he leaned back against the kitchen counter and crossed his arms.

Rose swallowed her nervousness at his reaction to what she wanted to say. On the outside she kept up her bravado, but on the inside her stomach churned with fear that he would turn her down again. "Here's the deal. I give you something precious, and in return, you do the same for me."

He frowned but said nothing.

She unfastened the chain bearing her Magic Knot. Niall watched silently. With every second he didn't speak, the fear inside her swelled. Rose drew a shuddering breath and reached to fasten the chain around his neck.

His expression softened, and the hint of a smile touched his lips as she carefully straightened her stones against the front of his clean brown shirt. "Have you got a date in mind, then?" he asked.

"A date?"

"The giving and receiving of Magic Knots is a symbol of handfasting. 'Tis like an engagement ring and a wedding ring rolled into one."

"Huh?" Rose stared at him with her mouth open as the words sank in. "So that means . . ." Her breath caught. "I've just . . . Crud." She slapped her hand over her mouth. Her ears buzzed as the blood drained out of her head, then flashed back, making her cheeks sting. "You'd better give them back to me." Just when she thought she was taking control and making progress, all she managed to do was make a fool of herself. How could she hope to help the piskies when she knew so little about fairy customs?

All the stress and fear of the last few days tumbled back. Her lip trembled, and she bit it in an effort to keep control as she reached up to unfasten the chain.

Niall caught her wrists and put his mouth to her ear. "How about next week? I want to make an honest woman of you."

She pressed her face against his neck and breathed in his scent. When he wrapped his arms around her, the tension drained away and relief flooded the void. Her eyes watered with happiness. After a few minutes Niall took her hand and pulled her out of the kitchen and up the stairs.

" 'Tis my turn now, lass." He drew her into his bedroom, closed the door, and sat her on the end of his neatly made bed.

Rose glanced at the laptop and remembered the other time she'd been in his room. Was it only a week ago? It felt like a lifetime.

He sat beside her, opened the small wooden box bearing the O'Connor coat of arms, and lifted out his Magic Knot. He stared at the stones cradled in his palm, then unraveled the leather thong and put it over her head. "Now 'tis official. We hold each other's fate by our hearts."

When she touched the stones resting between her breasts, they throbbed against her fingers, sending pulses of longing through her. A few days ago the Magic Knots had been a mystery. Niall had been a mystery. Now she and Niall were joined by the stones in a mystical way she still didn't understand.

He brushed the back of her hand, caressing her skin while his energy pulsed into the core of her being, sending spirals of heat radiating through her. A small, needy sound slipped from her lips, and she curled her hand into his.

He glanced over his shoulder at the bed. "Are you remembering the last time you were here?"

Memories of his body pressed against hers made her tremble. "Perhaps you should remind me."

He closed his box and placed it on the desk. "Last time I told you a wee fib."

"Did you now?"

"Aye." He gave her a self-deprecating smile. "Me arousal was not caused by friction."

Rose glanced down at his lap, her pulse skittering. "So friction had nothing to do with it, then?" She ran her palm up his thigh and rubbed the bulge beneath his zipper.

He sucked in a breath.

"I'd hazard a guess the friction helped."

He cupped her cheek and nuzzled her ear. "A little friction down that way would not go amiss."

Her blood sizzled as she sought his mouth. Kissing him in huge, greedy gulps, she pushed off his jacket, then broke away to tug the shirt over his head. With a shove she pushed him flat on the bed, then unfastened his pants, leaned back, and stripped off her dress. Niall gazed up at her, eyes dazed. "Crikey O'Reilly. Where's the fire?"

Rose grinned and ripped away her underwear. He blinked slowly and opened his arms to her.

With a squeak of excitement she leaped on him. He tried to roll her underneath, but she grappled for superiority, and they wrangled around on the bed, laughing, kissing, and touching until they were both gasping and trembling.

Finally they paused, Niall on top, the ebb and flow of their breath as one. He stared down into her face, his pupils huge and dark. "Want you."

A needy little sound escaped her as she pushed at the top of his pants with her feet, kicking them down his legs. Hot, silky flesh pressed between her thighs, blurring her mind. She grabbed at the firm muscles of his backside as her body bowed to meet his. Then he was inside her and moving. Niall's presence surrounded her, filled her body and mind. Passion stripped away his protective layers, and the raw ache in his core squeezed her heart. Could he believe she loved him? Would Niall conquer his fears and stay with her this time?

Rose opened her mind and let him sense her acceptance and love. She turned her lips against the sinewy strength of his forearm and tasted his skin.

He licked her neck, nibbled her ear, stroked her lips with his silky, hot mouth. She grabbed Niall's back, traced the length of muscle and strength of bone as he pressed her into the mattress. The stones around their necks tangled, pulsed as one. Rose sensed Niall sparking like electrical energy, ready to discharge. As he reached his peak, sensation blasted through her, a wild shock to the system that left her trembling and utterly complete. "God," she croaked into Niall's hair.

He lifted his head and smiled, eyes drugged with pleasure. "Fast and furious."

She grinned and stroked the damp hair off his forehead. "I love seeing you smile. You should do it more often."

Niall rolled off her with a sigh, pulled the covers over them, and gathered her against his chest. "You make me forget me woes, beautiful Rose."

"Did you sort things out with your father?"

With a shrug, he pulled her closer so she couldn't see his face. "Aye. Much as they'll ever be sorted. 'Tis you and me I be wanting to concentrate on now. We have to make plans to free the piskies."

Although she wanted to think about the piskies, sleep dragged down her eyelids.

Niall stroked her hair. "Sleep now, *a ghrá*. I know what must be done. We'll plan later."

"Knock-knock—make yourselves decent." Michael's voice sounded through her sleepy haze. Rose forced her eyelids up as he opened the door and peered in. The frown on his face sent a bolt of warning up her spine, jolting her awake.

Pushing himself up on his elbow, Niall asked, "What's the problem?"

" 'Tis Ana. She's gone."

Niall sat up and tucked the cover around Rose to keep her decent. "What do you mean, gone?"

"Someone's removed the wards. This here was nailed to the door." He held out a piece of paper.

"Great Danu." Niall jumped out of bed and grabbed the note. While Niall read, silent menace radiating from him in waves, Michael backed out the door. Niall balled up the paper and hurled it at the wall. "Tristan has her. He's wanting to trade Ana for your Magic Knot tarot paintings," he said as he yanked on his clothes. When he'd strapped on his knives, he glanced up at her expectantly. "How fast can you get the portraits shipped down?"

Rose swallowed and sat up, pulling the sheet beneath her arms. She couldn't sacrifice her whole troop to Tristan before she'd even tried to release them from the paintings. She reached out to Niall with love, hoping he'd understand her predicament. "Believe me, I really want to help Ana, but I can't give up the piskies.

I'm their queen. I have a duty to protect . . ." Her voice trailed away at the sheen of shock in Niall's eyes.

He dropped his head and stared at the floor.

She extended her senses toward him, and found a dark abyss of agony. Panic squeezed the breath from her lungs. "Niall?"

"I thought you'd trust me," he said so softly she had to strain to hear.

"I didn't mean—"

"Aye, you did." He raised cold, lifeless eyes to her. "You expected me to sacrifice the piskies."

Tears burned in her throat. What could she say? He must have sensed her feelings.

"I'll get the paintings sent down," she blurted, desperate to placate him. She wanted to trust him, more than anything in the world, but the warning on the Ten of Swords loomed in her mind. She clutched the sheet to her chest. Surely he wouldn't betray her after all they'd been through?

Unless he didn't have a choice.

Rose longed to heal the hurt between them. She tried to banish the doubt from her mind and reached for him mentally, but he blocked her out. Wrapped in the sheet, she stumbled out of bed and tottered toward him.

"If the druid's hurt me sister, I'll skin him alive." He cast her a sharp sideways glance as she approached, then turned his back on her. "You should have learned by now: I always look after me own."

Chapter Sixteen

Two hours later, Niall waited for Nightshade beside the entrance to Trevelion Manor. Staring into the inky shadows beneath the huge rhododendron bushes, he imagined the terror Ana must be feeling. He tried to send her reassurance that he was on his way to rescue her. But he couldn't sense his sister, because the second he relaxed the guard on his mind, Rose toppled in like a child leaning against a door.

Niall closed his eyes as her love and reassurance pulsed through him. Now that he'd cooled down, he realized he'd overreacted to her doubts about his plan for the paintings. Rose had known him for only a week. It was natural that she'd be cautious. The bond gave them both access to each other's thoughts and feelings, which could be a double-edged sword. Although now that he'd had a taste of her love, the idea of losing the connection was unbearable.

As soon as he returned to the Nest, he'd make up with her properly—all night. He smiled as his body tightened at the memory of Rose standing over him, eyes glittering with excitement as she ripped off her clothes. He couldn't get enough of her.

Swiping a hand over his face, he suppressed a throb of regret as he eased her loving presence out of his mind. This evening his discussion with Nightshade must be kept private. Rose liked to take control of situations, yet her sheltered human life had not prepared her to deal with the likes of Ciar or Tristan Jago. And she still did not understand fairy ways. Her ignorance had nearly cost her life while in Ireland. His plan to rescue Ana and release the piskies was risky, and depended on deceiving Tristan. There was too much at stake to confide in Rose and then depend on her acting skills for success. Far better she be genuinely surprised by his actions. Once the operation was in progress, Nightshade could explain to her there'd been no other way to pretend to meet Tristan's demands.

Branches rattled in a sudden gust of wind. The last dead leaves clinging to the surrounding trees fluttered loose and spiraled to the ground.

Niall glanced up as Nightshade descended out of the dark sky ten feet away. The stalker came a few strides closer and hesitated beneath a shaft of moonlight falling between the branches. "I had no control over your reaction to my bite, Irish."

A flame of humiliation flickered inside Niall, and he stamped on it. "*That* subject is not open for discussion. Now where's the bloody druid holding Ana?"

"Ana?" Surprise crossed Nightshade's face.

Disquiet rippled through Niall. When he'd called Nightshade for a meeting, he'd assumed the stalker would know what Tristan was up to.

"Tristan took me sister and left a note on the cottage door. He's wanting to trade her for the paintings."

"Shit!" Nightshade looked away and snapped his wings against his back. "He's said nothing. Maybe he no longer trusts me. One of the humans who sells him exotic animals to stuff could have fetched her. They'd do anything for money."

"Do you have any idea where he'd be holding her?"

"Beneath the manor. But it's strange I didn't sense her."

Niall shook his head. " 'Tis unlikely you would, unless you were looking for her. Me sister is bound closely to the earth."

"What are you going to do? Surely Rosenwyn won't give Tristan the paintings after all she's been through?"

Niall turned away and snatched a breath. Where did Nightshade's loyalties lie? Niall was going to have to play this carefully to save the piskies and get his sister back safely.

"Somehow I must work out how to free Ana without relinquishing control of the paintings to Tristan." He'd given the problem a lot of thought in the two hours he'd waited for Nightshade. "Me father told me the only way to rebind the piskies Magic Knots is with visceral blood from Rose." Niall palmed one of his blades and turned it in his hand, the thought of stabbing Rose sending a chill through him. "We must get all three parts of the piskies together with the Magic Knots if it's going to work."

"Tristan keeps the glass globes containing their minds and spirits in his workroom."

"And their Magic Knots?"

"They're in the workroom as well."

"The room where I found Rose?"

Nightshade nodded.

"Should have guessed. 'Tis a place of death, all right." Niall stroked the handle of his knife. "Everything we need is here except their bodies. It makes sense to bring the portraits to Trevelion Manor. Do you know if the piskies will need help to re-form?"

The stalker's eyes glowed in the moonlight. "When I leave my body and flit a long distance as a shade, I'm still aware of my heart beating and lungs breathing, and if I concentrate, I can see and hear what's happening around my body. Would not be safe to leave it otherwise. I guess it'll be the same for them. Although I doubt they've chosen to focus on their bodies while the portraits have been in storage. When the globes are broken, as long as their Magic Knots are then whole, I'm sure the piskies will find their bodies in the paintings."

"After all this time?"

"Time has no meaning when I'm a shade. I expect it's the same for them trapped between life and death. They won't have forgotten anything." Nightshade swallowed and rubbed his mouth.

A plan formed in Niall's mind. "What's Tristan planning to do with the paintings?"

"Arrange them around the walls of the great hall beneath the manor. The spirits in the globe can't see him, but he hopes they'll be able to watch from the paintings as he sacrifices Rosenwyn."

"Great Danu!" Niall took a threatening step forward. "When were you planning to reveal this minor detail?"

Nightshade stood his ground. "I haven't tried to hide anything. What do I have to do to make you trust me, Irish?"

Niall stared at the stalker. Although he'd carried Rose to safety, Niall still wasn't sure of his loyalty.

"You'll go and tell Tristan that I'm willing to trade. Tell him I've had enough of babysitting the pisky queen. I want to make another deal."

Nightshade's eyes widened, then narrowed dangerously.

"Wake up, laddie. 'Tis a ruse," Niall said.

The grim expression on Nightshade's face melted into a smile; then he laughed with relief and slapped Niall on the shoulder. Niall shook his head. How could anyone in his right mind believe he'd really betray Rose to Tristan?

Rose paced back and forth across the Elephant's Nest kitchen.

Michael watched her from the table where he cradled his morning cup of coffee between his hands. "You'll go wearing yourself out, darlin'." He flashed her a mischievous grin. "After that busy night you had, I'm thinking to meself you should be resting." When she cut him a sideways glance, he patted the wooden chair beside him. "Come sit yourself down and tell Uncle Michael what's bothering you."

She huffed in frustration. "I don't know. That's the problem." Halting beside the window, she squinted into the morning sun. "What the hell's Niall doing in the garden?" Kneeling in the backyard beneath the massive oak tree where they'd consulted the tree deva, Niall had buried both his crystal blades to the hilt in the earth and was waving his hands over them and chanting.

Michael shrugged and ambled across to stand beside her. "Who knows, darlin'? Niall was raised by leprechauns. The power of their earth magic is ancient as the dawn of time. Even the Tuatha Dé Danaan have never persuaded the wee folk to reveal their secrets."

"I've got a really bad feeling about today." Rose shivered, and Michael wrapped his arm around her shoulders.

" 'Tis probably just nerves."

Rose shook her head. "This plan Niall and Jacca have cooked up to rescue Ana and free the piskies is so naive, I can't believe Niall thinks it'll work."

Michael frowned. "Don't sound like me brother. He usually doesn't miss a trick."

Fiddling with Niall's leather thong around her neck, she glanced at Michael. "He reckons all we need to do to raise the piskies is free their minds and spirits from the globes and hey, presto"—she snapped her fingers—"they'll meld with their bodies in the paintings and come to life."

Rose shrugged off Michael's arm and paced to the table. "If it's that easy, why didn't he tell me before I traipsed over to Ireland and got fried by Ciar? And what about Tristan? If Niall thinks my father won't notice us waking a troop of piskies beneath his house, he's got another think coming."

Michael gripped her arms. "Listen, Rose, Niall can be a pain in the arse, right enough, but if there's one thing I've learned over the years, he always knows what he's about."

Although Michael's faith in his brother reassured her, she wished she could sense Niall's intentions. His thoughts and emotions were shadowed, as if he were hiding something. After his reaction last time she questioned his motives, she was reluctant to accuse him of keeping secrets.

A knock sounded on the kitchen door and the fair-haired barmaid popped her head in. "Delivery for Ms. Tremain, Mick."

Michael looked at Rose. "May the luck of the leprechauns be with you."

Rose glanced out the window at Niall and fluffed

her hair. "Better tell Merlin the Magician out there the pictures have arrived. I'll go and check them."

She strode through the bar to the parking lot and found the driver unfastening the back of his delivery truck. The man lowered the tail lift. Rose stepped on the metal platform, drew a breath, and steeled herself as he raised the two of them into the truck.

Each portrait stood over six feet tall. Rose stepped into the truck and stared at the stacked wooden cases containing the pictures as the man scanned the bar codes labeling each box. Part of her simmered with morbid fascination, wanting to open the cases and view the portraits. Part of her shied away. Jacca had told her the piskies could see out of the pictures and were aware of their surroundings. She couldn't get her mind around that concept—didn't want to. The thought of being shut in a dark, narrow space sent her pulse racing.

Niall walked up to the back of the truck. With an effortless jump, which left the delivery driver gaping, he vaulted up and wrapped a reassuring arm around her waist. "Don't go unpacking them here, lass. Wait till we get them to Trevelion Manor."

There were seventy-eight wooden cases. Seventy-two of the paintings depicted members of her pisky troop, and the remaining six, animals. The secret fear she'd kept buried since she'd learned what the pictures really were bubbled to the surface. Would they be angry she hadn't rescued them earlier?

She wriggled back into the comfort of Niall's embrace and laced her fingers between his. Solid and steady as a rock, his strength anchored her. "I hope they'll be a bit friendlier to me than Ciar's lot were," she whispered.

Niall cupped her chin and turned her face up. "They'll be sure to like you, me love. You are of sound body and good heart, and madness has yet to invade your brain." He smiled and touched his lips to hers. "I'm not at all sure what they'll make of meself, though."

The truck driver finished scanning the codes on the boxes. Rose signed to accept delivery of the paintings and the rental truck. As a taxicab drove into the parking lot, Niall pulled a roll of fifty-pound notes from his pocket and peeled off a wad. He counted the notes into the man's hand, then pointed at the cab. "That'll deliver you to the train station in Plymouth."

Twenty minutes later, Rose sat in the front of the truck beside Niall as he started the engine. Michael gunned the Porsche behind them and followed as Niall swung the vehicle out of the empty parking lot. They headed along the dirt track beside the estuary and out of the village toward the manor. Rose linked her fingers in her lap and took deep breaths to stay calm. The thought of facing her father again sent a prickling chill over her skin. And she couldn't shake the fear that Niall was keeping something from her.

"Niall." She watched for his reaction. "Are you sure there isn't anything else I need to know?"

His lips thinned; then he shook his head once. "No, lass. Not right now."

"It's just that the plan sounds too simple. I think you're underestimating Tristan."

Niall frowned and cut her a brief, troubled glance. "Don't you go worrying about things. Leave it to me."

She still wasn't happy, but Michael had assured her Niall would be well prepared. The image of the Ten of Swords floated into her mind. The more she tried to forget the prediction, the more the card plagued her. She reached beneath her shirt to clutch her stones for reassurance. When her fingers closed around the cool weight of the rings, she remembered they were Niall's and not hers.

Her stones were tucked beneath Niall's shirt against the solid warmth of his chest. The essence of her being rested in his control. When they'd exchanged Magic Knots, she'd found the idea romantic and arousing. Now she wasn't so sure. Fear of betrayal whispered in her head, stroked cool fingers down her spine. She shivered, pushed the thoughts away, and hardened her resolve to face her father. There was no room for doubts. She and Niall were a team.

As the delivery truck arrived, the front door of Trevelion Manor opened and Tristan stepped out, followed by Jacca.

When Rose opened her door to climb down, Niall gripped her hand.

"Hang on." His lips twitched in an attempt at a smile, but his eyes remained uneasy. "Whatever happens in there, trust me."

"You're king of the cryptic comment, you know," she said, but he'd already released her and was jumping out. Foreboding curled through her. She reached for him psychically and sensed dark tendrils of apprehension leaking around his mental shield. Why hadn't she pumped him for more information during the journey? Now they were out of time.

After jumping down from the vehicle, Rose jogged to catch up with him as he walked toward the house. For Tristan's benefit, she eyed Jacca warily, as if she didn't know him.

Niall gave her shoulder a brief, reassuring squeeze

as they halted, and he said, "We've got the paintings. Where's me sister?"

"Let's do this in a civilized manner." Tristan extended his arm, indicating that they should enter.

With a shudder of reluctance, Rose followed Tristan along the hall, Niall behind her, Jacca bringing up the rear. She hesitated before stepping into the drawing room, a premonition of disaster whispering in her mind.

Tristan looked her up and down and raised an eyebrow. "My daughter has blossomed since last I saw her." He gave Niall a speculative glance. "Your doing, I take it?"

Niall gripped Rose's elbow and pulled her to his side. "Where's Ana?"

"You do have a tediously single-track mind for someone with such a rich and creative heritage." Tristan held up a decanter. "Don't suppose I can tempt you?"

Niall scowled, and Tristan placed the decanter back on its tray with a sigh.

Rose leaned into the strong warmth of Niall. He obviously didn't intend to let Tristan separate them this time. Despite Niall's attempt to block her out, spikes of his anger darted into her as he glanced around the room.

Tristan crooked a finger at Jacca. "Bring the little creature in."

Niall's grip on Rose's arm tightened to the point of pain as he stared at the door. When Ana trotted in, dark curls bouncing around her wrinkled face, Niall released Rose and dropped to his knees. He took Ana's hands. "Are you hurt?"

"Naw, lad." She stroked his cheek, then smiled at Rose. "I'm right as rain now that you're here for me."

Niall stood, Ana's hand clasped in his, and glanced at the door. "Michael's waiting for you. I'll take you out."

"Not yet," Tristan said. "The girls stay with me until you've unloaded the paintings and taken them downstairs."

Niall cast Tristan a fierce look that made the hair prickle on the back of Rose's neck, but he didn't argue. He led Ana across to Rose. With a silent brush of caution across her senses, he gave her a meaningful look and put Ana's rough little hand into hers. "I'll not be long."

Rose glanced nervously at her father as Niall and Jacca walked out. She didn't want Niall to leave her, but he obviously didn't have any choice. She remembered now that the last time she was here her father had told her he wouldn't let her go. She'd never discovered why. Tristan smiled, razor sharp with victory, and her skin crawled.

Backing away, Rose pulled Ana to a leather sofa at the far end of the room. They huddled together in silence while Tristan poured a drink and sank into a chair by the fire.

"Me lad won't leave us for long," Ana said. She smiled again, folding her wrinkled brown face into a mass of crinkles. With a stubby finger, she brushed the bump of Niall's stones beneath Rose's shirt. "I do so love being right," she whispered, and chuckled. "That lad would have you thinking he's got no heart, but don't go believing him. 'Tis soft he is inside." She nodded to herself. "Aye, soft as thistledown, and equally fragile. You're a lucky lass. There's no finer fellow, believe me. He won't go letting you down, like some scoundrels."

Ana's total belief in Niall helped relieve Rose's

sense of unease, but didn't squelch it altogether. Chills of foreboding raced up and down her spine as Tristan watched her with an air of confidence that made her think he knew something she didn't.

Niall and Jacca seemed to take forever, but eventually the men returned to the room, looking dusty and hot. "All done," Jacca said to Tristan.

"Well, then, Niall. It seems you've fulfilled nearly all your part of our bargain. Nightshade will escort your sister out to Michael. You have my word she'll be safe now."

Rose stood at Niall's side and watched Jacca leave with Ana. "Aren't we going as well?" she whispered to him.

He cut her a quick sideways glance. "There's one more thing."

After downing the last of his drink, Tristan rose from his seat. Niall stepped behind her and curled his arm around her waist. Welcoming the reassurance of his presence with her father so close, she leaned against Niall.

Tristan's nostrils flared like those of a predator scenting prey. "I hope you haven't gotten cold feet, Niall," he said, his eyes sharp with anticipation.

Fear streaked through her. Something wasn't right. "Niall?" She pressed back against him, seeking safety.

"Shh, love," he whispered. "Trust me."

Before she could summon questions, Jacca returned and cast an apprehensive glance her way. She clutched Niall's arm and snapped her head around toward Tristan. He grinned with a tight malevolence that turned her blood to ice water.

"Someone tell me what's going on. Niall?" Out of the corner of her eye she caught the glint of a blade in

Niall's hand. With sudden horrific clarity, she sensed what he was about to do.

Still as death, Rose froze, the chill in her blood invading her heart. Time slowed. She opened her mouth in slow motion. Words bumped around her brain, but didn't make it past her numb lips. The Ten of Swords had spoken true.

"I love you," Niall whispered against her ear. His presence flowed into every cell of her body, overwhelming her senses. Despite her fugue, she felt pain lance her side, so hot and sharp it forced the air from her lungs in a keening wail. Fire invaded her belly. Ice filled her chest, splintering her heart and piercing her soul. Niall's essence floated away like mist on the wind as the room faded. Rose strained to hold on to him as darkness sucked her down toward oblivion. Betrayal hadn't required ten swords in the back. One knife in the side was just as deadly.

Chapter Seventeen

Rose opened her eyes. For a moment she wondered if she really had raised her eyelids or just imagined doing so, because the darkness was impenetrable. A flutter of cool, salty air brushed across her skin. Dense silence hummed in her ears. She moved and became aware of cold, unyielding rock beneath her.

For a few seconds she was disoriented; then the darkness pressed against her like invisible hands. Panic snatched her breath. Where was she? Underground? In a tomb? Instinctively she extended her consciousness, seeking Niall as the terror of being trapped tightened around her chest. The reassuring glow of his presence was close, but shielded from her. A little spurt of anger shot through her. Why did he always shut her out?

Then the memory of what had happened trickled back like ice water into her grave.

Tears sprang to her eyes, and Rose fought to breathe past the burn in her chest. Had Niall been working with Tristan all along? How bad was her wound? The pain had been horrendous when the knife went in. Now she couldn't feel anything. Gingerly she touched her side and found a dressing taped beneath her shirt.

She pressed her fingers against the gauze and was surprised the wound didn't hurt. Maybe they'd given her painkillers.

The tender words Niall had breathed against her ear as he'd made love to her the previous night fluttered in her mind. How could he stab her after all they'd been through together?

Righteous anger seared away her pain. She smacked her palm against the rock. *Damn him!* She'd kill him if he had betrayed her, and she'd bloody well kill him if he hadn't and this was all some ploy. Oh, yes, knowing Niall, that made more sense. No wonder he hadn't explained everything to her. He'd swamped her with his presence as the blade went in, probably trying to distract her from the pain. Well, it had still hurt like crap. She had half a mind to walk out and leave them all to it. Except there was nowhere she wanted to go.

Her bravado collapsed, leaving her hollow. Her human life, the career she'd worked so hard for, her past, all seemed like a dream. She belonged here now, with Niall and the piskies—or she'd thought she did. Although she'd tried to change and fit in, she still didn't understand how the fairy world worked. Ignorance had nearly gotten her killed in Ireland. Maybe now *it* would be the death of her.

Rose rubbed her eyes. Niall had never shown her the note listing Tristan's demands. Stabbing her must have been part of the bargain to release Ana. For a few seconds jealousy and anger swirled through her, overwhelming reason. Did Niall love Ana so much more than he loved her? Was it possible he'd sacrifice Rose's life to save his sister's?

But Niall had risked his own life to save her in Ireland. None of this made sense. The sweet memory of the previous night rolled through her. He loved her. He could not hide his emotion when they were joined physically, mentally, and spiritually. Why would he hurt her?

A faint scraping sound made her freeze. She opened her eyes and stared into the pitch darkness. Jacca's presence brushed her senses, darkly sweet like a blossom opening at twilight. A hand landed on her arm and she jumped.

"It's me, Rosenwyn," Jacca whispered in the darkness.

"And there's me thinking it was room service with the champagne and caviar." Despite her bravado, she tensed beneath his touch. What part had he played in her predicament? "I hope you haven't changed sides again."

"No." The edge of distress in his voice reassured her more than the word. "You're my queen. I'll protect you."

"Huh! I think your definition of *protect* must be slightly different from mine."

"Check the wound, Rosenwyn."

She frowned and pressed her fingers against the dressing again. "Niall stabbed me. I felt the blade go in."

"Wait." Cool air replaced his heat as Jacca moved away. An oil lamp flared to life on a scrubbed wooden table, illuminating the damp walls and gray dome roof of a small cave. He lifted the lamp and carried it closer, the light chasing ghoulish shadows across the speckled granite. "Examine your wound."

Rose shivered as she imagined what she'd find. His encouraging smile persuaded her to peel back the dressing and check. Her skin was pink, but showed no damage. She pushed up on her elbow for a better look and poked at the spot. "That's impossible."

"Niall's smoky quartz blades can be enchanted to cut away bad energy from people without leaving physical damage."

"He stabbed the blade into my side."

"Penetrating your body with the blade cleansed your energy field."

"Unbelievable." Rose sat up, ripped off the dressing, and tucked in her shirt. "He stabs me and you're trying to tell me it was for my own good. I wasn't born yesterday. Let's have the truth."

"Don't think too badly of him. Tristan had to believe Niall was going to betray you so he could stay for the ritual. Niall also needed your blood on the blade to raise the piskies."

"Why the hell didn't he warn me?"

Jacca gazed at his feet and shrugged. "He thought it would be worse if you knew what was coming. This way you didn't worry about it beforehand."

Anger at Niall's twisted male logic warred with the flood of relief that his motives were good. She stared at the flickering shadows cast by the oil lamp, and goose bumps rushed across her skin. If he did stupid things like this, how could she ever trust him again?

She crushed the wound dressing in her hand. "I thought he'd betrayed me." For a moment tears burned her throat. "It hurt."

"I'm sorry . . ." Jacca touched her hand. Anguish filled his eyes, sending a frisson of fear skating through her.

"There's more, isn't there?"

"I must take you to the great hall for the ritual."

"The one Niall wanted to stay for?"

Jacca nodded.

"To free the piskies?"

"We must play along with Tristan's plans. He wants to sacrifice you with a ritual blade before the paintings to show the piskies they have no hope of rescue."

Fear fisted in her belly. One taste of a blade was enough. She shook her head.

"Niall's planning to release the piskies while Tristan's occupied with the ceremony. We won't allow any harm to come to you."

Much as she hated the idea of putting herself at Tristan's mercy again, if her people were freed, it would be worth the risk. A rod of icy resolution straightened her backbone. "Okay, tell me what Niall intends to do so I'm prepared."

"I don't know. Niall said he'd give a signal when he wants me to fetch the globes containing the piskies' minds and spirits."

"Great!" Rose slapped her palms on the rock. "Tristan plans to sacrifice me, and Niall's going to wing it."

Jacca smiled apologetically. "We'd better go now. I'll leave the bonds loose when I tie you to the stone table. Relax and close your eyes. Tristan must think you're still unconscious."

Niall's presence nearby hummed like high-voltage cables. Whatever he planned, he was keyed up and ready. Despite his obdurate behavior, she was certain he loved her. She stood up and brushed off her clothes. All she could do was trust the man she loved.

When Jacca scooped her into his arms, she relaxed against his chest and remembered how terrible she'd felt on the flight from Ireland. She hadn't expected to face death again so soon. As they entered the dark corridor, she closed her eyes and pressed her cheek against his warm skin. This was her destiny. The lives of seventy-two piskies rested in her hands. Whatever it took to put right her mother's mistakes and her father's evil deeds, Rose was determined to pay the price.

Niall waited beside Tristan in the center of the great hall beneath Trevelion Manor. Every muscle in his body tensed when Nightshade appeared from the shadows with Rose's limp form cradled in his arms.

Extending his senses, Niall reached out to reassure her. She was conscious, but emotionally he sensed . . . nothing. Then a fog of fear and pain drifted between them, blurring his link with her.

He pushed harder, trying to strengthen their connection, let her know she was safe. No response. What was wrong? The stab wound should have healed within an hour, leaving her cleansed and strengthened to face Tristan. Apart from the initial pain, which he'd tried to alleviate, there should have been no adverse effects.

Niall stared at Nightshade until the man met his gaze and blinked, his expression unreadable. The stalker was supposed to have explained Niall's motives for stabbing her. Had she understood? Had Niall pushed her trust in him too far?

After Nightshade laid Rose on the stone table in the center of the chamber, he secured her wrists and ankles. She rolled her head and groaned, obviously pretending to regain consciousness for Tristan's benefit. Niall stayed inside her mind, trying to connect with her. She thrust him away and retreated behind sharp points of anger and hurt. Her name jumped to his lips and he bit it back. Tristan mustn't doubt his intentions. A chill settled in the pit of his stomach. Had he devised a plan that would save her people yet lose him her love?

Tristan shuffled over to where Rose lay and lit four black candles positioned on the corners of the stone table. When the druid gave her a malevolent grin, Niall suppressed the urge to race over and protect her.

Narrowing his eyes, Tristan surveyed the paintings of the pisky troop that were leaning against the walls. "Behind those frozen expressions they see everything." He stared at Rose as he withdrew a bone-handled knife from his robes. "Let's hope they enjoy our little show."

Rose shifted. She turned her head toward Niall. Unshed tears in her eyes glittered in the candle flames.

Niall's muscles vibrated with the effort to remain still. *Steady, love,* he whispered into her mind, and felt a flood of relief as she opened to him.

"We've come full circle, my dear," Tristan said. "Your mother lay here when I took her blood to destroy your people. Now you lie in her place as queen." Tristan passed his blade through a candle flame, a satisfied smile on his face. "The blood of the royal line condemned them. Only the blood of the royal line can restore them." He touched the ritual blade to his lips, then leaned over Rose, his face inches above hers. "On your death, the ungrateful wretches will be trapped forever."

Rose remained motionless, but Niall sensed her hanging on to their thread of connection like a lifeline.

Tristan raised his hands above his head. The wide sleeves of his robe fell back to reveal emaciated arms.

Time to give Nightshade the signal. Niall looked at the stalker, who nodded once in acknowledgment and slipped away to fetch the two glass globes and the wooden box containing the broken Magic Knots.

Niall flexed his wrist and let the bloodied blade he'd used on Rose slide into his palm. Timing was crucial. Although he didn't know how powerful Tristan was, Nightshade swore the druid's black magic was capable of killing them all. Niall had to wait until Tristan entered a trance state before he took action.

Tristan's Gaelic litany echoed around the underground chamber. Most Niall understood. He wished he didn't. Evil words from the mantra of eternal damnation hammered into his soul like rusty nails. Niall swallowed and concentrated on controlling his catching breaths. How much worse it must be for Rose. Yet she held on to their connection, trusting him. Her life in his hands.

He mustn't let her down.

When Tristan's voice dropped as though he were nearing the end of his incantation, Niall flexed his muscles, ready for action, and watched for Nightshade. The druid ceased speaking, face turned up toward the ceiling, eyes closed. Silence hummed in the room.

Come on, Nightshade. Where in the Furies are you? We need to act now.

Niall edged toward the door, counting off the seconds of Tristan's trance in his head. When Niall reached two hundred, Tristan sucked in a breath and looked down at Rose.

Dagda! They'd missed their best chance. With a wary eye on the tableau being played out on the stone table, Niall continued his silent steps toward the doorway where he expected Nightshade to reappear.

With the backs of his fingers, Tristan stroked Rose's cheek. Her dread tugged at Niall, but he couldn't be distracted now. *Hold on a little longer*, he whispered into her mind. Nightshade must return soon.

Tristan hooked his finger beneath the leather thong around Rose's neck and pulled out the Magic Knot. Niall froze, breath locked in his chest, every scrap of attention fixed on his stones. He hadn't foreseen this. Killing Rose was enough to put an end to the piskies. Why did Tristan want the stones?

Out of the corner of his eye, he saw Nightshade slide back into the chamber, dark as a wraith. *Grand bloody timing.*

If Tristan smashed Niall's stones, Niall would join the pisky troop in oblivion. A surge of pain swept through him. He was about to be rent asunder and he'd never actually told Rose he loved her.

Rose gasped. "Not the stones." She shot a panicked glance his way.

"Ah, at last you show some spirit." Tristan followed her gaze toward Niall and frowned when he noticed he'd moved. Then he turned back to Rose. "I thought you'd given up as easily as your mother. I expected more from you, since you carry my genes."

"Don't remind me," Rose spit.

The druid jerked the thong around her neck taut and whipped his blade across it. She cried out as the thin leather bit into her flesh before it snapped.

Tristan dangled the stones before her. "Say goodbye to your lover, my dear."

He hurled Niall's Magic Knot at the ground.

"Niall!" Rose screamed.

Niall leaped as the stones left the druid's hand. He caught them an inch above the ground and rolled over onto his feet. Tristan blinked in surprise, mouth agape. In the few seconds it took the druid to react, Niall pocketed his stones, turned, and sprinted toward Nightshade.

The stalker hesitated a second, then took off toward Niall, carrying the box of Magic Knots. Niall flipped the bloodied dagger blade out and held it ready. He concentrated on the box, imagined plunging the blade among the broken stones to rejoin them.

Five feet until he reached the wooden box.

Nearly there.

Pain pierced the base of his spine, exploding up and down, freezing every nerve, every muscle. He dragged breath into lungs heavy with cold, stumbled to his knees, and toppled forward, the side of his face smashing against the granite floor.

With agonizing effort, he lifted his head. Nightshade crawled toward him, pushing the box ahead. Niall dug his fingernails and boots into the granite and inched forward. Another foot and he'd be there. Once Rose's blood on the ensorcelled dagger touched the stones, the magic would take over.

With every fiber of his being, Niall willed himself on. Ice water ran where his blood should be. His teeth chattered. His breath misted before him. Muscles seized up. With a painful thud that sent stars spinning before his eyes, his head fell forward.

"What's happening?" Muffled and distant, Rose's voice reached him as if in a dream. Body useless, face pressed into the grit, he sought the warmth of Rose's love to chase back the chill invading his heart. He couldn't reach her. Tristan's spell must have locked him into his body. Nightshade had been right: the druid was dangerous.

Tristan's black patent shoes appeared a few inches from his face. "You nearly fooled me, but the way she looked at you tipped me off." He stooped and dragged the leather thong from Niall's pocket.

The druid dangled the Magic Knot before Niall's face and let the stones bump the toe of his shoe. The chill in Niall's body frosted his heart. He'd let Rose down, let the piskies down.

"So that means . . ." Tristan caught hold of the chain around Niall's neck and yanked it free. He crouched down and cupped Rose's Magic Knot in his hand for Niall to see. "These are my daughter's." He dropped Niall's stones into his palm before rolling the two sets around together. "I must say, I'm impressed by how fast you work. I had the impression your brother was the charmer. If I cared about Rose, I'd be pleased with her choice." He stroked Niall's hair and sighed. "Such a waste. Never mind, at least you have the consolation of knowing you'll die together."

Chapter Eighteen

Rose strained her neck to see what was happening behind her, but they were all out of sight. "Niall," she shouted. She could hear the murmur of voices echoing in the cavernous chamber, but no one answered.

Niall had sprinted away with purpose after catching his stones. Maybe he wasn't answering her because he was in the middle of trying to free the piskies. She gazed at the paintings dimly illuminated by candles on the walls. None of the pictures moved—yet.

Rose pulled on the straps Jacca had fastened loosely around her wrists. With a few tugs her hands slid free. Leaning up on an elbow, she peered into the gloom and saw Tristan crouched beside two prone bodies.

Niall! She probed for their link. A blast of mind-numbing cold hit her. The chill crawled into her core, crept along her limbs. What the hell had Tristan done to him?

She bent forward and fumbled with the knots at her ankles. Her body shook with each thump of her heart as she wriggled off the far end of the table and hid behind the hunk of rock supporting the surface. What could she do? At any moment Tristan might notice she wasn't where he'd left her. Rose dragged her hands through her hair and tried to get her brain in gear. Jacca had said her blood was needed to raise the piskies. How? *Damn Niall.* Why hadn't he told her what he planned to do?

Rose peered around the table to check what was happening. Niall and Jacca were both still motionless on the ground. *Oh, God, Niall.* She opened herself to him again, and at the icy touch pulled back.

Tristan stood and walked from Niall to Jacca. He halted, hands on hips, and shook his head. "I'm disappointed in you, Nightshade. I suppose I shouldn't be surprised. You betrayed your troop; now you betray me. They say a leopard doesn't change its spots."

Jacca had betrayed the troop? The thought puzzled her for a moment, but was knocked from her head as Tristan slammed the toe of his shoe into Jacca's gut. Rose jerked back and pressed her hand to her mouth to stifle her cry. Had Tristan kicked Niall as well when she wasn't watching?

She must do something. *Now.*

Rose crawled beneath the side of the table in the deepest shadows, getting a little closer. Perhaps if she ran away, Tristan would follow her and leave the men to recover. *Idiot! That's so lame.* She squeezed her eyes closed. *Come on, woman. Use your brain.*

Tristan unhooked the key ring holding the Magic Knot from Jacca's belt, then dropped the stones in his palm. It was a safe bet Tristan had taken Niall's stones as well. What about hers? Cold sweat prickled her body, and nausea swirled in her gut. She was certain the sick taint of his touch on her stones was causing her queasiness.

What had Niall planned to do? A box lay on the

ground between the two prone men. Rose squinted through the gloom. Was that a dagger in Niall's outstretched hand?

Tristan jangled the three sets of stones and smirked down at the men. "Do you know how I shattered the piskies'? It's ridiculously easy." His lips peeled back in a malevolent grin that spiked fear through Rose. "Let me give you a demonstration."

Tipping his hand, Tristan let the Magic Knots tumble to the floor. Blinding pain crashed through her skull as the stones hit. Rose clamped her hands over her head, clenching her teeth.

When she recovered enough to look up, Tristan was pushing one set of stones into a heap with his toe. He raised his heel above them. "I didn't think I'd have to do this to you, Nightshade." He released a deep, gusty sigh.

Tristan stamped down.

Jacca convulsed.

His animalistic cry echoed around the cavern. Her father raised his foot and examined the stones. "Tough guy, tough stones," he said, and crashed his heel on them again.

If Jacca were split up without a painting for his body to pass into, what would happen to him? She pressed her hands over her mouth as Tristan raised his heel a third time.

For God's sake, move. Do something. Anything. She blinked against the throbbing in her head and tensed her muscles. Dark waves of nausea rolled over her as she tried to stand. Clutching at the table, she collapsed back to the ground.

Tristan banged his foot down. Jacca's scream echoed with primeval horror that would stay with her for the rest of her life. His body shimmered, faded, and melted away into shadow.

Jacca! She pressed her hands over her eyes. He'd saved her life by flying her out of Ireland, and she'd sat here and watched her father kill him. Bile burned the back of her throat, and she fought the need to throw up.

Blinking back tears, she watched her father push the stones on the leather thong into a heap. "Not so superior now, are you, proud Tuatha Dé Danaan?" He crouched and angled his head to see Niall's face. "You always thought you were better than me, didn't you? Conceited as the bloody piskies."

She would not let Tristan do the same to Niall.

Rose swallowed hard and pushed herself to her feet. She blinked to clear her head and made herself walk toward Tristan. "You bastard."

Tristan glanced up and rose slowly to his feet. "Nightshade didn't tie you properly. I should have known."

Rose faltered to a stop ten feet from him and scanned Niall's body. She had no idea how to stop Tristan, but she couldn't let him break Niall's stones.

Tristan crossed his arms and smirked. "Have you just come to watch, or do you plan to try to stop me?"

Cool air carrying the scent of almonds feathered her skin. *Jacca?* Was he still here?

Rosenwyn, Jacca's voice whispered in her mind.

She tried to scan the room from the corner of her eye to see his shade.

Put Niall's knife in the wooden box. I'll distract Tristan.

Tristan raised his foot over Niall's Magic Knot.

"No!" Rose lunged at her father.

He lifted his hand. A dark nimbus of power danced around his fingers and shot out bolts of black fire. Rose lunged sideways, landing heavily, one arm numbed with cold from his attack.

Jacca's man-shaped shade materialized beside Tristan. The druid's eyes widened, and he backed away with his hand out. Black, smoky bursts flared from Tristan's fingers and passed through the shadow ineffectually. When her father turned to run, he managed two steps before he grunted and fell on his face.

Rose scrambled up, hugging her cold-deadened arm to her body, and ran toward Niall. Although desperate to check that he wasn't hurt, she forced herself to first pull the dagger from his limp fingers and throw it at the wooden box. The blade hit the side and bounced onto the ground. "Bloody hell!" Did everything have to be difficult? Rose crawled forward and snatched the knife up. This time she held the handle as she plunged the smoky quartz into the box.

Stone crunched against stone. It took her a moment to realize the box contained the piskies' broken Magic Knots.

Stirring the stone fragments with the dagger, she made sure every piece touched her blood. Rose gathered the pieces of Jacca's Magic Knot off the ground and added them to the box.

Close by, Tristan grunted, his limp body bouncing on the ground like a broken doll as Jacca's shade pummeled him. Pain etched his face into a white mask of death as he caught her in his malicious gaze. "You'll . . . pay. . . ."

Rose ignored him and touched the knife to Jacca's stones, then waited. Flickers of light jumped from the box, and the contents started to hum and sizzle. Rose dragged herself backward, worried the magic might be dangerous. A hand gripped her leg and she screamed.

Niall had pushed himself up onto all fours and crawled across to her.

"You're all right." Relief clogged her throat with tears. "God, I was scared." Rose put her good arm around his neck and pressed their cheeks together. For a second she drew strength from the solidity of him, the familiar scent of his skin.

"Globes," he forced out in a dry voice.

She pulled back, and her heart contracted as she examined his damaged face.

Gingerly she traced his cheekbone and forehead, both bruised purple and spotted with bloody pocks where grit was embedded in his skin. Licking his lips, he tried twice to get his words out. "Smash . . . the globes."

Rose followed his gaze toward a dark bundle by the wall.

On shaking legs, she walked around the wooden box, which was shooting out sparks like fireworks. She pressed the back of her hand to her mouth, a strange tingle of excitement and trepidation racing along her nerves. The piskies would soon be flesh and blood.

Rose eased down to her knees beside the bundle and pulled the brown animal-skin covering away. Blinding golden light pierced her retinas before she could throw an arm over her eyes.

"Smash them, Rose," Niall shouted. She peeped at him from behind her arm as he fell back to the ground, chest heaving with the effort of shouting.

Her father writhed on the floor close to Niall. As she watched, the shadowy form pinning him took on

Jacca's shape and grew solid. Her blood on the broken Magic Knots must be working. A heady burst of relief gave her renewed strength.

Rose balled the animal skin over her fist and, closing her eyes, smashed the first globe. She'd expected it to be tough, but it shattered like eggshell. Squinting to check her aim, she brought her fist down on the second globe. Careful of the glittering splinters of glass, she pulled the animal skin off her hand and collapsed back against the wall. She'd done all she could. Now it was up to the piskies to do the rest.

Two clouds of scintillating golden light rose from the shattered globes and swirled together. Instinctively she grabbed a breath and shielded her face as the light engulfed her. Images flashed in her mind of the people she'd known all her life from the tarot cards: smiling, laughing, dancing in this very place wearing bright, extravagant clothing. She saw their memories of her mother, young and beautiful, seated on a throne of twining branches beside a dark-haired man who must have been Rose's grandfather. Snippets of conversation drifted through her mind. *My queen, my queen,* repeated like a mantra in her head. After what could have been a few seconds or an hour, the cloud drifted away. A sense of peace and stillness filled her.

The twinkling light floated around Niall, and his body relaxed. Was he, too, seeing images of the troop? Once the cloud drifted away, he sat up and rubbed a hand across his mouth. Rose struggled up, made her way to him, and leaned into his welcoming embrace. With her cheek against his chest, she watched eddies of light brush across Jacca while he struggled with Tristan.

The cloud sharpened into a golden spear, plunged down, and arrowed in through her father's eyes.

Jacca jerked back as a strangled sound gargled from Tristan's throat. Niall's hand cradled her head and pulled her face against his chest. She concentrated on the steady thud of Niall's heart and the feel of his lips brushing her temple. " 'Tis over now, love. 'Tis over."

When she looked around, Jacca was sitting, ramrod stiff, eyes fixed on the glowing trails of light that issued from her father's body. The light fractured into points, making Jacca duck as the sparks zoomed past him, then shot off around the room toward the paintings.

Niall cupped her chin and turned her face up, his eyes warm and gentle. "I'm sorry, lass. I should have told you."

Her eyes filled with tears at the sudden release of tension. "Tristan's dead," she whispered.

"Aye. That he is."

She wasn't going to die. Niall wasn't going to die. His arms were around her, his heart beating strongly against her ear. The huge strength of his spirit surrounded her and filled her with love. They were together and would stay together.

"I'll forgive you this time." She clasped his hand and summoned a little lopsided smile. "Just don't do it again."

"Look!" Jacca called.

She peered out from the safety of Niall's embrace and watched, stupefied, as the figures on the paintings moved, filled out, then stepped from the pictures. Nearest to her, the young man in the Seven of Cups jumped down from his painting, shook out his red cloak, and flicked back long golden hair. He turned emerald eyes on her, and his mouth tilted into a wickedly sensual grin. The seductive pull of his glamour tightened deep in her belly.

She shook her head and gave him a reprimanding look. He pouted, then stepped forward and bowed with a flourish. "I am Thorn, beautiful Queen. I am completely at your service." It looked like Michael would have some competition.

Niall turned his head one way, then the other, gazing around the room. "We have some live ones." He dropped a kiss on her hair and helped her up. "Before we get caught up, there's something I've been meaning to say to you, lass." He rubbed his thumb over her bottom lip. "I love you."

She reached up and touched his face. "Then trust me. Don't shut me out again."

He lowered his head and stroked his lips across hers. "Never."

Jacca approached, went down on one knee, and offered them their Magic Knots. "My queen." He gave Rose hers. "My king." He handed Niall his.

Rose frowned at his subservience. "What's gotten into you? Get up. We're still the same people." The flash of fear in Nightshade's eyes shocked her. "What's wrong?"

Jacca looked over his shoulder, and Rose followed his gaze toward the multitude of brightly colored figures emerging from paintings around the room. "Will you speak for me? I worked with Tristan and . . ." He dropped his gaze and curled his fist against his thigh. "They'll banish me."

"Not if I've got anything to say about it." She surveyed the curious expressions turned her way. Her only experience of fairies en masse was at the Irish court, and no way would she allow her people to be that heartless. She looked at Niall. "You'll speak up for him, won't you?"

Niall cut her a sideways glance. "Don't suppose I've got a choice." When she glared at him, he huffed a breath. "We'll both speak for you, stalker. Now get off your knees, boyo, before I have to drag you up."

Jacca stood and tilted his chin with a return of his familiar arrogance. "You couldn't drag me anywhere, Irish."

Niall's eyes gleamed dangerously. "Aye, I could, and if you ever go telling anyone what happened in Wales, I will. You're a bloodsucking opportunist, but you carried Rose out of Ireland, and for that I'll tolerate you."

Jacca's nostrils flared; then his lips twitched and a mischievous sparkle lit his eyes. "Thank you, most noble King." He inclined his head. "If you'll excuse me, I think I'll go and find Michael." He glanced back over his shoulder as he melted into the crowd and added, "I'm feeling like a bite to eat."

Rose grabbed Niall's arm as he tensed. "Leave it," she whispered. They had more immediate matters to handle. With a soft rustle of fabric, the piskies collected around them on silent feet. Niall relaxed and surveyed the gathered troop. Rose followed his gaze.

A beautiful woman wearing a sumptuous blue velvet gown, her flowing dark hair restrained by a circlet of gold, stepped forward. All her life, Rose had known this woman as the Magic Knot tarot High Priestess. Suddenly the reality of what had happened knocked the breath from her lungs. She grasped Niall's arm as the woman came forward and knelt before them.

"My queen." The woman inclined her head to Rose in a courtly nod. "I am Cordelia, wise woman of the troop. On behalf of all, I welcome you and offer you thanks for restoring us. We have always trusted you'd find your way back to us." She turned to Niall, a small secret smile on her face that made Rose's hackles rise. "My king. You are most welcome. The noble blood of the Tuatha Dé Danaan will strengthen our royal line." She tilted her head and glanced up at Rose. "I first saw our king when he entered your chamber at night to steal a kiss."

"When was this?" Rose stared at Niall, her mouth open in surprise.

Niall frowned and fiddled with his cuffs. "I was only checking up on your welfare after the incident with Nightshade."

That was when she'd first arrived. "You kissed me while I was asleep?"

He shifted his feet and gave the wise woman a narrow look. She gathered a gray cat into her arms with a murmur of delight and smiled back innocently. Someone in the crowd giggled. Niall flexed his shoulders. "I can see I'll be having to watch me step with you lot."

"Did you kiss me?" Rose repeated. If he had, he'd been interested in her right from the start.

Niall tightened his lips. "Aye, but I did not take liberties."

Absolutely typical of Niall's warped male logic. He'd kissed her for the first time when she was unconscious and couldn't enjoy it. She wrapped her arms around him, ignoring his surprised look, and planted a kiss on his lips, right there in front of everyone.

She released a satisfied sigh and stared around at her people. Faces she'd known all her life nodded and smiled back at her. For the first time she felt complete. No doubt there would be trials ahead, but she loved Niall, and together they'd overcome the challenges.

Although she'd come to search for her father, she'd found something far better. She'd discovered who she really was.

All she had to do now was achieve the near-impossible task for which she'd originally come to Cornwall: help Michael sort out the financial muddle he'd made at the Elephant's Nest.

A few months later Rose sat in the office at the Elephant's Nest facing the new computer she'd given Michael at the piskies' December Yule celebrations. With a sense of satisfaction, she entered the details of another invoice into the accounting program and dropped the document onto the heap for filing.

Thinking about the state of his accounts had given her heartburn after the large New Year's meal they'd just finished. There was no better time than the first day of the year to start sorting the finances out.

The back of her neck tickled, and the familiar touch of Niall's presence brushed her senses. Licking her lips in anticipation, she swung the chair around to face him. He leaned against the door frame, arms crossed, mouth twitching as he fought his grin.

"What might you be doing closeted in here, lass, while everyone else is making merry in the bar?" As if to emphasize his question, she heard Michael shout the punch line of one of his bawdy stories, and a bellow of raucous laughter followed.

"Didn't you know? I'm waiting for you, Mr. O'Connor."

"Me?" he said in mock surprise. "And why would you be waiting for me?"

When Rose surveyed the way his smart black slacks

hugged his hips, desire tightened low in her belly. Provocatively, she crossed her legs.

Blue fire flared in Niall's eyes as her skirt crept up her thighs.

"Because"—Rose waggled her eyebrows—"you're the computer expert."

Niall grinned as he pushed away from the door frame, closed the door behind him, and turned the key.

"Are you going to help me?" she teased in a husky voice.

He sauntered forward and slid his palm up her leg. "Now, that depends on what you be wanting help with."

He leaned a hand on the chair back and tipped her into a reclining position. Rose squeaked in surprise, then giggled when he pressed his face against the red silk covering her belly and nibbled.

When he raised his head, she framed his smiling face between her hands and examined the fading scars speckling his cheekbone and forehead. Ironically, the imperfection accentuated his beauty. She pulled his head down and pressed her mouth to his, kissing lightly. As he sank to his knees beside her chair, she wrapped her arms around his neck and deepened the kiss. Time stopped. Rose forgot where she was. Her brain dissolved into warm mush, so she couldn't think clearly enough to remember her name, let alone process Michael's accounts.

Niall raised his head and snatched a ragged breath. "You're an expert when it comes to distracting me from me task."

He dug in his trouser pocket and pulled out a red

velvet bag tied with a tasseled gold cord. "I've a New Year's present for you, love." He took her hand and pressed the gift into her palm. " 'Twas passed down through the generations."

Rose weighed the bag in her hand. The velvet held something solid and surprisingly heavy. "You've already given me the bracelet and earrings and my favorite present." Rose turned her left hand into the light, and green fire flickered within the huge emerald adorning the ring he'd given her at their handfasting ceremony.

He closed his eyes and kissed her finger beside the ring. "This ring is more than a present. 'Tis a symbol of my love and commitment to you."

Rose stroked the glowing chestnut highlights in his hair, and love overwhelmed her. Ana had been right: Niall was soft as thistledown on the inside. The fact he trusted her enough to let her touch that part of him undid her.

"Check the bag, love. 'Tis a magical gift Troy sent over. If me father had loved a woman and bonded, it would have been passed to her, but Ciar never allowed him a wife. He wants us to have it."

Rose loosened the gold cord and tipped the bag's contents onto her palm. A single smooth stone the color of honey gleamed in the artificial light.

" 'Tis a cat's-eye. Sees into the heart, so they say."

Rose turned the stone in her hands, watching the light ripple through the crystalline layers. "Should I see things in it, like a crystal ball?"

Niall laughed and lifted the stone from her fingers. "No, lass. 'Tis not a tool of divination. Let me show you."

He stood and placed the warm stone against the

skin between her eyebrows. The familiar thread of connection between them suddenly became as focused and strong as a torch shining in her eyes.

"Cripes!" Rose blinked and gently pushed his hand and the stone away.

He grinned at her. "You'll get used to the feel. Wherever I am, you'll always be able to sense me and know me thoughts. Just wanted you to be sure you can always trust me."

"No more trying to protect me from the truth, then?"

He shook his head seriously, and love bubbled up, filling Rose. She'd forgiven him long ago, yet he still beat himself up over what went wrong the day they'd released the piskies.

"Does it work the other way around? Let you see into my mind?"

"Aye."

Rose gave him a mock grimace of horror. "I'll have to stop fantasizing about a threesome with Michael then."

Niall went deadly still, and Rose chuckled. "You're so easy to get a rise out of, Niall O'Connor." She patted his cheek. "I'm joking, darling. Check me out with the cat's-eye if you don't believe me."

He shook his head and dropped the stone into its bag. " 'Tis for you, lass. I never thought I'd say this to anyone except Ana, but I love you *and* I trust you." Turning her hand, he brushed his lips over her palm and, with a smoldering glance, kissed his way up her arm to the sensitive skin inside her elbow.

Rose sank lower in her seat with a sigh as he raised himself over her and pushed the chair back flat. She stroked her hands over the front of his silky blue shirt, savoring the hard muscles beneath. "I'm so glad you came to rescue me from the accounts."

He nuzzled her neck, and a delicious quiver rippled through her body. "Aye, I know a far better way to celebrate the start of our New Year as pisky king and queen."

Natale Stenzel

Author of *Pandora's Box* and *The Druid Made Me Do It*

Daphne Forbes always knew the world was an odd place. Unlike most CPAs, she grew up the daughter of a druid. Unlike her father, she eschewed the supernatural. But magic was coming to trip her up. In the form of an enchanted cornerstone, it was set to knock Daphne's socks off—or at least one of her shoes—and the rest of her clothes were soon to follow.

Magic filled Daphne, empowered her, shifted her shape and raged wild as a summer storm. Enter Tremayne. Whether the tormented newcomer was truly her guardian or something more sinister, one thing he wanted was clear. Daphne wanted him, too. She had spent her whole life with control but little power; this was just the opposite. She was suddenly between a magic stone and…someplace harder. And we're not (just) talking about Tremayne's abs.

BETWEEN a ROCK AND A Heart Place

ISBN 13: 978-0-505-52783-7

To order a book or to request a catalog call:
1-800-481-9191
Our books are also available at your local bookstore, or you can check out our Web site **www.dorchesterpub.com** where you can look up your favorite authors, read excerpts, or glance at our discussion forum to see what people have to say about your favorite books.

A Taste of Magic

Tracy Madison

"Fun, quirky and delicious!"
—Annette Blair, National Bestselling Author
of *Never Been Witched*

MIXING IT UP

Today is Elizabeth Stevens's birthday, and not only is it the one-year anniversary of her husband leaving her, it's also the day her bakery is required to make a cake—for her ex's next wedding. If there's a bitter taste in her mouth, no one can blame her.

But today, Liz is about to receive a gift. Her Grandma Verda isn't just wacky; she's a little witchy. An ancient gypsy magic has been passed through the family bloodline for generations, and it's Liz's turn to be empowered. Henceforth, everything she bakes will have a dash of delight and a pinch of wishes-can-come-true. From her hunky policeman neighbor, to her gorgeous personal trainer, to her bum of an ex-husband, everyone Liz knows is going to taste her power. Revenge is sweet…and it's only the first dish to be served.

ISBN 13: 978-0-505-52810-0